Temptation

Temptation

Jude Deveraux

WHEELER
PUBLISHING, INC.
ROCKLAND, MA

★ AN AMERICAN COMPANY ★

Published in Large Print by arrangement with Pocket Books, a division of Simon & Schuster, Inc., in the United States and Canada.

Wheeler Large Print Book Series.

Set in 16 pt Plantin.

Library of Congress Cataloging-in-Publication Data

Deveraux, Jude.
    Temptation / Jude Deveraux.
        p. (large print) cm.(Wheeler large print book series)
    ISBN 1-58724-021-1 (hardcover)
    1. Americans—Scotland—Fiction. 2. Housekeepers—Fiction.
3. Young women—Fiction. 4. Scotland—Fiction. 5. Large type books.
I. Title. II. Series

[PS3554.E9273 T38   2001]
813'.54—dc21

00-069485
                                                                CIP

To Lorna and Ron
with love

One

❧

"And in conclusion, ladies...and gentlemen..."
There was a murmur of amusement in the big
auditorium, for there were very few men who
attended Temperance O'Neil's lectures. They
couldn't stand to hear the truth of what Temperance said, couldn't stand to hear and see
what they had done to the American family.

"I say that the fight must continue, that we
have not yet begun to make inroads into this
problem, but we mustn't give up. We must continue!"

At that Temperance stepped back from the
podium and dropped her head so only the
wide wheel of her trademark hat could be
seen. It was an instant before the women
could get to their feet and start applauding.
Looking up, Temperance gave them a dazzling
smile; then slowly and with humility, she
walked off the stage.

"You were wonderful," said Agnes Spinnaker
as she put a small hand on Temperance's
shoulder. "As always."

"Let's just hope it did some good," Temperance said as she twitched the curtain aside

1

and looked out at the audience again. They were still on their feet, still clapping hard.

"You have to go back out," Agnes said loudly so she could be heard over the noise of the crowd. "You have to say something more. Do you have anything planned?"

"Oh, I have something planned, all right," Temperance said as she began pulling long pins from her hat. "Hold these, will you? I don't want anyone to get hurt."

"What in the world are you going to do?"

"Watch," Temperance said as she pushed aside the curtain, then went back onto the stage. As she stepped up on the little box that held the podium, she waited for the applause to die down; then when the room was quiet, she waited another few seconds. No one sat down, but the three hundred or so women stood in place, their hands ready to start clapping again; for whatever Temperance said, they were ready to applaud.

In the absolute quiet of the auditorium, Temperance looked down at the oak lectern in front of her, as though she were looking at notes and about to read from them.

But then, in one fast movement, she grabbed her big hat and threw it so it sailed high above the heads of the women, twirling, twisting, higher and higher. There wasn't an eye in the room that wasn't on that hat, one of *her* hats, one of Temperance O'Neil's hats.

The hat came down near the back row, and half a dozen women made a leap for it. Momentarily there was a tussle, with skirts rising above ankles, and buttoned leather shoes waving in the air. Then there was a squeal and a pretty young woman jumped up from the middle of the melee and waved the hat as though it were a flag won on a battlefield.

In the next instant the crowd went wild with excitement, clapping, yelling, stamping feet; there were even some whistles.

Temperance stepped down from the podium, gave a great wave to the excited young woman in the back clutching her newly won hat, then quickly left the stage.

"Oh, Temperance," Agnes said, "that was brilliant. Truly brilliant. I would never have thought of that."

"How many are out there?" Temperance asked as she walked briskly toward her dressing room, nodding toward the backstage door.

"Not too many. At least not as many as last time. After what happened last week, people are a little afraid of being hurt."

Inside her dressing room, Temperance reached down to open a hat box on the floor and grimaced. She knew that her theatrics helped her cause, and heaven knew that she needed all the help she could get, but she didn't like people to be hurt.

"How clever you are to have brought another hat. I guess you planned that gesture at the end."

"Of course," Temperance said. Agnes was a good person and she was useful, but she certainly had no imagination. "Is Willie out there?"

"Oh, yes. You know he'd give his life for you."

"Mmmm. Let's just hope he can get me out of here quickly tonight. My mother's ship arrived today. I haven't seen her in three whole months!"

"I'm sure she'll be very glad to see you. You look wonderful."

As Temperance glanced into the mirror, adjusting the replacement hat on her head, she smiled at Agnes. The newspapers alleged that Temperance surrounded herself with homely women so Temperance would look better by contrast. But when Temperance's mother had read that, she'd smiled and said, "But who wouldn't be plain-faced when next to you, dear?"

At that thought Temperance smiled at herself in the mirror. She had missed her mother so much over these last months. She'd missed having someone there when she got home, someone to listen to her escapades and triumphs. Even if some of the things that Temperance did frightened her mother, Temperance still told her about them anyway. "You're so much like your father, dear," Melanie O'Neil would say in that quiet voice of hers, then give a delicate little shiver.

Temperance's father, the beloved husband of Mellie O'Neil, had died when his daughter was just fourteen years old. But those few years had been long enough to instill in Temperance the fire that she needed to fight for women's rights for all the fifteen years since her father's death.

"How's that?" Temperance asked, turning to look at Agnes. "Am I presentable?"

"Oh, yes," Agnes said, clutching a program from tonight's lecture to her thin bosom. "You look wonderful."

"So do you," Temperance said, then gave Agnes a kiss on the cheek.

Blushing, Agnes looked down at her shoes. She was one of Temperance's "abandoned women," as the newspaper called them. Years ago Agnes had eloped with a handsome young man only to find out that he was already married. He'd abandoned her when he was told that her father had disinherited his daughter because she'd run off without his approval. When Temperance found Agnes, she'd been living out of garbage cans and her skin was covered with sores from poor diet and exposure. As Temperance did with hundreds of women, she had found Agnes a job, in this case, working backstage at the Kirkland Auditorium. As a result, Agnes would have walked across fire for Temperance.

"That's not *the* hat, is it?" Agnes whispered, looking at the huge hat that Temperance was adjusting on her head. It was black felt, with deep red silk roses all around the brim; magenta netting swirled over the flowers. It was the most beautiful thing that Agnes had ever seen.

"No," Temperance said, smiling, and making a mental note to buy Agnes a hat. "The mayor kept that hat. I think he nailed it to his office wall and throws darts at it."

Agnes's face screwed up into rage. "I'll—"

"I was making a joke," Temperance said quickly. "I heard he has the hat in a glass box in his house. In a place of honor." With each word she spoke, Agnes's face relaxed.

"He should. Everyone says that your hat got him reelected."

"Perhaps. There! Now it's on." Opening the door of the little dressing room, she went into the hall. "I'll see you again next month," she called as she ran toward the stage exit door.

Sometimes Temperance wished the incident with the mayor and the hat had never happened. Never mind that it had been good for both of them. Still, sometimes she wished she didn't have to spend every minute in public in a hat big enough to use as a wagon wheel.

But, as she'd told her mother, if it helped even one woman out of an intolerable situation, then it was worth it.

And her hats had helped many women. Or at least the recognition of the hats had helped them. It was nearly seven years ago, when Temperance was a mere twenty-two years old, that she had first encountered the mayor of New York and had arrogantly asked him what he was going to do about the Millon tenement. A week before, the four-story structure had collapsed on top of seventeen women and children, killing four of them.

The mayor, tired and frustrated, had taken one look at the flawless skin and dark green eyes of Miss Temperance O'Neil and decided she was one of those rich women who got involved in social issues for as long as it took before some equally rich man asked her to marry him.

In front of half a dozen reporters, the mayor looked at her and said, "If you can find a solution before I do, other than having your daddy pay for it, that is," he added, trying to inject some humor into what had become an inquisition, "I'll..." He hesitated. "I'll eat your hat."

It was obvious that the mayor hadn't expected anyone to pick up on his challenge, and certainly not the lovely young thing he made it to. But he had been surprised. The newspapers had no other worthy story at that moment, so they got the names of the people involved, then flashed the story all over the front page of every newspaper in America.

Temperance, fresh out of her all-female college, wasn't ready for the turmoil that hit her, but she made herself ready. She accepted the challenge.

And the race was on.

The mayor tried to get the people who had put him in office to erect another building to replace the one that had collapsed, but they, laughing, hesitated. They didn't especially like the mayor, but they did like the pictures they were seeing of the beautiful Miss O'Neil.

Later, Temperance openly admitted that she couldn't have done what she did if the mayor hadn't helped, but the City of New York rallied around her and they donated their services. People volunteered their time; stores donated building materials. With the help of gaslight and lanterns, volunteers worked round the clock, all with the result that in twenty-six and a half days, there was a new apartment building standing on the site of the collapsed one.

Some canny advisers had shown the mayor how he could use the entire situation to make himself seem more human, so he showed up for the ribbon cutting wearing a bib and carrying a two-foot-long knife and fork. He posed for half a dozen photos with Temperance's hat, looking as though he were about to eat it.

But the mayor, outwardly smiling but inwardly fuming, thought he was going to have the last laugh because he presented the deed to the building to Miss Temperance O'Neil, saying she was allowed to choose the new tenants and to run the place as she saw fit. Let her see how difficult it was to run a building in a slum area! he thought, smiling at the thought of her coming misery.

But the mayor's gesture was the beginning of Temperance's purpose in life. She filled that building with women who had been abandoned by men, and she came up with ways for them to support themselves and their children. She used her beauty, her newly acquired fame, the money her father had left her—whatever she had and could use—to find the women means of support.

By the time Temperance celebrated her twenty-third birthday, she was a celebrity and wherever she went in New York, doors were opened to her. Sometimes the men didn't want to see her, because visits from Miss O'Neil always cost them money, but Temperance had found out that there was always a woman who opened the doors that led to the men with the money—and women were always willing to help her out.

Now, outside the stage door, Willie was waiting for her, and Temperance gave a sigh. There always seemed to be a Willie in her life, some young man who watched her with big, adoring eyes and begged to be allowed to carry her umbrella. But after a couple of years, maybe only one year, when the young man finally got it through his head that Temperance was not going to marry him, he'd wander off to marry some girl whose father sold dry goods and they'd produce a few children. Just the other day Temperance had heard that the first "Willie" now had children in their third year of school.

Besides Willie, outside the auditorium there were about a dozen little girls, each looking up at their heroine, Temperance O'Neil. A couple of the older girls were wearing hats as big as Temperance's. When they saw her, they squealed and held out the photos of Temperance they had purchased at the five-and-dime, all the proceeds going to fund Temperance's projects.

Plastering a smile on her face, Temperance went down the steps and began to sign autographs and hear how the girls wanted to be just like her when they grew up.

Usually, Temperance enjoyed this time, but tonight she wanted to get home as quickly as possible so she could see her mother. She didn't know why it was, but this time she'd missed her mother more than usual and she was dying to sit down with her, kick off her shoes, and tell her mother all about the last three months.

Willie moved through the girls to stand close to her. "Can you get me out of here?" Temperance whispered. "I want to go home right away."

"Anything," Willie whispered back, and he meant the word. Like Agnes, he would have given his life for Temperance. In fact, just last night he'd purchased an engagement ring for her, and he planned to pop the question on Sunday.

Moments later, Willie had hailed a cab and had shooed the girls away so he could help Temperance into the carriage. Once inside, she leaned back against the seat and closed her eyes.

Mistake. Within seconds, Willie was kissing her hand and *making declarations of undying love.*

What she wanted to say was, Not tonight, Willie. But she just moved her hand away and asked him to ask the driver to go faster.

Willie had been through this many times, so he knew that if he pushed, he would anger Temperance. And her temper was not something that he wanted to unleash upon himself. After he'd ordered the driver about (and taken out his frustrations on the poor man), he turned back to Temperance and allowed himself a moment to stare at her. She was the most beautiful female he'd ever seen in his life. She had masses of dark auburn hair that she tried to tame, but no amount of pinning and twisting could contain all that hair. Constantly, it escaped from the upswept pouf that she wore under her big hats.

She had eyes the color of the finest quality emeralds, skin like porcelain, lips as red as—

"My mother is to arrive tonight," Temperance said, pulling Willie out of his trance. She had come to hate the puppy-dog way he stared at her. "I haven't seen her in three months."

He loved her voice, especially loved it when she spoke to him alone. "You are a saint," he said, his eyes wide. "You've given up having a family of your own to nurse your poor, weak mother. She is so fortunate to have a daughter like you to take care of her. Does she still mourn your father?"

"Every minute of every day. There will never be another man on earth like my father," Temperance said with feeling as she glanced out the window at the dark streets of New York. How much longer before they got home?

It seemed hours before they reached Greenwich Village and the brownstone that was her home. But it wasn't a home without her mother there, Temperance thought. Without Melanie O'Neil's presence, the house was just a heap of stone.

When the carriage finally pulled up in front

of the house and she saw that it was ablaze with light, Temperance broke into a grin. Her mother was home! She had so very much to tell her, so many things to share with her. In the last three months Temperance had accomplished a lot, but she was always thinking of what was left to do. Should she take on that project on the West Side? It was so very far away, all the way across the park. It had been suggested to Temperance that she buy a motor-car and travel about town in that. Should she?

There were many things that Temperance wanted to talk to her mother about. Next week Temperance had six meetings with politicians and the press. And there were four scheduled luncheons with men-who-had-money, men who could possibly be persuaded to fund Temperance's purchase of yet another tenement building.

Truthfully, sometimes Temperance felt so overwhelmed by what her life had become that all she wanted to do was put her head on her mother's lap and cry.

But now her mother was home and Temperance would at last have someone to talk to.

"Good night," Temperance called over her shoulder as she practically leaped from the carriage, not allowing Willie to help her down.

She ran up the steps two at a time and threw open the door to the house.

And standing in the entrance hall under the crystal chandelier was Melanie O'Neil, clasped tightly in the arms of a man. They were kissing.

"Oh, Temperance, dear," Mellie said as she broke away from the man. "I didn't want you find out until I'd had time to explain. We, ah…"

The man—tall, handsome, gray-haired—stepped forward, his hand outstretched, lips smiling. "Your mother and I were married in Scotland. I'm your new father. And I'm sure you'll be happy to hear that, day after tomorrow, the three of us are going home to live in the Highlands."

Two

Temperance managed to make it through dinner. The man, this stranger, sat at the head of the table—in her father's chair, her father's place—and laughed and chatted as though it were a given that both his new wife and her daughter were going to pack up and return to Edinburgh with him to live! All through dinner the man lectured on the glories of that foreign city.

Winking, and even once touching Temperance's hand, he told her that he'd be able to find her a husband in no time.

"I don't know what's wrong with these

American men," Angus McCairn said, smiling. "You still have your looks, and even though you might be a bit over-the-hill for most men, I'm sure we can find you someone."

"Can you?" Temperance asked quietly, looking at the man with hatred in her eyes.

He didn't seem to notice. "And we'll fatten you up on good Scottish beef. You're on the thin side for the taste of the men of the Highlands. Oh, we'll have a time of it. As long as I have my dear wife by my side, how can we fail to be happy?"

Temperance looked across the table at her mother, but Melanie O'Neil kept her head down, pushing the food about on her plate and refusing to meet her daughter's eyes.

"Mr. McCairn," Temperance said slowly and evenly so he'd be sure to hear what she was saying. So far the man seemed to hear only his own voice. "I do not know what you have been told about me, but obviously it couldn't have been too much." Her eyes bored into the top of her cowardly mother's head. How could you have done this?! she wanted to scream. She'd thought that she and her mother were friends as well as relatives.

But now Temperance tried to calm herself as she looked back at this large man who seemed so out of place amid all the delicate bric-a-brac that her mother so loved to collect. "Mr. McCairn, I—"

"You must call me Father," he said, smiling at her warmly. "I know you're a bit old to be given pony rides, but we can manage some-

14

thing." He looked at his new wife to share the joke he'd just made, but Melanie just lowered her head closer to her plate. Another minute and her nose would be in the roast beef.

Temperance had to unclench her fists. If the man made even one more reference to her age, she was going to dump the entire platter of brussels sprouts onto his head.

But she'd spent the last eight years dealing with difficult men, and she'd rarely lost her temper. "Perhaps it's a bit early for such familiarity, but what I want to say is that I cannot possibly live in Scotland."

"Canna go?" he said, looking from Temperance to her mother then back again. This announcement seemed to bring out the accent in his speech. "What do ye mean that you canna go? Ye are my daughter."

Temperance could see that there were little sparks of light beginning to flash in his blue eyes. Little sparks of temper. For her mother's sake, she'd better diffuse that anger.

"I have work to do here," she said softly, "so I must remain here in New York. If Mother must go—" Here she choked and again looked at her mother's head.

Melanie took a handkerchief out of her sleeve and put it to her eyes, but she didn't look up at her daughter.

"Now look what ye've done!" Angus McCairn said loudly. "You've gone and upset her. Come, come, now, Mellie, don't cry. She doesn't mean it. Of course she'll go. A daughter always stays with her mother until she's mar-

15

ried, so, with her bein' as old as she is, you may *never* lose her."

At that Temperance came to her feet. "Mother! How could you have *married* this insensitive lout?! Couldn't you have just had an affair with the grocery boy?"

When Angus McCairn got to his feet, Temperance didn't think she'd ever in her life seen anyone so angry. But she didn't back down from him, even when he raised his hand and she was sure he was going to strike her. She'd faced furious men before when she'd told them what she thought of what they were doing to their families.

"In my office," he said under his breath. "This is between you and me. I'll not upset your mother."

"My mother is a grown woman, and since she created this impossible situation, I think she *should* be involved in it."

Angus was now so angry he was shaking. When he pointed his finger toward the dining room door, he was trembling. "Go," he said under his breath. "Go."

Temperance looked down at her mother and saw that she was crying hard now, but Temperance had no sympathy for her, for she had been betrayed by the person she loved most in the world.

Turning on her heel, Temperance left the room, but in the entrance hall she halted. She was *not* going to enter her father's office and act as though she knew that now that room belonged to...to *him*.

16

Angus strode past her, flung open the door to the library, then stepped aside for her to enter. He took three strides to cross the room, then sat down on the green leather chair that had always been her father's chair. "Now we shall talk," he said, his elbows on the carved arms of the chair, his index fingers made into steeples as he glared at her.

Temperance decided that perhaps this situation called for a more subtle approach. "Mr. McCairn," she said softly, then waited for him to correct her. But he didn't.

Temperance took a seat on the other side of the desk. "I don't think you understand about my life, about who I am and what I do," she said with a modest little smile; then she ducked her head in a way that usually made men jump up and fetch something for her. But when she looked back up at Angus McCairn, he hadn't moved a muscle; there was still much anger in his eyes.

She gave him a smile. "I'm sure that you must be a delightful man or my mother wouldn't have married you, and, as much as I'll miss her..." Temperance had to pause or she was going to choke at the thought of her mother being gone forever. "I will miss her but *I* cannot leave New York. I am needed here."

Angus didn't say anything for several moments, but just looked at her. He was not going to tell her that tonight he had hidden in the back of the auditorium where she was making her speech and he had heard all of it. Never in his sixty-one years had Angus ever

17

been so disgusted. That a woman, any woman, could stand before people and give a speech was, in itself, going against nature, but what she had said was truly horrifying. She had encouraged women to *earn money*. She told the women that they couldn't depend on men to give to them but that women must find a way so they didn't *need* men in any way. "Except as the begetters of children," she'd said, and the hundreds of women in the audience had laughed and cheered riotously at that. Don't these women have families to take care of? Angus had wondered. What are their men doing allowing them to run around the city alone at night and listen to such sedition?

And now, here she stood before him trying to make him believe that what she was doing with all those poor women was something that he should allow her to continue. From Angus's standpoint, he was doing New York a favor by taking her away.

"Are you through with your play-acting?" he said after a while.

"I beg your pardon?"

"I have just spent three months with your lovely mother, and you are all she could talk about. I know all about your so-called 'work.' I know how you traipse through the slums of this city and how you interfere between men and women whom God has joined. I know all about what you do, little missy, and I am happy to say that now it has ended. You are going with your mother and me to Scotland, and that is my final decision."

Temperance wasn't sure she'd heard him correctly. "You are threatening me?" she said under her breath. "You have no idea of the people I know. Of the—"

Angus gave a guffaw in derision. "From what I can tell the only people really on your side are a bunch of women who've been discarded by the men in their lives. And I'm sure with good reason. As for important people, from what your mother tells me, even the mayor of the city would pay for your ticket out of here."

That was so close to the truth that Temperance thought she might explode from the anger that raced through her body. Coming to her feet, she leaned over the desk toward him. "I am a grown woman, and I will do what I damned well please. I'd rather starve than live anywhere near you."

"Then that's just what you'll do because you'll get no money from me," he said calmly, still sitting, still with his chin on his fingers.

Temperance stepped back from him. "I don't know what you think I am, but I can assure you that I'm not interested in your money. I have my own money and I—"

"No," Angus said softly. "The money you have belongs to your mother, and as she is my wife, it now belongs to me."

For a moment Temperance could only look at him, blinking. If she had been an innocent girl of eighteen or so and seen less of the world, she would have proudly told him she didn't need money, then turned and walked out of that room. But Temperance knew all too well how women fared in the world without a means of support. And, besides, how could she help people if she was spending fifty hours a week clerking in a ladies' shop or whatever?

"You married my mother to get at the money left us by my father," she said quietly.

At that Angus lost his calm. He came to his feet, his face turned red, and she could see that his emotions were so choking him that, for a moment, he couldn't speak.

When he did speak, his voice was tremulous. "The three of us will live on my earnings," he said, his back teeth clamped together. "I left my business for these weeks to pay my new wife's daughter the respect of fetching her in person. I could have sent you a letter ordering you to come to Scotland."

At that Temperance gave a snort. "And you think I would have obeyed such a letter?"

"No," he said, glaring at her. "I had heard enough from your sweet mother to figure out what kind of woman *you* are. No wonder no man will have you!"

"No man—" Temperance started, then closed her mouth. She was *not* going to tell this man of the suitors she'd turned down. If she'd kept all the engagement rings offered to her, she could have opened a jewelry store.

"Let me make myself clear," Angus said. "I'm giving you only two choices in this matter. You either return to Scotland with your mother and me or you remain here in New York. If you remain here, you will have no money and no home, as I may sell this place."

"You can't do that! This is my father's house!"

"Your father has been dead for fifteen years! Your dear mother has been *alone* all that time. She's dedicated her life to you for years, so now it's time she had some happiness of her own."

"*You* are to give her happiness?" Temperance sneered. "You are no match for my father. You are—"

"You know nothing about me," he said in dismissal. "Now, which is it to be? Do you pack or do you walk?"

At that Temperance couldn't reply. Her pride warred with her logic and with all the visions of what she'd seen in the years that she'd been working with destitute women.

As Angus watched her, he softened somewhat. "Come, girl, I know all this is a shock to you, but I'm not so bad a person. You'll find out. It's not that I've taken your money from you. All of it will be held in trust for you until the time you marry, then it will be turned over to your husband." His voice softened even more. "And I'm a fair man, so I'll make sure you have a small private allowance just for yourself so you can buy yourself some pretties."

This was all too much for Temperance to take in. It was as though, in one hideous night, she had gone from helping impoverished women to being one herself. "What about my work?" she managed to whisper.

Angus waved his hand in dismissal. "While

you live with your mother and me, you will be a dutiful daughter. You certainly won't spend your time traipsing all over the tenements of Edinburgh." He gave her a hard look. "Do I make myself clear?"

"Oh, yes, very clear," Temperance said, her eyes harder than his, but her mind was working quickly. Unfortunately, he had the law on his side. Temperance knew women who were fighting against such unfair laws that gave this usurper total control over a grown woman, but, so far, that particular battle had not been won.

She did her best to give him a smile, but it didn't reach her eyes. "Just for clarification's sake, could you define what you mean by 'dutiful daughter'? I don't want to have any misunderstanding between us."

Angus looked puzzled. "I don't know, whatever girls do. Tea parties, charitable causes, book clubs. Buy a few dresses and, and...gentlemen callers. I know you're a bit long in the tooth to make an ideal bride, but perhaps there would be a young or not so young man in Scotland who'd have you. You're presentable enough."

"Presentable, am I?" Temperance's voice was low. "Charitable acts and dresses? And I'm not to stray too far from home? Yes, I see. Perhaps that *is* the way," she said thoughtfully. Her head came up. "Yes, Mr. McCairn, I think I can promise you that I will be the most perfect daughter anyone has ever seen. I shall be the epitome of a good daughter and shall do only the most feminine things."

Had Melanie been there she would have told Angus to watch out when Temperance was being agreeable, but Melanie was upstairs hiding and couldn't tell anyone anything.

But Angus didn't seem to notice anything unusual in Temperance's smile. He'd expected the girl to give in. After all, what else could she do? And, besides, what he was doing for her would be, in the end, good for her.

He smiled warmly at his new stepdaughter. He'd told Mellie that all Temperance needed was a firm hand and she'd stop her nonsense and see reason.

"Good," he said, and there was relief in his voice. "I'm glad to hear something sensible come out of your mouth. I think perhaps you're more like your mother than she knows. Now, go and start packing."

"Yes, sir," Temperance said, then bobbed a bit of a curtsy to him. "Thank you, sir."

"No need to thank me. You just be a good daughter to your mother and that will be thanks enough."

An hour later, after Angus had told his new wife all about his little talk with his new "daughter," Melanie said, "Oh, Angus, I'm frightened."

"Mellie, dear, there's no longer anything to be afraid of. That's why I'm here, to take care of you both."

"But you don't know Temperance. When she's agreeable that's when she's most disagreeable."

"Don't be silly. All the girl needs is a man

23

to guide her. You mark my words, six months from now I'll have her married. Now come to bed, my little butterfly, and let me take all the worries from that pretty brow of yours."

"Oh, Angus…" Melanie said, then forgot all about her daughter's bad temper.

Three

SIX MONTHS LATER
EDINBURGH, SCOTLAND

Angus had to make his way through four giggling young ladies and six young men who were holding bouquets of flowers and boxes of candy. All ten of them were waiting for Temperance to finish the meeting she was in so she could attend to them.

As Angus handed his hat to the butler, he said, "How many today?"

"At last count, sir, fourteen, but then, it's only eleven in the morning. I believe there are more expected this afternoon."

"She's been told that I want to see her?"

"Yes. She said that she can spare you exactly thirteen minutes between meetings."

"Spare me!" Angus said in disgust as he threw his gloves into his hat then strode into his office.

The desk was piled high with bills, but he didn't have to open them to know what was in them.

Since he and his new family had arrived in Edinburgh six months ago, Angus McCairn had not had a moment's peace. Feeling as though he were being a good father, even if the offspring was nearly thirty years old, he had introduced his strong-willed stepdaughter to a friend of his, a lady by title, but without means. For a small compensation, she had been more than willing to introduce Temperance into Edinburgh society.

Angus had been prepared for a reluctant, sulking female; he'd expected fights and even tantrums, and he had mentally prepared himself for them. But he had not been prepared for what Temperance did: She threw herself into society with a vengeance.

And since the moment Angus had said the words, "Let me introduce you to..." he had not had a moment's peace. From early until late, his house was full of visitors. There were girls fresh out of the schoolroom, giggling and nervous, who came to have tea with Temperance. There were women in their forties, unmarried, who came on Thursday afternoons to chat about books. Three hospitals in Edinburgh had weekly meetings in his house. Last week he returned home to find that his library had been recruited for bandage rolling. There wasn't a moment when the household was awake that both parlors of his house weren't full of young women who were having a meeting to discuss some good works they were planning.

25

At the end of the first month, Angus had told Temperance to have her meetings outside his house. But Temperance had told him in the sweetest tone imaginable that a good daughter stayed at home and didn't leave her family. Temperance said that she wouldn't be a "dutiful daughter" if she flitted about Edinburgh unescorted.

Angus had gritted his teeth, but his pride wouldn't allow him to throw her or her zealously good friends out.

Besides the earnest women, there were the males. As far as Angus could tell, Temperance had allowed the word to spread that she wanted to get married, even that she was desperate to get married. To Angus's eyes, Temperance's age was a handicap to a man who wanted to start a family, but Temperance's beauty, her trim figure, and her inheritance seemed to make up for her age. The result was that there were as many males in Angus's house as there were females. Boys and men, ranging in age from nineteen to sixty-five, were courting her.

And, Angus thought with his fists clenched at his side, she fluttered her lashes, gave coy little smiles, and encouraged all the males to outdo themselves in their courting techniques.

There was the time at three A.M. when Angus was awakened from a sound sleep by a young man who was serenading Temperance. He sang in a creaky, but very loud, voice while a band of Italian guitar players backed him up. Angus had to threaten to shoot them all to make them go away.

Three times Angus had been awakened by rocks thrown at his window in the wee hours. He'd had to sling open the window and shout at the suitors that they had the wrong room. Once was a mistake, he thought, but three times? He knew that Temperance had purposefully told the men the wrong room.

At work Angus was deluged with men using every excuse in the world to get in to see him to try to persuade him to put in a good word with Temperance. Angus had twice lost business because he had been so sure that the men asking about drapery fabrics were really after Temperance's hand in marriage that Angus had shoved the men out of his warehouse.

Now, looking back at his desk, he grimaced. And there were the bills. Temperance offered food and drink to every committee member, every do-gooder she invited to Angus's house. She fed all the men who came to her, no matter how many times a day they showed up. Angus was sure that at least half the men "courting" Temperance were just poor students who were there for the free food.

And what could Angus do? Send them all away? Every day there were letters in the mail telling him what a wonderful job he was doing with this committee and that committee. It seemed that Temperance refused to take any credit for herself but gave all the glory to Angus, saying that he was the one who really did everything. So if Angus threw them all out, he would look like a monster and he'd lose what business he had left.

Besides the food bills, there were bills for Temperance's clothing. She'd managed to spend thousands of pounds on outfits by Worth and Redfern, Paquin and Drécoll. At first it had bewildered Angus how Temperance could find the time to buy so much when she was constantly in one noble meeting after another. But it seemed that his busy stepdaughter could do half a dozen things at once, as Angus found out when he'd accidently walked in on a meeting of women dedicated to saving diseased cats or some such, and Temperance had been in her underwear trying on some lacy thing that cost the earth.

There were bills for luggage, a couple of bicycles, a typewriter, even motion picture equipment, which she used to show historical films to a group of orphans who came every Friday afternoon and ate their weight in sandwiches and cakes.

So far Angus had had to hire three new maids to help cook, clean, and serve.

And in the six months since he'd been at home with his new bride, they had not had a single moment of quiet calmness together. He couldn't eat breakfast alone with his new wife because Temperance always had some downtrodden group of women to join them. "They so want to meet the man who has made all of this possible," Temperance purred at her stepfather.

The result of Temperance's vow to be "a good daughter" was that, one way or another, Angus was going to go bankrupt. He figured that at the rate Temperance was spending, he could last another two years at most. And truthfully, he was so agitated about his disruptive home life that he couldn't concentrate on his business and consequently found himself making stupid decisions that were costing him money.

On the other hand, if he threw all these soulful-looking, down-on-their-luck people out of his house, all of Edinburgh would rise up against him and he'd never have another customer.

Either way, he was going to go bankrupt—or lose his mind—he thought.

But for the last two weeks he had worked on ways to solve this dilemma. He could go traveling with his wife and stepdaughter. But who would run his business? He could give his stepdaughter her freedom, which, of course, he fully realized was what she was after; but Angus couldn't do that. He had been raised in a time when men looked after women and he would never be at ease in his own soul if he allowed a woman under his care to live alone. For all that Temperance had become the bane of his life, she was a woman and she was his responsibility.

On the other hand, his first responsibility was to his wife, and Temperance was making his household so chaotic that Melanie was a heap of nerves. So perhaps Angus should modify his original stand when it came to his stepdaughter. But to save his own pride, maybe he could work a compromise with her.

And maybe he could use her ability to...to manage people, shall we say, to do something for him that he'd been working on for years but without success.

So Angus had worked out a solution: He'd send Temperance to be under the care of his nephew, James McCairn, for a while. But he knew he'd have to give Temperance something to occupy her busy mind while she was there or she'd drive James mad, just as she was driving him, Angus, insane. And since there was a problem he'd been having with his nephew for a number of years now, maybe he could kill two birds with one stone.

When the knock sounded on his library door, Angus drew in his breath and let it out slowly. The last time he'd had a private conversation with his stepdaughter had been in New York. And the result of that little talk was that he was now drinking half a bottle of Scotch every night.

"Come in," he said.

"You wanted to see me, Father dear?" Temperance said as she demurely sat down on the edge of the chair on the other side of Angus's desk. Still smiling, she looked at the watch pinned to her lovely bosom. "I think I have a few minutes before my next charitable meeting."

Angus knew that that watch had been made in Switzerland, handcrafted by a company that had been in business for over two hundred years, and that it had cost as much as the yearly salaries of two of his clerks.

Might as well get to it, he thought as he stood and clasped his hands behind his back. How could his sweet wife have given birth to this virago? "I want to offer you a job."

"But a dutiful daughter would never take employment outside her home. A dutiful daughter—"

He gave her a look that cut her off mid-sentence; then he saw her look down at her hands in an attempt to hide her smile. "You can stop the acting while you're alone with me."

"Whatever do you mean?" she asked sweetly. "I have merely tried to be what you asked of me."

He ignored her challenge. He was not going to lower himself to argue with her about whether or not she had done what he wanted. "If you complete this job to my satisfaction, I'll give you an allowance and a modified version of freedom."

"A what?" The false sweetness was gone from her voice; this was the woman he'd first met, the one he had secretly heard give a speech of such force that, had she been a man and talking on an appropriate subject, he would have admired her for.

"If you successfully complete this job, I will give you access to your inheritance, but it will be supervised by my banking contacts in New York. And I will allow you to live in your mother's house in New York but with a,

shall we say, companion chosen by me."
When she started to speak, he held up his
hand. "And you will be allowed to continue
your..." He could hardly say the words. "Your
work with the underprivileged in New York."

"And if I refuse this job?"

"You will remain here and be a daughter to
your mother. I shall put it about that she's ill
and there're to be no more visitors to the
house."

"This is blackmail," Temperance said under
her breath.

"And what have *you* been at these last
months in hell?" Angus half shouted, then had
to take a breath to calm himself.

Temperance leaned back against the chair.
"All right, I'm listening. What's the job?"

"I want you to find a wife for my nephew."

"A what?" she said as she sat upright, then
drew her mouth into a tight line. "You're
trying to marry me off, aren't you?"

"You!" Angus said loudly, then looked
toward the door. He could hear more women,
more men being shown into his hall. Qui-
eter, he said, "No, I do not want *you* to marry
my nephew. I like my nephew. No, actually,
I love my nephew. His father was my older
brother, and we—Anyway, the last thing I'd
do to my nephew is saddle him with a termagant
like you."

"I shall take that as a compliment," Temperance said. "What's wrong with the man that
he can't find his own wife?"

"Nothing is wrong with him. He's the laird

of a clan here in Scotland, and he's very hand-some."

"But...?"

"But he lives in isolation and he works hard to save those people under his care, so he doesn't have time to look for a wife."

"So I'm to go to this place and parade a lot of young women in front of him and he's to choose?" Pausing, she considered this for a moment. "I don't think that'll be too difficult. I've met many unmarried women here, so I'll just invite them—"

"No. James mustn't know what you're up to. He's a bit, uh...headstrong and if he were to know that I was interfering in his life, he'd throw you off the place and he'd..." He looked at Temperance.

"Your nephew would end up like me," she said, glaring at him. It seemed that every word out of the man's mouth offended her in some way. She had to consciously swallow her pride.

"If I'm not to introduce him to marriage-able women, how do I find him a wife? May I assume that you have a plan?"

Angus dug about in the unopened bills on his desk. "I want you to go to him as his housekeeper."

"His what?"

Angus held up a letter. "James has written to me asking me to find a new housekeeper for him, as the last one died. She was eighty-something, I believe, so it's no wonder. I want *you* to go as the housekeeper and to get

33

him married to a woman of good station in life. Certainly not one of your down-on-her-luck women that would take any man. A *good* woman. You understand me? As soon as you do that, you're free to return to New York."

For several minutes, Temperance sat there looking at him. "You couldn't just forget this charade and give me what is mine by rights?" she said, trying to keep the bitterness out of her voice.

"I could, but I have a job that is particularly suited to your, ah, talents and I don't see why you can't do it. Why should I give everything and you give nothing?"

At that Temperance stood up, her hands clenched into fists, and leaned across the desk toward him. "Because you are a thief and a scoundrel, that's why. You took what was left to my mother but intended to be shared with me, but because of unethical laws that are straight out of the Middle Ages, you have the legal right to take—"

"Do you want to do the job or not?" he said, his eyes blazing in rage as he leaned across the desk from the other side toward her. "Because if you decide not to do this, I shall pack you and your mother away to some remote village in…in the Himalayas and keep you there for as long as I live."

"Which wouldn't be for long, I can assure you," she spat back at him.

At that they were interrupted by a knock on the door and the entry of the butler. "Miss Temperance is late for her meeting, and the young ladies were wondering if they should start without her."

"Start eating my food is what they mean!" Angus shouted, then looked back at Temperance. "What is your answer?"

"Yes," she said, but her teeth were clamped shut when she said it.

⁓◦◉◦⁓

"Temperance, darling, I know that Angus's ways might seem foreign to you and somewhat harsh, but—"

"What about in bed?" Temperance persisted, her eyes boring into her mother's. "Couldn't you persuade him while you're in bed together?"

At that Melanie O'Neil had to stop pulling clothes from the drawers in Temperance's room and sit down on the chair by the open window and fan herself. "You know, dear," she said breathlessly, "that a lady doesn't talk about..." She couldn't bring herself to say the words; but then her head came up and she gave her daughter a sharp look. "And, besides, you're unmarried, so what do you know of such things?"

"I've never harpooned a whale, but I've read *Moby Dick,*" Temperance shot back. *"Can* you do something with him?"

"I...I..." Melanie looked at her daughter, then stood up and went back to choosing what clothes were to be packed. "I'm not sure I want to. A summer in the Scottish Highlands will be good for you, much better than all that smelly air in New York. And now with those motorcars on the streets, well, I don't see why horses aren't good enough."

"Mother, perhaps you prefer the smell of horse manure to gasoline fumes, but I don't. I have work to do at home."

"Temperance, I can't understand what I ever did to make you see life as so...so..."

"Unromantic?" Temperance asked. "Mother, if you'd ever visit a tenement with me, you'd see—"

"No thank you, dear. I think New York has enough to handle with one O'Neil taking care of it. Temperance, I was wondering if you've thought of the paper you could present in New York when you return there. Six months in a Scottish village. Surely, the village would have a poor section where you could save people. Or maybe it doesn't and you could present a paper on how not to be poor."

At that Temperance couldn't help but laugh. "Oh, Mother, you do say the most amusing things. 'How not to be poor.' What a ridiculous idea. My impression of Scotland is that it's very rural and—" Suddenly Temperance's eyes opened wide. "Cottage industries."

"What, dear?"

"Cottage industries. Those remote places have cottage industries—you know, weaving and knitting, that sort of thing. Maybe I could..."

"Observe and learn, then teach your poor young ladies back in New York?" Melanie tucked another pair of gloves into a little leather case propped open on the bed.

"Exactly. Mother, you read my mind."

"But what about your job of finding a wife for Mr. McCairn? Won't that take most of your time? And you'll be the housekeeper too."

"What time does housekeeping take? I'll order the staff in the morning, and in the afternoon I shall observe and learn. I won't interfere. No, I'll think of this as a...a..."

"University course?"

"Yes. Exactly. I'll think of it as a university course. I'll make daily records of what I see and learn, and when I return to New York, I'll publish my findings. Yes, that's what I'll do. I'll—"

"What about Mr. McCairn?"

Temperance waved her hand in dismissal. "Oh. Him. As far as I can tell, every woman in the world except me is dying to get married. If the man is ugly as a warthog, I'll still find someone for him."

"But what if *he* doesn't want to marry *her*?"

Temperance rolled her eyes in exasperation. "Mother, have you learned nothing from living with me? Marriage is for men. Married men live longer because they have everything given to them. And all men are susceptible to a pretty face and a trim ankle. Besides, I'll leave that part of this assignment to you."

"Me?" Melanie dropped the silk stockings she was holding.

"Yes. You're good at this. Didn't you try to match me with every eligible man in four states?"

As she bent to pick up the stockings, Melanie sighed. "Yes, but look what a good job I did. You liked none of the men I introduced you to."

"True. But that still didn't stop you, did it? So now's your chance. Send me some pretty young ladies. Not too smart, though. It's my experience that men don't like smart women. And no education. Except for painting and singing, that sort of thing. Yes, send me a few of them and I'll see that he marries one."

"How can you be so sure this man wants that type of wife?"

"Mother, I've seen— Never mind all I've seen, but men marry one type of woman. She's—" Abruptly, Temperance cut off her words, then gave a guilty look at her mother.

"Like me, dear? Pretty? Helpless? Needy?"

"Mother, you're a darling and I love you very much. It's just that marriage—"

"Isn't for you. I know, dear. You've certainly told me often enough. And I know that saving people is a worthy cause, but as you get older it's nice to have someone to come home to. Temperance, dearest, I know what I'm talking about. I was married for sixteen years, alone for fifteen, and now I'm married again, and I can assure you that married is better. You don't want to remain alone forever if—"

"Alone? Mother, you've never been alone. You had Father for sixteen glorious years, and since then you've had me. Haven't I been a dutiful daughter? I've never left you, have I?"

Melanie gave a sigh. "No, dear, you've never left me. But—"

"But what?" Temperance said with some agitation in her voice and no little hurt. Then she calmed herself and said more softly. "But what?"

"Temperance, you're so strong, so sure of yourself. You're so like your father, so...so perfect, that sometimes I wish you were just a little more human."

"Human? I'm not human?" Temperance was stunned. "Isn't what I've dedicated my life to very human? I can assure you that—" She stopped. "You have one of your headaches, don't you? Lie down and I'll call Marie."

"Yes, dear, you do that. And please call Angus."

"Him? No, I'll stay with you. We can finish our discussion and—"

"Please." With her hand to her head, Melanie staggered to the fainting couch on the far side of the room and had to push half a dozen dresses aside to make room for herself. "Just Angus. Just my husband."

With a grimace, Temperance left the room. It hurt to have lost her mother so completely.

Four

⚜

"I hate him. I hate him. I hate him more," Temperance said as she brushed a wet strand of hair out of her eyes. "I hate him more now. I will hate him more tomorrow."

With each declaration, she lifted a foot and set it back down in the mud, then she had to pull up on her leg with all her might to keep the sucking mud from pulling her down again as she made another step forward. The spines of her umbrella had broken within minutes of her leaving the village, and now she used it as a crutch to balance on.

"I hate him with all my might," she said, then pulled up a foot. "I hate him with the might of my...*ancestors!*" She said the last word with force as she leaned on the umbrella staff, then wrenched her left foot out of the ankle-deep mud.

It was late at night and she was alone on a deserted muddy track that some man at the post office had told her was called a road. The thing didn't deserve such an accolade.

"I hate him into eternity," Temperance said, then pulled up her right foot.

All the people at the post office had been driven into hilarity when Temperance asked them about transportation to the McCairn estate.

"McCairn?" the man behind the counter had said. "'Estate,' is it?"

If the corner of his mouth hadn't been twitching, Temperance would have thought she was in the wrong place. But wasn't this James McCairn supposed to be the laird of a clan? Temperance didn't know too much about Scottish history, but wasn't that something important?

But, based on the amusement of the postmaster and the four other men in the store, Temperance was saying something that was mightily funny to them.

"This is Midleigh, Scotland, isn't it? The driver didn't let me off at the wrong place, did he?"

"Oh, aye, this is Midleigh and ye're in Scotland, but..." His secret joke so overcame him that he had to turn away for a moment.

Temperance was cold and hungry and angry. The last twenty-four hours of her life had been hell. Up until the very moment that her mother saw her off in the heavily laden coach, Temperance had not believed that this was happening to her. She thought that her mother would suddenly find her spine and say, "No, Angus, what you are doing to my beloved daughter is *wrong* and the three of us will return to New York *now!*"

But nothing close to those words came from her mother's mouth. Instead, Melanie seemed to gain strength as the day of her daughter's departure drew nearer. For the first six months of their stay in her new husband's homeland, Melanie had hidden in a darkened room and taken headache powders four times a day. But during the two weeks before her daughter's departure, the woman had been a dynamo of energy. She'd organized the packing of Temperance's bags as though she were sending her daughter off to be gone, well, forever.

"I can't believe I'll need a ball gown," Temperance had said as she watched her mother clean out a wardrobe. "I'll be gone only a few weeks."

"One never knows," Melanie had said cheerfully. "Remember that Angus's nephew *is* the laird of a clan and he does live in a castle, so I'm sure there will be wonderful parties. And now don't forget, dear, that I can send you anything you need. Except money. Mr. McCairn has forbidden me that, but anything else you need, just let me know and I'll send it."

"You can send me what my money can *buy*, but you can't send me my money. Is that correct?" Temperance had said.

"You know, dear, I feel one of my headaches coming on. Perhaps you could—"

"Fetch your husband?" Temperance said, but her mother didn't seem to hear the hurt or bitterness in her daughter's voice.

For her part, Temperance had spent the two weeks before departure discontinuing her meetings, telling people that she was returning to the U.S. very soon. "After a bit of a holiday,"

42

she'd said as airily as she could manage. She'd roast in hell before she told anyone that her stepfather was blackmailing her.

So eventually the horrible day when she was to leave had arrived, and even at the last moment, Temperance still expected her mother to save her. As Temperance walked down the steps and saw the coach, heavily loaded with her trunks, she felt like a prisoner walking to her execution.

But her mother hadn't saved her. In fact, Temperance hadn't seen her mother looking so cheerful in years. There was a flush on her cheeks and a tiny dimple at the corner of her lips. And that odious man, Angus McCairn, was standing beside her, his arm around his wife's plump waist, and he was grinning ear to ear.

"Write me," Melanie said to her daughter. "And don't forget that if you need anything—"

"A pardon?" Temperance said, coming as close as her pride would allow her to asking for a reprieve. There was part of her that wanted to go on her knees to Angus and beg to be allowed to stay. For all that she was a grown woman "past her prime," as Angus constantly reminded her, she had never been away from her mother except for the three to six months a year when her mother went away to "rest." But those separations didn't count, Temperance told herself. Only distance had separated them then. Now, Angus McCairn separated them.

But Melanie didn't seem aware of her

daughter's misery and acted as though she hadn't heard her. "I have a gift for you," she said happily, "but don't open it until you're on the road. Oh, my, I can't believe the time has come so soon. Well, dear, I..."

When Temperance saw tears come to her mother's eyes, she knew she had a chance, but then Angus put an arm firmly around his wife's shoulders and led her away from the carriage. "Yes, Daughter, do write us," he said over his shoulder as he led his wife into the house before she could say another word. Once inside the entrance, Melanie turned, gave a quick wave, then was pulled away, and Temperance was left alone to get into the carriage by herself.

Then, once seated with some hope still in her heart, she hurriedly opened her mother's gift. Maybe there would be a letter inside saying that Temperance didn't have to go after all. Maybe the fat little package contained steamer tickets back to New York. Or maybe—

It was a copy of Fannie Farmer's cookbook.

And at that sight, all hope left Temperance. She really was being sent away to a strange place among strangers to do an absolutely absurd job.

After a long, exhausting trip, two hours before sunset, the carriage had unloaded her and her trunks at the post office in Midleigh.

"But where's the castle where the laird lives?" she'd asked the driver as she looked around at the little thatched-roof houses.

But the driver only said that this was where he'd been told to let her off and he hadn't been paid to go so much as another mile.

Her mountain of luggage and the face of a stranger had caused what seemed to be the entire population of the small village to stop what they were doing and go stare at Temperance. And, based on the way they were gaping at her hat, current fashion had not reached Midleigh.

But, with only her pride holding her erect, Temperance had walked into the post office and asked to hire transportation to the castle of the laird of McCairn.

And that simple utterance had seemed to cause great mirth among the villagers. As soon as the words were out of Temperance's mouth, one of the men lounging against a wall had run outside, and she was sure the man was going to spread the word of the stranger's strange—and hilarious—request.

It took thirty minutes to get through to the postmaster what she wanted. The man was either stupid or having such a great time laughing at her that his brain had shut down, but, whatever his problem was, it took Temperance that long to get any directions out of him.

And by that time, Temperance's pride was the only thing holding her upright. Smirking, the man said she should stay the night in Midleigh before setting out in the morning. "And where is the nearest hotel?" Temperance had asked, and her question had caused even more laughter.

"About fifty miles down the road," the man said. "Back the way ye came."

"Ye can spend the night with me," a man behind her said.

"Or me," said another.

Temperance had braced her spine. "How far is it to the town of McCairn?" she'd asked, thinking that she'd have to barricade the door of anywhere she stayed in in Midleigh.

"Four miles," the postmaster said, "but it's too rough goin' for a lovely American lass like yourself. You should stay with me and the missus."

Maybe he was being nice and maybe Temperance should have accepted his invitation, but there was a twinkle in his eye that made her want to get away from him fast. She wondered if he even had a wife. "No, thank you," she said. "Where can I hire transportation to take me to McCairn?"

"None to be had," said the postmaster. "If Jamie didn't send someone to pick you up, then you walk."

"Walk four miles in this rain?" she'd asked, incredulous.

"I told you Americans were weak," said a woman's voice behind her. "She is good for nothin' but holdin' up them fancy clothes."

Maybe it was her pride or maybe it was the insult to her country, but Temperance picked up her small leather case and said, "If I may leave my trunks here, I think I will walk."

So that's how she had tricked herself into being up to the middle of her calves in mud in the rain and on her way to the castle of the laird of Clan McCairn. And when she arrived, she planned to give James McCairn the sharp side of her tongue. He may think she was only the new housekeeper, but even housekeepers deserved the courtesy of transportation.

She couldn't see her watch under the heavy mackintosh she wore, but she was sure that it was at least midnight when she finally saw a light ahead. The postmaster had loved telling her that if she veered off the road by so much as a yard, she'd find herself in the sea.

"Then I'll have to swim, won't I?" she'd shot back at the man, making the entire room laugh.

But now she'd made it, as, with each step she took, the light came closer. Through the driving rain and the mud that splattered her face, that single, dim light was the most welcome thing she'd seen in her life.

She was exhausted, nearly at the end of her endurance as she pulled her feet out of the sucking mud and tried to slog forward. Maybe the laird had thought his uncle had hired a carriage that would drive Temperance all the way to the castle and that's why he hadn't sent anyone to meet her.

Maybe the light she saw now was a fire. A big fire roaring in an open hearth. Maybe there was a table there and it had a bowl of warm soup on it. And bread. With butter. Freshly churned butter. And milk straight from the cow.

Temperance could hear her stomach rumble

even over the sound of the rain and the mud. There was part of her that wanted to fall facedown in the mud and remain there until someone found her or she died, and, truthfully, right now, she didn't care which one happened.

"Get hold of yourself!" she said out loud. "Think of something good."

She used all her might to try to conjure an image of their former housekeeper, Mrs. Emerson, and her room at home in New York. Temperance had spent many hours of her childhood in that cozy room, with its big fireplace and the chintz curtains. Mrs. Emerson always ate her meals alone in that room, and she often shared them with young Temperance. They used to giggle over the fact that the cook often made delicious things just for them, things that were never put on the table in the dining room, for Temperance's father had been a stickler about economy.

"So they have leftovers, while you and I get the pick of the seasons," the housekeeper used to say to Temperance, her finger over her lips in secrecy.

Temperance never told either of her parents of the lovely little extras that she shared with the housekeeper. Nor did she tell them of the hours that Mrs. Emerson spent dozing in her fat chair before the fireplace in her room. "A good staff, that's the key, my girl," Mrs. Emerson would say. She said that her talent was in hiring good people and because of that talent she had "a bit of leisure."

So now Temperance was going to be living

in the castle of the laird of a Scottish clan and she was going to spend her evenings in a cozy little sitting room like Mrs. Emerson's. And the memory of that room gave Temperance the strength to pull one foot out and put another foot in.

By the time she reached the window that held the light, Temperance was too exhausted to remember much of anything. There was a door with a heavy brass knocker in front of her, and she managed to lift her hand to it. But her fingers were so frozen that she had to hook them over the ring of the knocker rather than curl them around it.

Somehow, she managed to lift the ring and let it fall again. One, two, three times; then she waited. Nothing. She couldn't hear anything over the rain, but there didn't seem to be any noise coming from behind the door.

Slowly, she lifted her frozen hand up again and managed to bang the knocker again. One, two, three, four times.

Again she waited, but there was nothing.

She was not going to give in to tears, she told herself. She was not going to collapse. If she had to bang that knocker from now until doomsday, she would. Biting her lip to give herself strength, she raised her hand again.

But before she could touch the knocker, the door was thrown open and a man blocked her vision.

"What the hell do you want?" bellowed a voice that drowned out the rain. "Can't a man have any peace in his own house?"

Part of Temperance wanted to give in to fatigue and faint on the doorstep, but she had never been the fainting type and she wasn't going to start now. "I'm the new housekeeper," she said, but she could barely hear her own voice.

"What?!" the man shouted at her.

She hadn't much strength left, but she managed to lift her head up to look at him. The light was behind him and the rain was drizzling in her face, so she couldn't make out much except that he was big and dark. "I'm the new housekeeper," she said somewhat louder.

"The what?" he shouted.

Was the man stupid? she wondered. Had there been so much inbreeding within the clan over the centuries that the man was retarded? Maybe she could write a paper on this...

"I'm here for the job of housekeeper!" she shouted up at him, using one of her misshapen, frozen hands to wipe water off her face. "Angus McCairn sent me."

"You?" the man said, looking down at her. "You're no housekeeper. You can go back where you came from and tell Angus McCairn he can go to hell. And you can tell him that I don't care how pretty the strumpets he sends me are, I'm not marrying any of them."

With that he slammed the door in Temperance's face.

For nearly five full minutes Temperance stood there, rain running down her face, staring at the door, and utterly unable to comprehend what had just been done to her. Her mind

50

seemed to fill with a motion picture of this long, horrible day, starting very early this morning with leaving her mother. There had been a long, jolting carriage ride that had given her a couple of painful bruises; then there was that encounter at the post office. And to top it all off, a four-mile wade through mud that had tried to devour her.

And now this! She'd had a door slammed in her face by a man who *had* to be Angus McCairn's nephew. There couldn't be two men like him by coincidence. No, only breeding could produce two of those jackasses!!!

If this James McCairn thought that he was going to get rid of her that easily, he had another think coming. She raised her hand to knock again and found that her hand had thawed a bit. Anger certainly did produce warmth!

She pounded away at the door with renewed strength, but the door wasn't opened. To her right was the window where she could see the light, and she thought that if she had to, she'd break the glass and get inside the house that way.

But it was when she went to take a step that she found that her mackintosh was caught in the door. So, she thought as she tugged on the thick wool, it was either get inside or spend the rest of the night trapped in front of this door.

She grabbed the knocker with both hands and began to pound. And pound, and pound; then she pounded some more.

It was a good twenty minutes before the door was opened again.

"I told you you can go back to where—"

Temperance wasn't going to let him slam the door on her again. Slickly, she slid under his arm and into the room. The light she'd seen was no fire. There was a single candle on a rough wooden table that sat before a fireplace that looked as though it hadn't been lit since Edward I came through Scotland.

"Out!" the man said, the door still open, his arm raised as he pointed toward the black, rainy night.

Temperance had had enough!

She grabbed the curved handle of her umbrella and jammed the four-inch-long steel point into his chest. "No!" she yelled, using a voice that had been trained to carry to the back of huge auditoriums. "I am *not* going out in that godforsaken rain and mud again. So help me, if you throw me out I'll come in through the window or down a chimney. Whatever I have to do, but I'll not go out into that again." She narrowed her eyes at him. "And if you murder me, I'll *haunt* you."

As she was advancing on him, he was looking down at her in amazement. He was a big man, with shaggy hair that fell down over the back of his collar. He had dark, fierce eyes and black eyebrows that peaked in the middle in a way that made her think of the devil. The bottom half of his face was covered with a scraggly beard and mustache, but she could see that he had full lips under the hair.

The truth was, if she'd had to draw a picture of the devil, she'd have drawn this man. He was handsome but in a way that looked wicked.

But with the way Temperance was feeling, she was ready to take on the devil himself.

"I don't know what you have in that small mind of yours," she said, "but I am here for a job and nothing more."

Suddenly something in her snapped and she was back in New York in a tenement and she *was* one of the many women whose tragic stories she'd listened to and tried to change.

"You think I'm too *pretty* for this job? Is that what you think?" She was pushing at him with the umbrella, and she knew he could have taken it from her, but he didn't. Instead he watched her with the fascination of a cobra following a flute.

"But it's this pretty face that has caused me all my problems from…from you…men!" She spat the word at him, and as she pushed, he backed up. "I hate you. All of you for the things you've done to me. I have a husband, but do you know where he is? No, of course you don't. Nor do I. He left me alone with three children to feed. We were thrown out of our apartment and all my children died of scarlet fever, one right after another. I prayed to go with them, but I was left on this earth for what purpose I don't know.

"So your uncle Angus married a rich American woman and he told her he had a job in Scotland for me, so I returned with them to this cold wet island that no one would want if you tried to sell it, and I had to walk four bloody miles in mud nearly up to my knees, and now I get here and I'm told I'm too damned pretty for your bleedin' job."

He was still watching her, listening to her, and backing up when she pushed at him with the umbrella. When she gave one great push, the back of his knees hit a chair and he sat down hard, still watching her in fascination.

"Let me tell you something," Temperance said, bending over him. "I don't want to marry you, and I can't see why anyone would want to marry you and live in this cold place, but I happen to *be* married already—although if I ever saw the worthless, philandering imbecile again, I can assure you that I'd soon be a widow—so, now, do you need a house-keeper or not?"

For a moment the man just looked at her wet face without saying a word. "Uncle Angus sent you, but you don't want to marry me?" he said in a tone that said that he couldn't believe this fact.

She blinked at him. "You're a bit slow, aren't you?"

At that one side of the man's lips curved upward in what Temperance thought was maybe a smile. "You're not like what my uncle usually sends me." He ran his hand over his beard and looked at her as though he were considering the matter. Now that he was sitting and she was standing, their eyes were on a level with each other.

While she waited for him to make up his mind, Temperance took off what had once been a very nice hat and wrung it out onto the stone floor. Now that she was beginning to look around, she could see that the room was filthy. Cobwebs hung from the ceiling. The table had dried food on it that had hardened into lumps that would take a hammer and chisel to remove. She wasn't worried about the water that was puddling on the floor around her feet because it could only help to wash the place.

When she looked back at the man, he was looking her up and down. She'd seen that look before. "Mr. McCairn—you are James McCairn, are you not?"

The man nodded, still silently looking at her in speculation.

"I need a job, and you obviously need someone to...to..." She looked around the room. What could she say? He needed someone to... "The Aegean stables were cleaner than this," she muttered.

"And you are Hercules?" he asked.

She turned back to him, her face showing surprise since he'd understood her reference to a Greek legend.

Abruptly, he stood up, then turned his back on her. "All right," he said over his shoulder. "Breakfast is at four. But if you make one attempt to marry me, I'll throw you out on your delicate little ear. Hear me, Mrs. Hercules?"

Temperance wasn't given time to answer because he disappeared through a door at the far end of the room.

When she was alone, it was as though all her courage left her and Temperance sat down on the hard wooden chair that he had sat on and put her head in her hands. She didn't know what had made her act as she had and certainly not what had made her lie like that. In her years of working with destitute women, she'd heard one woman after another say that she'd been driven to lie, to steal, or into prostitution. In what she now realized was a very superior manner, Temperance had always told the women that there were alternatives.

But today, in just one day of cold and hunger, when she had been faced with the prospect of spending the whole night in the rain, she had easily formed a lie that would get her a warm bed for the night.

As she thought that, a shiver went through her body. Now that she was "safe," so to speak, and no longer had rage coursing through her veins, she was cold. She looked at the candle on the table. Where was the house-keeper's room? For that matter, where was the kitchen so she could get something hot to eat before bed?

Quickly, she jumped up and went through the door where the man had gone, but she was in a dark hallway, facing a staircase that looked as though it had... Now she was seeing things. The staircase looked to be littered with bones.

Going back into the room with the table, she picked up the candle and started to make her way through the house in search of a warm bed.

Five

"Mmmmm," was all Temperance could say as she snuggled against the warmth. Even half asleep, she could smell that the sheets needed changing, but the bed was soft and warm and she was oh so tired. Last night the single stub of a candle had burned out before she could find her way around the house, so she had ended by feeling her way along cold plastered walls until she came to a door.

After several tries, she'd given up on finding a kitchen with a cheery fire banked for the night and so much as a piece of cheese for dinner. Instead, she'd turned and gone up the stairs toward what she assumed were bedrooms, and when she'd touched a mattress, she'd stripped off her wet clothes down to her combs, her combination garment, and climbed under a coverlet that must have had a six-inch loft. Within seconds she was asleep.

But now, it was dark in the room, and she was too sleep befuddled to open her eyes, but there was something...

Someone was holding her, holding her in a way she'd never been held before, and against her cheek she could feel the warmth of another human being. Mother, she thought, then snuggled closer. But a hand ran over her body, down the back of her. With her eyes still closed, she moved even closer.

"I like this part of your job," came a soft, low voice in her ear, and Temperance smiled in her half sleep as the hand ran over her hip and down her thigh.

There was a bare shoulder under her cheek, and she felt the texture of warm skin under her lips; then she moved her leg so it was between two large, heavy thighs that drew her closer still.

"Yes," she whispered as the hand moved from the back of her body to the front. Her combinations had an opening that extended from just below the waist in the front to the waist at her back; the hand found this opening and moved inside, over her bare hip.

It was when the man moved on top of her that Temperance awoke fully. The unaccustomed weight of a man on her made her eyes fly open, and she looked up...

Only she could see nothing. There was no light within the room, no light outside, and all she could see was blackness. But she could feel that a man, a very large man, was in the bed with her and was now—

Temperance let out a scream that made the doves, sleeping on the roof, awake with a start. Then she started fighting with all her might, hitting out with her fists, kicking, and screaming all the while. It's what she'd been taught when she'd once attended a six-course session on how women of virtue could defend their honor. Temperance had felt she needed what the male instructor could teach, since she was often in places where men did not conduct themselves with propriety.

"Bloody hell," she heard the man say as he rolled off of her and she was free of him. Within seconds he had found a match and lit a lantern by the bed.

James McCairn was leaning over her, and he didn't have a stitch of clothing on.

"What do you think you're doing?" she demanded, pulling the coverlet up to her neck, and there was real fear in her eyes. She knew what men could do to women. Hadn't she seen broken noses? Broken arms? Hadn't she heard tales of—

"Me?!" he shouted. "You are in *my* bed. Lord, woman, but I think you've broken my rib. What possessed you to come at me like that? And after you'd made the invitation?"

Right away Temperance saw that everything was her own fault. Obviously, last night she'd been too tired to check if the bed already had an occupant. So now, should she apologize? Grovel even? Somehow, she doubted that any etiquette book covered this specific situation. Better to brazen this out, she thought.

"Would you please put on some clothing?" she said, with her chin up and her eyes averted.

So that was lust, she thought as she stared at the faded wallpaper on the opposite side of the room. That's what women were talking about when they said they "couldn't help themselves," that they "forgot" everything else when a man took them in his arms.

And that's how women ended up poor and alone and with three children to feed, Temperance thought.

She could feel that he wasn't moving, but she still couldn't look at him. He seemed to be waiting for her to speak.

"You want to tell me what you were doing in my bed?" he asked. "If you aren't looking for a new husband, then why—"

That did it! Naked or not, she turned to glare at him. "I made a mistake, that's all. A simple mistake. I was tired, hungry—am still hungry—and the candle went out and I groped my way down the hall to the first bed I found and I got into it. Could you please tell me what makes you believe that every woman wants to *marry* you?"

He still stared down at her, still made no attempt to put on clothes. "Do you swear that you didn't come here to try to persuade me to marry you?"

"I told you that I already have a husband," she said, the lie making her throat swell up so she wouldn't have been able to swallow if she'd tried.

"*Hmph!*" he said and she couldn't tell if he meant that he did or didn't believe her.

She was trying not to look at his nude body, but he was beautiful, like a Greek statue from the museum come to life. He had broad, muscular shoulders, a wide chest that was molded with muscles. Whatever this man did all day, it wasn't sitting behind a desk writing letters.

"I can assure you that I do not want to marry you," she said, pulling her eyes away from him. She was finding it impossible to keep her eyes on his and not look downward. Her previous visions of the male member had been on children and those statues at the museum. Her mother had not wanted her to see those statues.

He stood there a moment longer, looking at her; then he turned and pulled a tartan garment from the back of a chair.

Temperance tried with all her might to keep her eyes averted, but she couldn't resist looking at the back of him. His massive, muscular back tapered down to a slim waist and buttocks that were hard and firm and round. She'd once heard a woman say about her lover that you could "bend a nail on his bum"; then the other female listeners had laughed raucously. At the time, Temperance had put her nose in the air and walked away. Thoughts like that were what got a woman into trouble in the first place.

But now she could see what the woman meant.

He fastened a thick kilt over his hips, and Temperance blinked a couple of times at the realization that he wore no undergarment under the kilt. A big cotton shirt was pulled on over his head, and as he began to tie the cuffs, he turned back to her.

"Then why did my uncle send *you?*" he

asked, but as Temperance opened her mouth, he held up his hand. "I know you're an American, and I know that you think we're backward Scotsmen, but please, for all that we have a country no one would want, according to you, some of us do have a bit of a brain. You're no housekeeper. You have the hands of a lady."

He looked up from the tie on his cuff, and his voice lowered. "And you've not had three children. Not with that flat belly."

Temperance had no idea that a person's entire body could blush, but hers did. She turned red from her toes to her hairline. For a moment she looked away to give herself time to recover. Fast! she thought. She had to come up with an answer very fast. If she told him the truth, he'd send her away; then Angus McCairn would make her live forever in Edinburgh and she'd never see New York again.

She turned back to James McCairn, standing beside the bed wearing the big shirt, open at the throat and showing muscles and hair. He had looped a wide leather belt about his waist, fastening it with a heavy silver belt buckle that she was willing to bet hadn't been made in this century.

At the thought of Agnes, Temperance had an idea. "I was a lady," she said softly, looking down at her hands, "but I..."

"You what?" James snapped. "I haven't got all day."

"I ran off with a man and my father disinherited me; then when the man found out about my father—"

62

"He skedaddled. Right. You poor fool of a woman."

Temperance had to bite her tongue to keep from setting him straight on that one. No man had ever come close to making her forget that she had a purpose in life, a purpose that she meant to get back to no matter what she had to do!

She swallowed, then took a breath. It was difficult for her to try to look helpless. "Your uncle's new wife helps women in my situation, so she—"

"Ah, a do-gooder. I wouldn't have thought that Angus would be attracted to such a woman," James said thoughtfully as he reached for a heavy sweater from the chair. "Angus likes women who are sweet and gentle, not those half-male kind that can't keep their minds on their own business."

Temperance thought she might choke.

"Go on explaining!" he ordered. "Or do you want me to send you back to him?"

Temperance gave a shiver that was genuine. Anything but that! "Your uncle has given me six months to bring order into your life. If I don't succeed, then he'll send me back to New York to fend for myself."

"I see. With no man to care for you. That's not a life for a lady, is it?"

There was almost sympathy in his voice, and maybe she should have been grateful, but she wanted to scream that she was nearly thirty years old and she had never had a man "take care of her" and that all she needed was her own money.

As James pulled the sweater on and as his head popped through the opening, he said, "You know, of course, don't you, that Uncle Angus means for you to marry me?"

"No," Temperance said with her teeth clenched. "I know no such thing. Would you mind, if it's not too much bother to you, could you please tell me why you think that any woman who speaks to you, even if it's to apply for a job, is out to marry you? Are you so very great a catch?"

At that James sat down on the bed at her feet, but not in a sexual way, in a chummy sort of way, as though they were two friends having tea and a chat.

"No, I'm not, and there's the mystery of it. Oh, aye, I'm a fine-looking man, there's no denying that, and I can give a woman a lusty time in bed. And she'd have fine sons from me too, what with all my ancestors and all, but..."

Temperance was blinking at him. The man's vanity was fascinating. "With such a pedigree, what could be wrong with you?"

He gave her a sharp look to see if she was making fun of him, but Temperance, still sitting on the bed, the coverlet now just covering her breasts, gave him a sweet smile of encouragement.

"The life here is too hard for city women. They can't take it. They're too soft. I wear them out. Oh, not what you're thinking, in bed where it's good to wear a woman out, but out there." He pointed toward the curtained window. "It's lonely here, and only the strongest of women can take it."

Temperance let go of the coverlet and leaned toward him. "Surely you can find a woman who'd like to be married to the laird of a clan and live—"

At that James snorted in derision and got off the bed. "Is that the romantic nonsense that my uncle filled you with? Oh, aye, I'm the laird all right, but Clan McCairn is the smallest and the poorest in all of Scotland. Do you know how I got this body?"

Temperance's eyes widened. The man seemed to have no sense of what was proper and what wasn't. But then, they were alone in his bedroom and she was under the covers in just her underwear and... All in all, she thought she'd better not look at the circumstances too closely. "How?" she asked.

"I'm a sheepherder. And I drive cattle. I muck out barns, and I repair roofs. I go out fishing with the men and we sell our catch."

"But I thought you had a castle, and this house seems to be huge."

"Castle! It's a ruin on the hill. We use the stone to repair the houses in the village. And as for this house, my great-grandfather built it." He narrowed his eyes at her. "He married a pretty little thing that wanted the comforts of London, so he tried to give them to her and he built her a house that cost too much."

"So now you hate all women," Temperance said with such sarcasm that her mouth turned downward.

"Oh, no," James said, wide-eyed. "I love them too much, but as I've told you, they can't take the life here. Too hard for them. Now, I've no more time to explain my life to you. I think you should go back to my uncle and tell him you'd rather return to New York and take your chances. We have no jobs for ladies here."

Temperance didn't move. "I somehow doubt that life here is more difficult than life in a New York tenement. If you don't mind, I think I'll remain here."

"Suit yourself," James said as he walked toward the door, then turned back, his hand on the latch. "Do you mean to sleep with me every night?"

"Certainly not!"

"Ah, pity," he said, then left the room.

For several moments Temperance sat there blinking. "What an extraordinary encounter," she said aloud, then got out of bed. And the only thing she had to put on were the still-damp garments she'd worn the day before.

Six

By two o'clock in the afternoon, Temperance was ready to admit defeat. She was sure she could clean up the tenements of New

York City, but the household of James McCairn was already defeating her.

The house was large, with many bedrooms and four reception rooms, and Temperance could tell that when the place was built, it had been beautiful. There was evidence of plaster ceilings, hand-painted silk wallpapers, inlaid floors. There were lighter places on the walls where she was sure paintings had once hung. Dents in the floors showed where furniture had once stood.

But now the house was a filthy wreck. Cobwebs hung everywhere, mold crept up the once-beautiful wallpapers, animals had eaten holes in the floors. Four of the bedrooms had holes in the ceiling from the roof, and the rooms were full of pigeons and, in one room, chickens. What furniture there was, was grimy and damaged.

But there wasn't much furniture. In fact, there wasn't much of anything in any of the rooms. And it didn't take great skills of deduction to figure out that what had been in the rooms had been sold to pay debts.

"Even the rich can be poor," Temperance muttered as she closed the door of a bedroom where half a dozen hens were sitting on their nests. After seeing the state of the house, she had great sympathy for James McCairn and his attempt to remain living in the wreck of the house.

She still hadn't had anything to eat since the day before, so she went in search of the kitchen and the cook, but when she opened a door she found herself in a courtyard—and it was as though she'd stepped from hell into heaven. In contrast to the filth and neglect of the house, the courtyard was clean and beautiful. The paving stones sparkled as though they had just been washed, and there wasn't a weed to be seen.

Frowning in puzzlement, Temperance walked the short distance to what looked like a stables and peered inside. What she saw made her blink. Under a long slated roof were six horses, and although Temperance didn't know more about horses than that they pulled carriages, she could see that, while two of the horses were for work, the other four were for something else. The four animals were divinely beautiful: sleek, glossy, radiant with health.

In the hour and a half that she'd spent wandering through the house, she hadn't seen another person, but here she saw three men and a tall, half-grown boy, each busy at the tasks of polishing a harness, cleaning an empty stall. One man was throwing buckets of clean water on the already clean stones. The boy was feeding apples to one of the horses.

Not one of the people looked up at Temperance, or seemed to show any interest in her.

"Excuse me," she said, but none of the men looked up. "Excuse me," she said louder, and the boy turned to look at her. One of the men glanced up from the harness, then spit before he went back to his work.

Temperance walked toward the boy. "I'm

the new housekeeper, and—" She stopped because one of the men gave a derogatory sound that made Temperance turn toward him.

"I beg your pardon," she said. "Did you have something to say to me?"

The man glanced up at her with a half smirk on his face. "Housekeeper," he said. "The new one."

Had Temperance been younger and less experienced, the man's attitude would have made her turn away, but she'd dealt with hostile men for years. She moved to stand in front of him, and with her hands on her hips, she glared at the top of his head. "If you have something to say, I'd like for you to say it to my face."

The man looked up at her, a smirk on his face, and he opened his mouth to speak, but the boy put himself between Temperance and the man.

"We've had a few housekeepers," the boy said quickly, "and they don't last long. McCairn throws them out."

"Or they run away," the man said from behind the boy.

This startled Temperance as she had been under the impression that she was the first woman to be offered the job since the former housekeeper had died. Ignoring the man behind the boy and the other men, who had now stopped working to look at her, she said, "How long ago did the other housekeeper die? The older woman? And how many have been here since then?"

For a moment the boy blinked at her without saying a word. He was a handsome child, and for all that he was nearly as tall as Temperance, she didn't think he was much older than about twelve. Obviously, *he* was being fed.

"Six," the boy said at last; but when the other men snickered, he blushed a bit and said, "More like a dozen." He seemed to offer the words in apology.

"A dozen women have tried this and failed?" Temperance asked, eyes wide. She wasn't going to say so, but no wonder the men in the stable yard paid no attention to her. They probably thought she'd be gone by evening.

"And what made them fail?" she asked, the anger that had risen in her now gone as she looked around the boy to the men and waited for an answer.

"The McCairn," one of the men said.

Temperance looked at the man with a shovel full of horse manure. "Aye, the McCairn," the man said.

The third man just nodded, then swished the water on the stones with a wide broom.

Temperance looked back at the boy. "The McCairn," the boy said with a bit of a sigh, as though in resignation.

"I see," she said, but she saw nothing, and, suddenly, she felt that she should defend her entire race. "This morning Mr. McCairn told me that the women he met were too soft, that the life here for them is too hard. I think I should say that I'm not a soft woman, that I've seen and done—"

She cut herself off because the men were laughing at her. At first they had just exchanged smiles with each other, as though they knew something that she didn't; then they put down their shovels and brooms and harness, and flat out *laughed* at her.

Temperance's anger returned. Since the boy was the only one who wasn't debilitated with laughter, she turned to him, her brows raised in question. But the boy couldn't seem to say anything either. All he could do was shrug his shoulders and say, "McCairn," and that seemed to be all the answer there was.

With her hands made into fists at her side, Temperance turned on her heel and went back inside the house. And when she flung open a small wooden door, she found herself in what had once been a magnificent kitchen; but, now, like the rest of the house, it was dirty and empty.

Pulling out a scuffed wooden chair from the big table that sat in the middle of the room, Temperance collapsed on it. There was nothing like extreme physical discomfort to make a person want to give up. She hadn't had anything to eat in nearly twenty-four hours, and her clothes were wet and cold, and the people here were set on laughing at her for no reason at all.

Hearing a sound, she looked up to see an old woman shuffle into the kitchen. Her gray hair and skin were so pale and the long plaid skirt she was wearing was so old and faded that for a moment Temperance thought she was

71

seeing a ghost. A house like this could have any number of ghosts and no one would notice, she thought. But then, Temperance doubted if even ghosts would want to live in this dirty, crumbling heap.

"Are you real?" Temperance heard herself whisper as the woman approached.

At that the woman let out a cackle of laughter that could have cracked crystal. Not that there was any crystal in the house, and certainly not in that cold kitchen.

"Oh, aye, I'm real," the woman said. "So you've seen the house, so I guess you'll be leavin' us now. Aleck will take you back to Midleigh. There'll be a coach come by in a day or two."

And do what? Temperance thought. Live with my stepfather forever? Continue to pester him with meetings that I despise? If she had to listen to another brainless woman discuss the merits of Mr. Dickens's works, she'd go mad.

Temperance made herself stand. "No, I'm not leaving. The place is horrible, but with the staff's help, we can do something with it. I'll need—"

"No staff."

"I beg your pardon?"

"There's no staff," the old woman said louder. "Just you and me and Eppie."

"And Eppie is?"

"My older sister."

Temperance sat back down on the chair. "*Older* sister?" she whispered, looking at the woman. There were rocks that were younger than the woman standing before her.

How was she expected to persuade a respectable young woman to marry Mr. McCairn if he lived in a house like this one? If a woman had any choice at all, she'd run away from this mess.

But then, there was Mr. McCairn himself, Temperance suddenly thought. For all that there seemed to be some joke among the men, he was, as he described himself, beautiful to look at. Surely, a woman might fall for his appearance and overlook the house.

All Temperance had to do was get enough of the house cleaned up that she could invite a woman to a nice dinner, then let Mr. McCairn charm her.

If he didn't think she wanted to marry him, that is.

Temperance looked back at the old woman standing before her. "Where is the cook?"

"Buried these last seven months," the woman said, and seemed to be delighted at the joke.

"All right," Temperance said as she stood up, "we'll just have to get the men in here to help us. They'll—"

"No, the men work on the horses. No men help in the house. McCairn's orders. He don't want to waste time on the house."

"I could have guessed that. But it's unlimited money on the horses, is it?"

"Oh, aye, anything for his horses."

The old woman's eyes were twinkling, and

she was enjoying Temperance's misery. "Aleck'll take you back to the city," she offered again.

For a moment Temperance looked about the kitchen. There was a huge old-fashioned fire-place, big enough to roast an elk whole, but from the look of the bird droppings on the hearth, it was now a pigeon roost. The floor hadn't been cleaned since the house was built, and the table had three tarnished copper pans tied to it by inch-thick spiderwebs. Temperance really hoped she never saw the spider that could weave such a web.

"Where does he eat?" she asked, looking back at the woman.

"With Grace."

Temperance didn't understand. "With prayers?"

Again the old woman cackled. "No, Grace. His light-skirt."

"His...? Oh. I see," Temperance said, then turned her red face away, but she could feel the old woman laughing at her. No wonder the man didn't want to marry. Why bother if he already had everything that a man needed from a woman?

Taking a deep breath, Temperance turned back to the woman. She'd better stop looking on the negative. First, she had to identify the problem, she thought. Better to sort out things now. "Let me see if I understand this. To take care of this whole enormous house, there are just the two of you, but the horses have three men and a boy to take care of them. Is that correct?"

"Well...young Ramsey isn't exactly..."

"Yes, yes," Temperance said, still looking about the horrible kitchen. At that moment she could quite cheerfully have *killed* the man her mother had married. "The boy is too young to be considered of any real use, but we can get him to polish things and maybe he's small enough to be a chimney sweep."

Temperance's head came up as she had an idea. "If the stablemen can't be used to clean, can the boy be sent to deliver messages? Does he have that freedom? Do you think I could get permission from his father to, say, ride one of those horses? I can't imagine that Mr. McCairn can give four horses enough exercise."

The woman was looking at her with dark eyes that told Temperance nothing, but she seemed to be saying that this was a new request. None of the other housekeepers had asked such a question.

"Young Ramsey has permission to exercise the horses," the old woman said, looking at Temperance in speculation. "What do ye have in mind?"

Temperance opened her mouth to answer but closed it. It was better that she didn't confide in anyone. No, she was going to tell her mother the truth about the situation that that horrid man she'd married had put her in. Surely, if she told her mother the truth, Melanie O'Neil would get her out of here.

"I need pen and paper," she said to the old woman, and when she just stood there, Temperance raised one eyebrow. "Pen and paper," she said again, not any louder, but in a tone that made the old woman turn and leave the room.

Thirty minutes later she returned, and put a thick stack of old, but excellent quality, writing paper, a cut-glass inkwell, and, heaven help her, a quill pen in front of Temperance on the big kitchen table.

For a moment, Temperance could only look at the quill pen. A feather? she thought. A *feather?* It was the twentieth century and she was supposed to write a letter with a feather?

With a sigh, Temperance picked up the pen, then told the woman to find something for her to eat. "Anything," she said over her shoulder.

Dear Mother,

This is an impossible situation, she began; then slowly, as writing with a blunt-ended feather was not something one could do quickly, she described in detail what she had been put into.

This is not something I am good at, she wrote. *I think someone else would be better qualified.*

Temperance put her twenty-nine years of training into that letter to her mother, using everything she could think of to persuade her that Melanie had to get her daughter out of the country. Guilt, tears, pleas, were things she used on her mother.

In conclusion, Temperance wrote on page twenty, *it is my firm belief that you* must *send me the money to return home.*

Yours in love, your only child, who loves you so very much,
Temperance.

She sealed the letter with old-fashioned sealing wax and a heavy brass seal, then gave the letter to young Ramsey and asked him to deliver it to her mother in Edinburgh as fast as possible.

❧◈◈❧

Temperance had to admit that the horses were fast. And the boy, Ramsey, was no shirker. Within twenty-four hours, Temperance had an answer from her mother.

With hands that shook from anticipated relief, Temperance opened her mother's letter.

My dearest daughter,
Use the cookbook I sent with you. Men will do anything for a decent meal. I am sending you a quarter of a cow, half a hog, and some other things. The men don't eat until they have worked all day for you.
With much love,
your mother.

Out of the letter fell a steel pen.

Seven

Four days, Temperance thought as she dipped the mop into the bucket. For the most horrible four days of her life, she had cleaned and scrubbed until her hands were raw and cracked.

"You want somethin' powerful bad, don't you?" the maid, Grissel, said at the end of the first day, after she'd watched Temperance attack the kitchen with, first, broom, then mop, then a knife when ancient encrustations wouldn't come off.

Temperance didn't say anything to anyone except to give orders. Her one and only goal was to get *out* of this horrible place and away from these people, whom she did not like. The men in the stable yard smirked at her as though she were the biggest joke they had ever seen. The two ancient maids stood back and watched her as though she were there for their entertainment.

But no matter what Temperance said, no one made any effort to help her clean up the filthy old house.

As for James McCairn, she hadn't seen him since the morning she awoke in his bed.

"Maybe he's with Grace," said one of the maids with a shrug, as though it meant nothing.

For all that Temperance had spent her adult life working with distressed women, she couldn't help being shocked at this open sinning. Wasn't the countryside supposed to be full of wholesome people who believed in right and wrong?

And what about this poor woman, Grace, who had been forced into being the man's mistress? What misfortunes had befallen her that she had to take this way out?

On the second day that Temperance was in the house of James McCairn, the wagonload of goods arrived from her mother, and with it the trunks full of her clothes. Temperance had never felt such joy in her life as when she saw those trunks, for she'd been wearing her never-dry traveling clothes since she'd arrived. There were also three huge wooden tubs full of melting ice, and inside were parcels wrapped in cheesecloth and paper. There were two crates full of vegetables and fruits, even a few bottles of wine.

Of course all the people who "worked" at the McCairn house gathered around when the wagon arrived and peered inside in curiosity.

"Is that beef?" asked a man she now knew was named Aleck, his tone casual, as though he didn't care what was in the wagon.

Temperance was already tired and fed up, and she had no courtesy left inside her. "You want some, you help me," she said in a tone that would take no argument.

In the next second, she was brushed aside as the three stablemen began to pull the big parcels from the tubs of ice. But when the men left her trunks in the wagon, she stood there with her hands on her hips and glared at the back of them so hard that they turned around.

Manus pulled a heavy trunk to the edge of the wagon, then bent and slid it onto his back. "Where you want it?" he said to Temperance.

"She's stayin' in the queen's bedroom," old Eppie said, amusement in her voice.

At that Temperance looked aghast. That horrid old room she'd found after that first night was the *queen's* bedroom? What queen? she wondered. Which century?

The other men took the remaining trunks inside, then carried them up the stairs to the dirty bedroom that Temperance had made her own. There was an empty room off the kitchen that Grissel called the housekeeper's room, but Temperance refused to stay in there with the broken window and absence of furniture. So she'd found a room upstairs that had an old four-poster bed, and she'd fallen into it at night, too tired to care whether it was clean or not.

"Only four of the others stayed this long," Ramsey said softly to Temperance after the others had entered the house.

"Four other what?" she asked.

"Housekeepers," the boy said. He was as tall as Temperance, so she looked him directly in the eyes. "Most of 'em left after the first day. When will *you* leave?"

"When I finish my job," she said quickly, then clamped her lips shut.

"Ah...." the boy said. "So you *do* have a reason for being here. Do you want to—"

"So help me, if you ask me if I want to marry McCairn, I'll deck you right here."

At that the boy smiled in such a way that Temperance knew that someday he was going to cause a lot of problems to a lot of females. She narrowed her eyes at him. "Do you think you know how to wash kitchen floors, or must there be horse manure spread on it before you Scots males will wash it?"

Ramsey lifted his hands, palms up, in surrender. "Only two housekeepers ever washed anything."

"Then it must have been years ago," she snapped at him before returning to the house.

Inside the wagon was another letter from her mother, informing her daughter that Miss Charmaine Edelsten would be arriving in two days.

She knows her role and about the secrecy, her mother wrote. *I believe you will find that she is exactly what you asked me for.*

At that Temperance had to think about what she had asked for in a wife for a man she'd never met. Ah, yes: pretty, not too smart, and little to no education. Now, looking about the place, Temperance hoped the young woman was nearsighted as well.

So for the next two days, Temperance scrubbed and cleaned and scraped as best she could. She ordered the three men, two old women, and the boy about as much as they would allow her, and she paid them with the beef her mother had sent. And it seemed that her mother was right, that the way to get a man to move was through his stomach.

Temperance thought about this as she took the sharp edge of an axe to the kitchen table to scrape off the hardened bits. Maybe when she returned to New York, she could use this knowledge to get some funding from some of the more difficult residents of the city. Or maybe she should use this technique on the straying husbands of abandoned women.

Suddenly she stopped scraping. What about cooking courses for women in the tenements? Maybe they could learn how to use what little they had to better advantage. *Mmmm,* she thought as she began scraping again.

It certainly was odd that her mother had come up with this cooking idea. Temperance hadn't realized that her mother could be of help in some situations. In her eyes, since she was fourteen and her father had died, Melanie O'Neil was someone who needed to be taken care of, not the other way around.

As the day dawned that Miss Edelsten was to arrive, Temperance began to grow nervous. She'd managed to get four rooms clean: the kitchen, the entrance hall, the dining room, and one small bedroom in case the woman was to spend the night. Of course it was good that the rooms would be lit only by candlelight or she'd see the state of disrepair they were really in.

Although, Temperance had to admit, now, as she looked at the clean rooms, she was proud of what she'd accomplished, and the old house seemed prouder now that parts of it were cleaned.

Standing in the doorway of the entrance hall, Temperance ran her hand along the doorpost. Beautiful, she thought, looking at the ceiling where she could now see that cherubs peeped from around painted clouds.

"This is a house a person could love," she said softly, then shook her head to clear it. She had too much to do to think of beauty.

Now she had to get Miss Edelsten together with James McCairn and...

When it came to that part, her mind was a blank. What did she know about love? She'd never come close to feeling that "falling in love" sensation that seemed to make morons of people. Truthfully, Temperance didn't understand the feeling, and from what she'd seen of it, she had no desire to understand it.

However, get James McCairn together with his future bride, she must, and if the cooking worked with the men in the stables, why wouldn't it work with their master?

But Temperance didn't know anything about cooking, and, as far as she could ascertain, neither did the two maids; but, she thought, how hard could it be, especially since she had a set of directions? Using Miss Farmer's cookbook that her mother had given her, Temperance sat down and—using the steel pen her mother had sent her—she wrote out a menu, then had Ramsey deliver it to Mr. McCairn, wherever he was.

Cream of Watercress Soup
Fricassee of Lamb
Riced Potatoes   Stewed Tomatoes
String Bean and Radish Salad
Apple Pie

An hour later, Ramsey returned, breathless, to say that the McCairn would be here for dinner as soon as it was dark. The boy then pulled a cute little lamb from across his saddle and tossed it into her arms. "For dinner," he said, then turned the big horse he was riding and rode away.

Temperance looked at the lamb, it licked her face a couple of times, then she set it down on the clean stones in front of the stables, but it followed her into the kitchen. When the lamb looked up at her with big eyes, she poured out a bowl of milk and set it before the tiny thing.

Temperance took her copy of the menu for that night, crossed out "Fricassee of Lamb" and wrote, "Salmon with Cucumber Sauce," then called to Ramsey to find a fishing pole and bring her back a fish.

Temperance then set about figuring out how to follow a recipe.

⚜

By the time the sun set and James McCairn arrived for dinner, Temperance was in a bad temper and quite nervous. Where *was* the woman her mother was sending? she kept wondering. Had she encountered the residents of Midleigh and given up? If no woman ever showed up, then Temperance would never get a wife for McCairn, so she'd never get out of this place. She'd spend her life living with these people who thought she was a joke. Or would she have to return to Edinburgh and live under the rule of Angus McCairn?

When James entered the kitchen, slamming the door open and letting in a great draft of wind, she snapped at him. "Close that door! And why did you come in through the kitchen? Don't you know that you're the laird, so you're supposed to enter through the front door?"

"I thought you said you *weren't* applying to be my wife," he said, his voice amused.

Temperance couldn't help but laugh. She had on an apron, but she still had flour and pieces of salmon skin on her clothes. One thing was for sure: *She* wouldn't be giving cooking lessons.

For a moment James stood blinking at the kitchen as though he'd never seen the room before. There was a fire in the hearth of the huge old fireplace, and the old oak table in the middle of the room was sparkling clean and laid out with an array of pots filled with food.

"Is that the dinner I sent you?" he asked, looking at the lamb sleeping on a sheepskin at one side of the hearth.

"More or less." Temperance ducked her head so he wouldn't see her red face. What kind of housekeeper couldn't deal with slaughtering animals for the table?

The room seemed large, but when he was in it, it seemed to shrink. He was muddy and he was wearing his ratty old kilt, but maybe the woman who was coming—if she ever got here—would think his bare knees were romantic.

"Dinner will be served in the dining room," she said, turning her back on him as she picked up a tureen of soup and carried it through the door.

After setting the tureen down on the table in the dining room, she turned around to see him standing in the doorway, his big body filling it. His mouth was open in astonishment as he looked about the room.

"How'd you do this?" he asked, meaning the clean room, the silver candlesticks, the beautifully laid, clean table, the fire glowing in the grate.

"The men helped," she said brusquely as she started to go back into the kitchen, but he blocked her way.

"Why is there only one place setting? And where did you find the dishes?"

"If I told you, you wouldn't believe me," she said in exasperation.

"I have nothing else to do but listen," he said quietly, looking down at her. "And I can't eat alone. At least not fricassee of lamb."

It suddenly went through Temperance how

much she'd like to have a conversation with a person. All she'd said since she'd come to this awful place was, Get me this, Do that, Move those. And she was tired. She wanted to get off her feet and sit down for a while. And if the idiot woman ever did show up, Temperance could certainly excuse herself.

"All right," she said. "I'll join you."

"Behind the cabinet?" James asked as he finished the last of the salmon.

"I could see that the bottom wasn't as deep as the top of the cabinet, so I knew there was some hidden space. Young Ramsey used a crowbar to pull out the boards and the dishes were inside. They're Wedgwood."

"Worth anything?" he asked, picking up his bread-and-butter plate and holding it up to the light.

"Depends on the pattern and the age. These are in pristine condition, so they might bring something. Why do you think they were hidden like that?"

He took a sip of the wine that Temperance's mother had sent. "My grandmother loved to spend money." He looked away when he said it, and his lips were tight. After a moment, he looked back at her. "When I was a boy my father told us kids she'd bought things and hidden them so her husband wouldn't find them."

"I had a friend like that," Temperance said. "She was thirty-five years old and unmarried because her father had turned down eleven suitors for her hand, so she... Well, she bought things."

"You women do have a way of hurting us men," he said with some bitterness.

"Us!" Temperance nearly came out of her seat. "If you had any idea of the things I've seen, of what has been done to women by you...you, men!"

"Ha!" James said. "I can top any story you can tell me. *I* have a friend with eleven children."

Temperance waited for the punch line, but he took a bite of green bean salad and said nothing more. "Well?"

"He had an accident when we were boys. I won't give you the gory details, but he can't have children."

Temperance blinked at him; then she smiled. "Oh, I see. If he tells people the children aren't his, then he has to explain how he knows for sure. But if he lets people think they're his, he's considered a great stallion."

"It is a dilemma, isn't it?" James said, smiling back at her. "What would you do?"

"If I were the man or the woman?"

"Which do you want to be?" he shot back at her; then they laughed together.

It was at that moment that there was a pounding on the door, and it was all Temperance could do to keep from saying, "At last!" She threw down her napkin on the table. "I wonder who that could be at this hour," she said as she went running into the entrance hall and opened the door.

Standing in the doorway was one of the prettiest young women Temperance had ever seen in her life. She had a small, heart-shaped face with big blue eyes and a tiny nose set above full lips that seemed to be set in a little pout. Beautiful blonde ringlets escaped from under her turquoise blue hat that exactly matched her eyes. This lovely head was set atop a body that was short, with a tiny waist and an enormous bosom, and she couldn't possibly have been more than eighteen years old. She was exquisite, and Temperance knew that no man on earth would be able to resist her.

But then she opened that adorable little mouth and spoke.

"Oh you must be Temperance and I'm Charmaine but all my friends call me Charming because that's what I am and your step-father said that you were an old maid but you're prettier than I thought you would be even though you do have lines around your eyes but my mother said that if I never squint or laugh too much I'll never get those lines but I can tell you that my mother has them but she says that she spent a lot of her childhood laughing so that's why I never laugh at any-thing but then I don't find too many things funny and is he here because I've never met royalty before but your mother said he wasn't exactly royalty but in America where I come from but oh you come from America too don't you so is he wildly handsome and it's just too too romantic isn't it and that's why my driver had to take a hammer to the wheel on the carriage to get it to come off so it looked as though we were stuck here and what's for dinner but then the food in this country isn't very good is it but I mean that at home I can have anything I want but don't you think spring weddings are nice and do you think the king will attend and is he here?"

It took Temperance several moments to realize that the girl had indeed stopped talking. "Is the king here?" she asked.

"No," Charmaine said slowly, as though Temperance were stupid. "Him. His lordship. Lord James."

"Oh." Temperance was feeling as if her head had been emptied of everything and now there was nothing inside.

"I want to meet him and make him like me but then all men do like me and your mother said that I was exactly what he wanted or what you wanted him to have but then I'm not sure which but when I do marry him I don't want to have to live in this awful place so I wish we could go over everything before I meet him so I could know exactly—"

"Charmaine!" Temperance said so loudly that she glanced toward the door to see if James had heard her. "Let me do the talking, would you? I mean, not that you aren't—"

"Charming that's what I am and everyone says so but I'll let you do the talking because you're so much older than me so I'll pretend that you're my mother because you're very like her but you really should do something about those lines at your eyes so I'll give you some cream I have with me but at your age you really should use the salve my mother uses because she says—"

"Quiet!" Temperance hissed, then put her hand on the small of Charmaine's back and shoved her toward the dining room.

What in the world had her mother been thinking of when she sent this scatterbrained idiot? Temperance wondered. How could a man fall in love with this?

But then Temperance saw the way the girl walked, with her hips swaying beneath her teeny tiny waist, and she thought maybe, if she could just get her to keep her mouth shut, a man might like her. But, on the other hand, men always went for beauty over brains, so maybe she had nothing to worry about.

As Temperance followed Charmaine into the dining room, she glanced at a mirror hanging on the wall. The backing on the mirror had yellowed, but it was clear enough that Temperance could see the lines at the corners of her eyes that Charmaine had been going on and on about. "Bother!" she said in disgust, then hurried forward so she could enter the dining room before Charmaine did.

Temperance looked at Charmaine, put her finger to her lips, then opened the dining room door. "It looks as though we have a guest," Temperance said brightly. "May I present Miss Charmaine Edelsten? Lord James McCairn." Temperance had no idea if there was a "lord" in front of James's name, but at the moment it sounded good. "Miss Edelsten's carriage broke down and she saw the lights, so she came here. Would it be all right to offer her dinner while her man repairs her carriage?"

Temperance saw that James couldn't take his eyes off the girl, and thankfully, Charmaine was modestly looking down at her hands.

"Of course," James said cheerfully, then jumped up to pull out a chair.

He didn't pull out a chair for me, Temperance found her-self thinking, then reminded her-self that his gentlemanly behavior toward Charmaine was good. Temperance had dishes ready on the sideboard, and she was thankful that she'd found the beautiful Wedgwood dishes. However, when she opened the big covered server, she saw that there was no more salmon. She had prepared enough for more than two, and she was horrified to realize that she and James had sat there and talked and eaten *all* of the fish.

"How about some soup?" Temperance said, then ladled what was left of the cream soup into a bowl.

"And what brings you all the way out to McCairn?" James said in that teasing way that men talk to beautiful women.

Charmaine opened her mouth to speak, but Temperance said loudly, "Scenery! And history! Miss Edelsten just loves both of them, isn't that right, Miss Edelsten?"

Again, Charmaine started to speak, but James, looking at Temperance, said, "How do you know she loves history? Have you met her before?" There was suspicion in his voice.

"I never saw her before tonight," Temperance said sweetly and honestly. "But she told me all about herself while we were in the hallway."

"So, if you don't mind, let her tell *me* now." James looked back at Charmaine, and his face softened again. "Now, where were we?"

Charmaine opened her mouth to speak.

"She loves the history of the clans," Temperance said loudly. "But then, so do I. Maybe tomorrow the three of us can go walking, and you can show us where the battles took place."

James turned to look at Temperance as though she were crazy. "What battles are you talking about?"

"I thought there were battles all over Scotland. Clan against clan, that sort of thing. Didn't Bonnie Prince Charlie do something here? Wasn't the Norman Conquest near here?"

"No," James said quietly, "Bonnie Prince Charlie didn't do anything here." His voice was rising. "Nor were the Normans conquered here. In fact, Miss O'Neil"—he was nearly shouting now—"the Norman Conquest was in *England!*"

"Oh," Temperance said, but when she saw that Charmaine was about to speak, she said quickly, "I bet Miss Edelsten knew that. She's really a great history person, aren't you, Miss Edelsten?" But she didn't give Charmaine time to answer. "I think that tomorrow you, as the laird, should teach us all about whatever did happen in this part of Scotland, and—"

"Miss O'Neil," James said quietly, "if you don't let this young lady talk, I will put you on a horse and send you back to my uncle. Tonight. Do I make myself clear?"

At that Temperance took a deep breath and sat down at the table, then gave James a weak smile.

He turned back to Charmaine. "Now, Miss Edelsten, tell me about yourself."

"Oh no one calls me Miss anything because I'm Charmaine to everyone and my mother says that I'm well named because I could charm the birds out of the trees if I wanted to but I don't know if I'd want to do that because birds can be really frightening things can't they and I don't know anything about history so I don't know why Temperance made that up because I want to represent myself to you as I am because what with you being a lord and all I know you'll see right through me and I mean see through my mind that is and not my clothes and oh I made a joke but I can't laugh or I'll get lines like Temperance has and I can't do that because—"

James turned to look at Temperance for a moment, but she couldn't meet his eyes. Of course he didn't know that it was Temperance who'd asked for this young lady and that it was Temperance's mother who had sent her, but his lack of knowledge didn't clear Temperance's conscience. I'd never make a good cardplayer, she thought while looking straight ahead at the darkened windows and not looking at either person at the table.

"—and I really would like to see all of this place and especially meet this prince because I wonder what it means when you call him bonny because does he wear a bonnet but oh my I made another joke so you can see that it's sometimes difficult for me not to laugh when I have such a sense of humor and my mother says that I should write what I say down because I make so many jokes but—"

Temperance turned when James got up from the table. He's going to leave the room; she thought, but instead, he went to the window and opened it wide. It was a bit stuffy in the room, but maybe that was because she was having difficulty breathing.

"—do your servants call you lord and I was wondering that because I wondered what your wife would be called by the servants who work in the castle but then this isn't a castle is it but then I've never been in a castle that anyone lived in before but do you think they would call your wife Mrs. Lord or do you think she'd be called oh my goodness you *are* in love with me aren't you your highness but then lots of men react to me like this and—"

In openmouthed astonishment, Temperance saw James McCairn bend over and swoop Miss Charmaine Edelsten into his arms, then carry her toward the open window. To give her her due, Charmaine didn't so much as pause for breath. Maybe men picked her up every day and it was a common occurrence to her, Temperance thought.

"—but my mother says that a man can't help

falling in love with me because I'm so charming that all I have to do is open my mouth and men will love me so much so she said that I might as well become a Mrs. Lord or a Lady Lord or whatever your wife would be called because—"

James tossed Charmaine out the window with exactly the same heed that he would have given to a sack of potatoes. She landed with a surprisingly heavy thud for so small a person.

James then shut the window and pulled the heavy red damask curtains closed, making dust fly up into the room.

As though nothing had happened, he sat back down at the table and looked at Temperance, his dark eyes daring her to say anything.

"I think those curtains need to be washed, don't you?"

For a moment he turned away, and Temperance saw a tiny smile play at his lips. When he looked back at her, she said, "Do you want your pie warm or cold?"

"I want it *quiet,*" he said, and they both burst into laughter.

∾⧉∿

Dear Mother,

The charming Charmaine didn't work out. Perhaps you could send someone just as pretty but not quite so unintelligent, and maybe she should have a little *education. And it might be better if she were a bit older.*

Yours in love,
Temperance

Eight

It must have been at six the next morning that Temperance awoke with a start and thought, I should *ask* him what he wants in a wife.

It didn't seem like a thought that was going to set the world on fire, but in its small way, it was revolutionary. Her experience had been in trying to get men away from women. She dealt with men who drank away their meager earnings, leaving a wife and children destitute. She tried to find work for women who had been beaten and abused, then abandoned by the man in their life.

It had never crossed Temperance's mind to try to get a man and woman *together*.

As she dressed, she kept her eyes focused on the clothes in her trunks, refusing to look at the room. Last night she'd heard noises that sounded suspiciously like mice gnawing. She was *not* going to think of the word "rats."

At least now I can face the women in the tenements, she thought, because what was this place but a huge tenement?

She put on a wool skirt that reached only to her ankles ("Scandalous!" her mother had declared it), a long-sleeved cotton blouse, a

97

wide leather belt, and sturdy ankle boots, then went downstairs.

"So where does he spend his days?" Temperance asked as soon as she entered the kitchen. Now that she, Temperance, had cleaned the room, it was amazing how it had become a center of activity. She couldn't walk into the kitchen without finding one or both of the old women in it and, usually, at least one of the men. Ramsey had started feeding the lamb with a huge baby bottle; he'd even named it, calling it Isaac after the story in the Bible of the child who wasn't slaughtered.

Today, two women, two men, and one boy opened their mouths to answer Temperance's question.

"If one of you says the word 'Grace,' there'll be no dinner tonight."

All five of them put their heads down and closed their mouths.

Temperance silently counted to ten, then said slowly. "He said that he herds sheep and fishes. Where does he do those things?"

Five faces full of relief turned back toward her. Ramsey, sitting at the kitchen table, holding the wriggling lamb while it ate, said, "Top of the mountain. He'll be up there all day. But you can't go up there, if that's what you mean to do."

"Why not?" she asked, and dreaded hearing the answer. Since "the" McCairn, as they called him, seemed to have absolute rights in this place, did he hold orgies up there? He and Grace?

"Walkin's too tough for a city lady," Aleck said.

At that, Temperance threw up her hands in disbelief. She had never in her life met such snobs as these people. They believed that if a woman had grown up in a city, she was utterly useless.

She smiled at the lot of them. "I'm sure you're right, but if you'll point me in the right direction, I think I'll take a leisurely, citylike stroll that way. After I make something for lunch," she said.

An hour later she had filled a canvas rucksack with Cornish pasties and oranges and an earthenware bottle of watered wine. While she'd chopped meat and vegetables and rolled out dough, all the people in the kitchen had watched her with interest that they tried to hide.

At seven A.M. she said, "Ramsey, I'm ready," then put her arms through the straps of the rucksack so it rested on her back.

Somehow, she wasn't surprised to walk outside and see a big, nervous-seeming horse saddled and prancing about. Even though not one person had entered or left the kitchen, they all seemed to know everything that she did or planned to do before she did it.

Temperance thought she'd choke before she asked how they'd signaled for the horse to be ready. Instead, she waited until Ramsey mounted, then took his arm as he helped her climb on behind him; then she held on to the saddle as they rode.

Since she'd arrived in the night to this land

99

of Clan McCairn, she'd not been but a few feet outside the house, so now she looked with interest at the countryside. When Ramsey led the big, skittish horse up a narrow, rocky path that had a steep hill on one side and absolutely nothing on the left, Temperance had to fight the temptation to scream that she wanted *off!*

Ramsey must have felt her fear because he twisted about in the saddle and smiled at her. "Nothing like this in the city, is there?"

"There are a few tall buildings," she said, trying to sound as though she weren't scared half to death. One false step of the horse and they'd fall to their deaths. But even though her hands on the saddle were white-knuckled, she kept her face turned toward the solid hillside on their right and refused to allow the fear to overtake her.

"There, that's McCairn," Ramsey said softly; then, to Temperance's horror, he halted the horse.

She had to take a deep breath before she could turn and look to her left, and when she did, the beauty of what she saw overrode her fear.

Below her, spread out like a picture in a children's fairy story, was a beautiful little village. There weren't more than twenty houses, all arranged on both sides of a narrow road that meandered up toward the base of the mountain they were now on. The houses were whitewashed, with thatch roofs. Smoke twirled from out of a few chimneys; chickens wandered about in the road. She could see a few people, women carrying baskets; children played in the street.

Each house had what looked to be a garden in the back, and she could see a few barns and a couple of fenced animal enclosures.

"It's beautiful," she whispered; then she looked farther out and saw that there was only a narrow strip of land that connected this little village to the mainland. Actually, the place was little more than a mountain on what was almost an island. On one side were the village houses and on the other side was James McCairn's rotting old stone house, and in the middle was the mountain.

"It's so isolated," she said. "Do the children leave this place when they grow up?"

"Oh, aye, they do," Ramsey said as he urged the horse to move again, and there was great sadness in his voice.

"But not you?" she asked.

For some reason, this seemed to amuse the boy. "No, not me," he said as though that were a joke. "You're not like the other ones," he said after a minute.

"Can I take that as a compliment?"

In answer the boy just shrugged and urged the horse forward, and Temperance gritted her teeth as she held on to the saddle. Heaven forbid that she'd get a compliment out of these people. Never mind that they so liked the cleanliness of the kitchen that now they wouldn't leave it, but she was sure that each of them would die before saying, "Good show, old girl," or whatever they would say in Scotland.

After what seemed to be hours, they reached what looked like the top of the mountain, and the boy halted the horse.

"You have to get down here," he said as he turned to help her down. "The McCairn can't see the horse up here."

As her wobbly legs tried to hold her up on the rocky ground, she looked up at him. "Why not?"

At that the boy smiled as he reined the horse around to go back down the path. "Too dangerous for his prize horses. They could fall; then what would he race against the other lairds? We don't have much, but we win the races," the boy said; then, with a wicked glint in his eyes, he kicked the horse and tore down the steep, extremely narrow path at a speed that took Temperance's breath away.

"If he were my son, I'd..." She trailed off at that thought because how did one control a boy as big as Ramsey?

For a moment Temperance stood still as she looked about her at the meadow with its spring flowers and listened to the call of birds and smelled the fresh, pure air.

"Not like the city, is it?"

Temperance nearly jumped out of her skin at the voice behind her, then turned and saw James standing not four feet from her. With her hand to her heart to still it, she said, "No it's not like the city, but then the city has its own merits. We have the ballet and the opera and—"

James turned on his heel and walked away from her.

Temperance, tripping over rocks and clumps of grass, tried to keep up with him. "So tell me, Mr. McCairn, are all Scotsmen rude, or is it just the people on this island?"

"We're not an island. Not yet," he said over his shoulder. "And which horse did that boy use?"

"Horse?" Temperance said, not wanting to get Ramsey into trouble.

"Are you going to try to make me think you *walked* up here?"

"I don't see why all of you think—"

Halting, James turned to glare at her. There was no use trying to lie. "Big one, reddish coat, white spot on its back right leg."

After a quick nod, James started walking again, and Temperance hurried after him.

"So why did you come up here today?" he asked. "What do you want from me?"

What could she say? I want to know what kind of woman would make you ask her to marry you so I can mail-order her from my mother so I can get out of this place? Not quite.

"Oh, just bored," she said. "Thought I'd see the place."

"*Hmph!*" James snorted. "And do all you Americans think we Scots are stupid?"

"Just me hoping," she said before she thought, but when she heard his laughter, she smiled. "What do you do all day? Are you alone up here?"

At the last question, he stopped and turned to look at her, one eyebrow raised. "Is that why you came up here? To be alone with me?"

"You can only wish," she said; then he smiled and started walking again.

Following him, she walked down a little valley, then up again, and at the top she could hear sheep. When he stopped, she looked around him to see that the southern side of the mountain was covered with what looked to be hundreds of sheep. Here and there she could see a dog running about, snapping at the heels of the sheep, and there were a few men walking on the steep side of the mountain.

"Alas, we're not alone," she said, sounding very unhappy. "No ravishment today."

For a second James looked at her in astonishment, then he threw back his head and laughed so hard she could see the veins in his neck standing out. He was certainly beautiful, she thought, and if she were the kind of woman to indulge in affairs, he'd be the first one she'd run to.

Below them, two of the men heard the laughter and stopped to look up. Temperance raised her arm and waved to them, and that seemed to make them freeze.

"Bet they can't believe I'm not Grace," she said. When James said nothing to that, she turned to look at him and he was staring at her with a frown.

"They gossip too much."

"If you mean that lazy bunch of louts you have sitting around your stables and your house, about all they do is gossip. Is it legal for a laird to flog people?"

James laughed again. "You Americans,"

he said. "What ideas you have about us. Well, now that you're here, what do you plan to do?"

"Not clean anything!" she said emphatically.

"All right, then how about helping me with this?" he said as he led the way further down the path.

Behind a little hedge of bushes was lying a huge sheep and she was panting.

"Is she dying?" Temperance asked, looking up at him.

"Not if I can help it. Now you get at that end, and I'll take the business end, and we'll help her out."

It took Temperance several moments before she understood what he meant; then it dawned on her that the sheep was giving birth. "Oh," she said. "Oh. I see. Maybe we should call a veterinarian."

"Oh, aye. And he'll send us a bill. No, here it's the McCairn who's the vet. Ready? Hold her. This baby is breech, and I need to turn it."

What happened in the next hour of Temperance's life she would never have believed. When James tried to put his arm up the birth canal of the ewe, he found that there were twins inside and there wasn't room for him to get his huge arm inside.

Sitting back on his heels, he looked at Temperance. "Not enough room for me. You'll have to do it."

"Me?" Temperance said. "I can't—"

"Take off your fancy shirt so it won't get dirty and put your arm up inside her and get those lambs out. If you don't all three of them will die."

"Take off my—"

"Come on, woman, get busy. There's no one about to see you."

"There's you," Temperance said, blinking at him over the panting sheep.

"And you think I've never before seen all that a woman has?" He gave her a look of disgust. "Have it your way then. Get the blood and birth all over your shirt, but come on, girl, and *do* it."

Maybe it was the way he'd called her "girl" that made her obey him. After Charming Charmaine from last night, Temperance needed to think of herself as younger than a mother to an eighteen-year-old.

As quick as she could, Temperance unbuttoned her blouse, pulled it out of her skirt, and tossed it on top of the bushes. She had a quick thought that she was glad she'd charged so much to that odious Angus McCairn and she now had on a lovely little camisole. It was all white, but it was pin-tucked and had an exquisite little design of hand-sewn eyelet flowers all across the top.

"All right, what do I do now?" she asked as she moved toward the other end of the sheep.

It took her forty-five minutes of hard work to turn the first tiny lamb inside the ewe. And every few minutes the ewe's uterus would give a violent contraction and Temperance's arm would be squeezed so hard that tears of pain would come to her eyes.

"You're doin' well," James said softly from behind her, and she could tell that his emotions were involved in this for his accent thickened. He put his big hands on her shoulders and kneaded them while the contractions strangled her arm. "Just relax. Breathe," he said softly into her ear.

When the contraction relaxed and she could feel her arm again, he talked to her about what she was feeling inside the ewe's uterus. "Feel for the foot. There, got it now? Now pull. No, you won't hurt her. She's in too much pain now to know what you're doin'. There, good. Pull. Slow, now. There! Pull again. Harder this time."

All of a sudden the lamb popped out of the ewe and into Temperance's lap. It was wet and covered with blood and a sac of mucus, but Temperance didn't know when she'd ever seen anything so beautiful. Holding the little creature, she looked up at James in wonder.

"There's another one," he said, smiling at her. "Get it; then we clean them up and try to get the mother to nurse."

After the first lamb the second one was easy, but Temperance could feel that the contractions were much lighter now, and she looked up at James in alarm.

"Just get the lambs out. We'll worry about the mother later."

In another few minutes there was another lamb in Temperance's lap, and she watched as James grabbed handfuls of grass and tried to clean the afterbirth off the new lambs.

Without thinking what she was doing, Temperance grabbed a white cloth from off the bushes and began cleaning the second lamb.

The lamb James had, by instinct, went to its mother to nurse, but the ewe just lay there, still panting.

"She's dying," James said softly to Temperance. "Sorry for this to happen on your first one."

"My first *sheep*," Temperance said emphatically as she put her lamb next to its sibling, then put her hand onto the big ewe's stomach. "I've had to attend to the births of human women three times," she said as she put one hand over the other and began to knead the ewe's stomach. "One time the afterbirth got stuck and the midwife pushed and pushed on the woman's stomach until—"

She was working so hard that she couldn't talk anymore.

James pushed the lambs aside, then knelt beside Temperance and helped her knead. And after several moments the sheep expelled the huge afterbirth, which dropped onto the ground with a wet splat.

James and Temperance sat back and watched for a moment. The sheep seemed to stop breathing for a few moments; then she opened her eyes, moved her head upward, then lifted her legs.

"She wants to stand," James said, triumph in his voice.

They got off their knees, helped the big ewe to stand, and after a few wobbly seconds, she ran off, her lambs running after her.

"Ingrates!" Temperance said, laughing, as she looked at James. He'd stepped away from her and was now holding up what had once been her clean shirt. It was now covered with what she'd removed from the lamb.

"I told you I should have left it on," she said, smiling, and taking it from him with the tips of one finger and her thumb. "Now what do I wear to go back down the mountain?"

Still smiling, James removed his own shirt, quickly untying the cuffs and pulling it over his head, exposing his bare chest to the light.

Temperance took the shirt from him and put it on, laughing when the cuffs covered her hands by inches and the tail reached to her knees. James lifted her hand, pushed the sleeves upward, then tied the cuff about her wrist. When he was on the second cuff, he nodded toward her rucksack, lying on the ground where she'd tossed it when she first saw the ewe.

"Anything to eat in there?"

"Cornish pasties. They're—"

"Even here in backward Scotland we've heard of such foreign food," he said, smiling at her. "Come on; I know a place to eat."

Without hesitation, she ran along behind him as his long legs ate up the ground and he moved away from the side of the mountain where the men were looking after the sheep.

There was an ancient tree holding on to the side of the mountain, and the ground beneath it was covered with what looked like lethally sharp rocks, but James climbed straight down the mountain for a couple of feet, then reached up his arms to her. She started to take his hand, but he wouldn't let her.

"Jump and I'll catch you," he said. "It's too steep for that skirt."

She started to tell him that that was absurd, but the next moment she felt her body falling forward into his arms in complete trust. He caught her about the waist, swung her around, then set her down on a path. Sort of a path, as it was only about six inches wide. One misplacement of her feet and she'd fall straight down.

"If you're scared, hold on to my belt," he said as he started walking.

"Shirt off; hold on to your belt," she said. "No wonder you don't want to get married when you lead all the girls about with *those* requests."

She smiled when James's laughter floated back to her. She really *must* stop being so outrageous! But, truthfully, it was a relief to be around a man who wasn't begging her to give up what she wanted to do in life and marry him. Sometimes Temperance thought that she was a challenge to men, rather like climbing the highest mountain. How many men had said to her, "Come away from all this and be my wife. Bear my children"?

Because of where they always seemed to lead, Temperance had had to keep humorous remarks to herself. At least she'd never been able to share them with any man.

But now she could. James McCairn was a man she could laugh with and not fear the consequences. As a result, she felt herself becoming more outrageous by the minute.

James stopped so abruptly that Temperance had to put her hand on his bare back to steady herself. His skin was certainly warm! she thought as she reluctantly removed her hand.

"What do you think?" he asked, turning back toward her.

Temperance put her back to the rocky side of the trail and looked out. Below them was the village, the same breathtaking view she'd seen with Ramsey on the horse. To the left was what looked to be a little cave. "It's beautiful," she said honestly.

In the next second, James disappeared around a corner, and she lost no time in following him. It was a cave, about six feet deep, eight feet wide, and inside was a rough plank bed covered in sheepskins and a little stone circle where she could see there had been many fires.

When she looked back at him, he had an expression of a boy, as though he really, really wanted her to like his secret place.

"Cleaner than the house," she said seriously.

James smiled as he put the rucksack down on the ground. "Have a seat," he said cheerfully as he tossed a sheepskin to the ground, "and tell me all about yourself."

"Well..." she began, her eyes twinkling in mischief as she watched him rummage inside the canvas sack. "—but Mother says that I'm so adorable but then I know that because all the boys tell me that so that's why I want to marry a lord and become a princess and—"

Smiling, James took a pasty from the sack, leaned back on one elbow and bit into it. "I don't think a woman has ever made me laugh as much as you do," he said thoughtfully.

Temperance suddenly had a dose of reality. They were very alone in the little cave, and he was half naked, and...

"So why are you really here?" he asked, looking at her with squinted eyes.

"You need a housekeeper, and I need a job." She was glad to think of something else besides his bare body.

With his head turned toward the front of the shallow cave as he looked out over the village, he snorted. "You're as much a housekeeper as I am a clergyman. What did my uncle actually say to you about me?"

Temperance couldn't think quickly enough to make up a lie, so she just looked out at the village in the distance.

"So what's he want of me this time?" he asked, looking at her profile. "Did he think that I'd be so overcome with your beauty that I'd end up *having* to marry you?"

"Most certainly not!" she said *much* too fast.

"Ah, but there is something more to this than you cleaning my old house."

She opened her mouth to speak, but he held up his hand in dismissal. "No, no, don't tell me; I like a puzzle. Bloody little to think about in this place. So what would make an American city woman like you come to a remote place in Scotland and scrub floors? It's not the romance of the Highlands, is it? Getting to live near the laird of a clan, that sort of thing?"

"Not likely." Temperance looked down at her pasty. It was beef and onions and potatoes wrapped in pastry, then baked. If she did say so herself, it was delicious. Maybe she did have an aptitude for cooking after all.

In spite of her pretense of being uninterested, listening to him try to figure out the puzzle was the most interesting conversation she'd had since she'd arrived in Scotland.

She had to keep from smiling as he looked at her hard and tried to piece together what little he knew.

"Shall I give you a hint?" The words were out of her mouth before she could stop herself.

"Ha! The day I can't figure out what a woman's up to is the day I give up."

She had to turn away to hide her smile; then she looked back at him. But that was a mistake. All he had on was a kilt, a wide leather belt, and some soft boots that reached to mid calf. She decided it was safer to keep looking at the village.

"Would you mind telling me what this is between you and your uncle? He seemed as though he cared about you, but he also seems to do things that you hate."

Sitting up, James leaned over her to reach the rucksack, and Temperance couldn't breathe while he was so near. Now I'll be able to tell my women that I know what it's like to lust for a man, she thought. However, I *must* also be able to tell them that I controlled my raging emotions.

"...and marriage," James was saying.

"I beg your pardon, I didn't hear you." She had to try to remember where she was and not transport herself back to New York every few minutes.

"I said that my uncle is determined to marry me off, and I don't want to get married."

"Why ever not?" Temperance asked, turning to him, her interest in his answer overriding her senses.

"Once you get married, you have no freedom. She wants you home for dinner every night. She wants you to...to... She wants you to go shopping with her in Edinburgh." He sounded as though he were going to be sick.

Temperance couldn't keep from laughing. "Oh, you poor tortured man. What do you expect her to do? Climb a mountain with you and help deliver lambs?"

"Yes," he said so softly that Temperance barely heard him.

When she looked into his eyes, they were fierce and dark, and she had difficulty looking away from him.

When she spoke, her voice was light. "If you fall in love with me, McCairn, you're going to get your heart broken. Your uncle is paying me well to do this job, and as soon as I have enough money, I'm going back to New York. I have a job to do there. People need me."

James smiled at her in a way that made sweat break out between her breasts. "I don't want to marry you; I just want you back in my bed."

"You, me, *and* Grace? Won't that be a bit crowded?" she said without blinking.

At that James laughed and moved back onto his elbows. "You know, I think I like you. You're not like other women. All right, so what is it you want to know about me so much that you came all the way up here?"

That nearly threw Temperance. He was a bit too perceptive for her to be able to hide too much from him. So, the closer she stayed to the truth, the better off she'd be. "I don't know a lot more about *why* he wants you to marry than you do. Actually, I had only one conversation about the whole matter with your uncle. He told me that if I would be your housekeeper for..." She hesitated. "Six months, for the summer..." Truthfully, Angus hadn't given her a time limit, and sometimes that frightened her. What if she didn't find James a wife for ten years?

"...for six months," she continued, "he'd give me passage back to the U.S., and he'd even donate to one of my causes."

"Your causes?"

"I help destitute women."

"Ah. Like yourself. So destitute that you'll take a job as a cleaning woman."

When she turned to look at him, there was genuine anger on her face. "Your uncle is a low-down, lying scoundrel who refuses to bend or listen to reason or—" She opened her eyes wide in horror.

"Oh, aye, he's all that, all right, and more. You can't tell me anything about him that I don't know already. But what has he done to *you?*"

"He made this job seem wonderful: laird of a clan, a big house in the country. I thought I was going to be directing a houseful of servants and that it'd take me only a few hours a day."

"But instead you got us," James said, his voice full of amusement.

"Why do you keep your stables so clean and that house so...so..."

James shrugged and reached for another pasty. "The house means nothing, but every year I win races and money, so the horses are worth more to me than the house. What do I need with a big house? I live up here."

"But if you did get married—"

"Once is enough for me."

"Oh," Temperance said with a slow smile. "Now I understand." She pulled her knees up to her chest and hugged them to her as she looked back at the village. "Now I see everything. You were hurt in love, so now you despise all women. I think I've read that book."

When James didn't say anything, she turned to look at him. He was staring at her in an odd way. "You and my uncle didn't get along, did you? He doesn't like women who see things as they are."

Temperance laughed. "Not well, no. So, are you going to tell me about your wife?"

"No," he said. "You have it all figured out, so why bother?"

Temperance could have bitten her tongue for having been so flippant. If she'd asked him nicely, maybe he would have told her something about his marriage that she could use. "Why is your uncle so set on getting you married? Because you need an heir?"

At that James smiled. "Oh, aye, there's a great fight over who gets this heap when I die."

"Then why does your uncle insist that you marry?" she persisted.

James took a moment to answer. "I think that Uncle Angus likes marriage. He wrote me that he married again just recently. I haven't met her, but he says she's the best of all his wives, a very kind woman, sweet-tempered. Angus likes sweet women."

"And what kind of women do *you* like?" she shot back at him.

"Ones that aren't too nosy," he said quickly. "I have to get back to the sheep now," he said as he started to stand up.

"But—" She couldn't think of what to say— that he couldn't leave because she hadn't yet discovered what she meant to find out? "What's Grace like?" she asked as she got to her feet.

"What's your interest in Grace?"

"None. It's just that I hear her name so

often, and you must be in love with her if you... I mean, if you..."

He was standing outside in the sunlight, and he looked down at her. "I think people talk too much and you listen too much. You going to bring me lunch every day?"

"Will you get me some help in cleaning up that house? I can't repair the roof or get rid of the chickens in the bedrooms."

"What does it matter to you if the place is clean? Why not just take my uncle's money and sit out your six months' sentence?"

What could she say? That any of the prospective brides her mother sent would turn tail and run at the sight of the place? "Angus McCairn is likely to send inspectors to see if I've done my job."

"I doubt that, and I don't believe you think he will," James said softly as he looked at her in speculation.

Temperance had to turn her face away to hide its redness. She could see that he knew she was keeping something from him, and he was trying to figure out what it was.

She followed him along the narrow path; then he climbed up ahead of her and helped her up the steep hillside to stand under the old tree.

"Go straight down the wide path, don't get off of it, and you'll come to the village. Take a left and you'll wind up back at the house."

"What about your shirt?" she asked, holding out her arm. He was bare-chested, and she was certainly an odd sight in his big shirt that reached to her knees.

"I have another one," he said, motioning his head back up the hill. "Now go, you've taken up enough of my time."

"And mine as well," she said, annoyed at his attitude that she was being a nuisance. Quickly she turned and started down the hill, and all the way down she thought about nothing but what was going on between James and his uncle about the marriage. Was it money? In her experience in the tenements, everything seemed to come down to money or sex, or both. So what was behind Angus McCairn's insistence that his nephew marry?

"I'll find out," she whispered aloud, then started composing a letter to her mother in her head.

But when she reached the bottom of the steep path and looked at the split path, all thoughts of her mother left her. To the left was that dirty house that needed months more of work to make it habitable. To the right was the village. Were the cottages full of women knitting sweaters that they sold in Edinburgh? What could she learn from these people that she could take back with her to New York?

Nine

As Temperance neared the head of the road that led into the village, she halted. She couldn't very well walk down "Main Street," such as it was, wearing the shirt of the laird. It would take about two seconds for everyone to start talking about who she was and what she was doing—or what she and James McCairn had *been* doing.

"Bother!" she said, then turned off the path and headed toward the rocks that she knew were on the edge of the sea. Maybe a stroll along the water would help her think.

"I found four!" she heard a girl say as Temperance stepped onto a rock and looked down to see a tall, slim woman and a girl just on the edge of womanhood digging for something in the rocky beach along the edge of the water.

And when Temperance saw the woman, she felt at home because she recognized the way the woman walked, the way she tilted her head. She was one of what the newspapers called, "Miss O'Neil's abandoned women."

Feeling as though she were seeing an old friend, Temperance hurried down the rock. "Hello!" she called out.

The girl, startled, ran to stand beside her

mother and watched Temperance approach with curious eyes.

"I'm Temperance O'Neil," she said to the woman, putting out her hand to shake, but the woman just stood there staring at her. "I'm the new housekeeper at the...the...well, at the house," she finished lamely.

"We know who you are," the woman said softly, but she had stepped in front of the girl in a protective way, as though Temperance might try to take her child away from her.

"And what's your name?" Temperance asked, smiling at the girl.

But the girl didn't answer, just kept looking at Temperance with wide eyes; then she stood on tiptoes and whispered something to her mother.

Turning back, the woman looked at Temperance. She was a pretty woman, but her skin had seen too much weather. In another five years she'd be old.

"My daughter wants to know why you have on the McCairn's shirt."

"I helped him deliver a couple of lambs and my blouse got covered in blood, so he lent me his shirt." Temperance was smiling, but neither of them smiled back.

"I'm Grace," the woman said, her jaw fixed and rigid. "I expect you've heard of me."

Temperance had had much experience with moments like this. All the women in the tenements were sure that since Temperance was a "lady," she was going to judge and condemn them. Now she gave a big smile. "Oh, yes, I've heard of little else. It's Grace this and Grace that all day long."

The woman's expression of hostility changed to puzzlement. "But did they tell you that I..."

"That you're a friend of McCairn's? Oh, yes," Temperance said cheerfully. "And does he take care of you? If not, I might be able to help some. Has he given you a snug house? Is it warm? You two have lots of food?"

"I, uh..." the woman sputtered.

"So do *you* know why he refuses to marry?"

For a moment the woman stared at Temperance with big eyes, blinking rapidly, then she grew still and she seemed to be considering something. "He doesn't have time to *talk* to me," she said at last, and her eyes were twinkling.

Temperance laughed, and when she did, so did Grace. But from the way the laugh sounded, it wasn't something she did often.

"So what do you have in that pail?" she asked the little girl. "Is it something good to eat?"

"Would you like us to show you?" Grace asked softly.

"Oh, yes," Temperance said, "I'd like that very much. And I'd like to hear all the gossip. And in return, I'd like to talk to someone about those men at the house." Grace and her daughter started walking, Temperance beside them.

"Which ones?"

"All of them, from McCairn on down. I

have to bribe them to help me clean that big old house. And McCairn says that only the horses are worth his attention. Do you have any suggestions?"

"And why do you want it clean?" Grace asked softly.

At that Temperance stopped walking. "How trustworthy are you? Can you keep a secret?"

Grace's handsome face was solemn. "I have secrets that will go to the grave with me."

Part of Temperance's success had been in being able to judge women. She wasn't great with men, but with women, she was almost clairvoyant. In her line of work, she had to be. For example, she had to be able to ascertain if a woman really wanted to stop being a prostitute or if she was just trying to get benefits from Temperance.

Now, looking into Grace's careworn eyes, Temperance knew that Grace could use some friendship.

"Are you in love with him?" Temperance asked, for she knew that nothing could be done when a woman said she was "in love" with a man.

At that Grace smiled.

"Good, because my secret is that I'm trying to find a wife for him. Heaven only knows why his uncle wants his nephew to marry, but it seems to be of utmost importance to him. And since his uncle has married my mother and taken control of the money my father left me, that McCairn marry has become important to me too." Temperance turned to look at Grace. "Since you know him best, what does he like in a woman?"

"One who doesn't bother him with her problems," Grace said quickly, and Temperance could detect bitterness in her voice.

"I see. I take it that means you get no cozy little house with a table full of food."

"Hmph!" Grace said in answer, then pointed to a lone cottage set halfway up the mountain. "It used to be a sheep herder's hut."

"But he *does* keep the place in good repair for you, doesn't he?" she asked.

"I don't expect it of him," Grace said in answer, then seemed to need to defend herself. "I was an orphan in Edinburgh and my husband brought me here, but he drowned three years ago and after that I had no one. And I had young Alys to care for, so what was I to do? There's no money to be made here, and I have no skills, and—"

Temperance put her hand on the woman's shoulder. "You wouldn't know how to cook, would you?"

"As well as anyone," she said cautiously.

"Then you shall come live with me at the house. I've just hired you as the cook."

"You canna do that," Grace said, backing away from Temperance. "He'd go into a rage."

But Temperance caught her hand. "If there's one thing I'm used to, it's the rages of men. I could tell you stories of what I've had to deal with that you wouldn't believe."

"You? But you're a lady."

At that Temperance had to laugh. She was

wearing the stained shirt of a man, her hair was straggling about her neck, and her skirt was muddy. How could anyone mistake her for a "lady"?

Temperance looked down at the girl standing just behind her mother. "Would *you* like to live in the house? If we clean up a room, you can have something beautiful."

The girl backed against her mother, but she looked up at Temperance with wide eyes, eyes that told that she'd love to live elsewhere.

"Well?" Temperance said to Grace. "Do you accept the position or not?"

"I think I will," Grace said. "Aye, I will."

"Good!" Temperance said, then reached out to shake Grace's hand.

⁂

Dear Mother,

I haven't much time to write now, but I need a few things. I need to know the truth about why your husband so urgently wants James McCairn to marry. My instinct tells me there's a secret. See what you can find out.

Second, I need the man's authorization to hire a cook. He may have to pay her a salary, as I doubt McCairn will want to pay her, since he's used to the woman in another capacity.

How is the bride-hunting going? She needs to be a rather athletic person, as he likes a woman who can climb mountains and deal with sheep.

By the way, I think I may have made a friend here. And, oh, yes, McCairn and I delivered twin lambs.
    Yours in love,
    Temperance

As Temperance looked at the letter, she smiled at the last sentence. Let her mother figure *that* one out!

⌒⌒⌒

"You did what?!" James McCairn bellowed at Temperance over the dinner table. "You hired *who* to be the cook?"

"Grace," Temperance said calmly. He was standing, but she remained sitting. "Would you like more potatoes?"

"No, you interfering woman, I don't want more bloody potatoes. I want that woman out of my house."

Temperance put a big mouthful of the buttery potatoes into her mouth. "Too bad. They're delicious. Not only is Grace a great cook, she's also a fount of knowledge. She knows how to get food from the village. She knows who has cows and can supply butter and—"

"I want her *out!* Do you understand me?"

Temperance looked up at him in wide-eyed innocence. "And why is that?"

"She is— You don't know but she's—"

"A woman of low moral character because

126

you go to bed with her without the benefit of marriage? Or is it not just you but all the men in the village who don't have wives?"

At that James looked almost shocked. "She does not—"

"Oh, then it's just you?" Temperance said.

James sat down and stared at her. "You are a cool one," he said, looking at her in speculation.

"Why? Because I can understand what she's been through and why she's had to do what she's done? More beans? No?" She put the bowl down and looked at him. "All right, what better way to take this little sin from the village than to put her to work under your watchful eye?"

James's lips narrowed as he leaned toward her. "But I don't *want* this 'little sin,' as you call it, taken from the village. I want to *keep* this particular sin."

"Is that your personal opinion or the opinion of all the villagers, women included?"

"The women don't count," James said quickly. "At least not in this matter."

"But this is the very heart of women's matters. And do you want everyone to know that you fired Grace because you could get in bed with her but you wouldn't allow her into your kitchen?"

"How about if I send you back to my uncle with a note pinned to your chest saying, 'No thanks'?"

"You could do that, but then there'd be no

more meals like this one and the rats would soon be back in the house and no one would take pasties up to you on the hill and—"

When James leaned back in his chair, Temperance knew that she'd won. He was going to allow Grace to stay. "Now what am I to do for my...needs?" he asked softly.

"Get a wife?" Temperance said sweetly. "You could always marry Grace, you know. Nice woman."

"You're beginning to sound like my uncle. And why are *you* so interested in my marrying anyone?"

"What woman isn't interested in marriage?" she said quickly. "When I heard that poor woman's story, my heart went out to her. You should hear about what she's been through, being orphaned as a child, then falling madly in love with—"

She broke off because James got up from the table and left the room, and Temperance smiled. Years ago a man had shouted at her that she'd ruined his life. She'd told him the sad story of why his mistress had been driven into prostitution, and it had made him feel so sorry for her that he'd not been able to go to bed with her again.

However, the story had a bad ending, because the next day his former mistress shouted at Temperance that she should mind her own business and save only those people who wanted to be saved and that now she was going to have to find another rich gentleman to take care of her. From that Temperance had learned to help only the women who wanted to be helped.

And, happily, Grace, who had taken over the kitchen as though she'd always been there, had wanted help.

Ten

"Reverend," Temperance said, smiling, as she opened the door to the powerful knock. "How nice that you should call on us and—"

The man, short and built like the bull he resembled, pushed past her to enter the hallway. Except that he was wearing the robe of a clergyman, Temperance would never have guessed him to be a man of the cloth. He looked more like the man who delivered ice to her house in New York.

"You'll not be bringin' your immoral city ways to McCairn," the man said as he glared at Temperance, then looked her up and down in a way that made her want to slap his heavy-jowled face.

"I beg your pardon," she said, but she knew exactly what the man was after. This wasn't the first time that a man had hidden behind the trappings of the church as he tried to force her to his own will. Temperance knew he was after Grace, and Temperance was going to defend her new friend with her life if she had to.

The man raised his arm and pointed toward the back of the house. "You have brought immorality into this house. You have—"

Temperance was still smiling, but it was an icy smile. "I assume that you mean Grace."

"Yes. You *should* pray for Grace."

"She can do her own praying, and she's a great deal better off here than where she was."

At that the man looked at Temperance as though she'd lost her mind. "Gavie's Grace?" he said at last.

It took Temperance a moment to figure out that Gavie must have been Grace's husband's name. "Isn't Grace what we're talking about? About her and James McCairn?"

"I know *nothing* about Grace and James McCairn," the man said, tight-lipped.

Talk about hiding your head in the sand! Temperance thought, then leaned toward the man. "What *are* you angry about?"

"You! You do not attend church services. Your skirts are indecently short! The women in this village are beginning to want to imitate you. Soon we'll have—"

"Women who drive cars! Smoke cigarettes. Control their own money! Women who *speak their own minds!*"

When she finished speaking, she was nose to nose with the man. There was anger flashing in his little eyes, and she was so close she could see the hairs in his nose vibrating as he took deep, angry breaths.

"You will regret speaking to me in this manner," the man said, then turned on his heel and left the house.

For a moment Temperance stood in the entrance hall glaring at the closed door. What an odious little man, she thought; then she turned when she heard a sound behind her. Grace stood there, flour in her hair, watching Temperance.

"What's his name?"

"Hamish," Grace said, still watching Temperance.

Temperance was very angry. She had been attacked before but never quite so personally. "Why was he attacking *me?*" she asked. "You were...were..." She didn't want to offend Grace, but still...

Grace shrugged. "My husband grew up here. He was one of their own, so they—"

"By default you're also one of 'their own.' But I'm—"

"An outsider."

"I see," Temperance said, but didn't really see. "I'm a corrupting influence, but if I'd grown up here, I would have been accepted."

"If you'd grown up here, you wouldn't be the person you are," Grace said softly, a twinkle in her eye. "I think that maybe Hamish is worried that you will single-handedly turn this place into where you came from."

"Couldn't hurt to make some improvements," Temperance muttered, then decided that the best thing to do was dismiss the man from her mind. "You know, I've not seen all this house. Maybe we should take a tour and see what work needs to be done on it. Maybe I can think of a way to persuade McCairn to part with some money to repair it. He definitely needs new curtains in the dining room." She said the last with a smile, but when she was halfway up the stairs, she turned to Grace and said, "Tell me, does McCairn attend church services and listen to that man?"

Grace tried to hide her smile. "I don't think the McCairn's ever been inside the church. Not that I know of, anyway."

"But the rest of the village goes?"

"Oh, yes. Even me. I can't imagine what he'd do if someone of McCairn other than James missed his services."

"Probably lecture them to death," Temperance said with a grimace as she started back up the stairs.

There were eight bedrooms upstairs, each one in a horrible state of disrepair.

"These were once beautiful, weren't they?" Grace said, holding up a curtain of shattered silk. "The colors are beautiful."

"I wonder who decorated these rooms? Whoever it was had taste," Temperance said as she looked in one room at the few remaining pieces of furniture that had once been beautiful. There was an elegant little dressing table against the wall that she thought might be valuable, but, sadly, there was white rot running up the legs. For herself, she didn't know one piece of furniture from another, but her mother did. Maybe she should see this, Temperance thought. Maybe her mother...

"His grandmother," Grace said.

"What?"

"You asked who furnished these rooms and it was the McCairn's grandmother."

"Of course. The Great Spender."

"According to James," Grace said quietly. "But then, he saw her from an accounting point of view."

"What does that mean?"

"It's the duty of the laird's wife to take care of the villagers, and the McCairn's grandmother took very good care of the people. My husband's family speaks nothing but good of her."

As Temperance left the room and walked down the hall, Grace beside her, she said, "I got the impression the woman was crazy. I've found things that she bought and hid."

"Probably to keep her husband from gambling all the money away."

"Ah, now that's interesting. I thought she—"

"Drove Clan McCairn into bankruptcy? No, there's a weakness for gambling in the family. James's brother has it. If he'd inherited the island, he would have lost it in a bet an hour later."

Temperance turned the knob of another door, then had to put her shoulder to it and shove to get it to open. Inside, a flurry of doves made the two women put their arms up in protection as they backed out and closed the door.

"Roof," the women said together, then laughed.

"How do you know so much about the family? Or does everyone know?"

"My husband was the estate agent for James."

Temperance grimaced. "And the laird certainly took care of you after your husband's death, didn't he?"

"I think you should be less harsh with James. Truthfully, the first time I..." Trailing off, she looked down the hall, not meeting Temperance's eyes.

From experience, Temperance guessed that Grace carried the great secret that she had made the first moves toward McCairn. "Loneliness makes us all do things we sometimes regret," she said in dismissal. "Shall we look inside that room?" Temperance asked, nodding toward a door at the end of the hall. "Tell me more."

"The gambling seems to skip generations and people. James's grandfather had it, his father and Angus didn't. James doesn't, but his brother, Colin, does. It's a good thing for all the people who want to live here that James was born the oldest."

"I can't get this door open," Temperance said as she pushed against it.

As Grace put her shoulder to the door to help, she kept talking. "Even though James's father

134

didn't gamble, he considered himself a gentleman, so he spent what was left of the McCairn fortune that the old man hadn't gambled away. The younger brother, James's uncle Angus, was better off, as he didn't inherit the burden of this place, so he was free to run off to Edinburgh and make his fortune in the drapery trade."

"And Angus was *never* a gentleman," Temperance said under her breath as she pushed on the door. "Wait a minute," she said, then disappeared into a bedroom and returned with a fire poker, which she used on the rusted hinges of the door.

As Temperance worked, Grace leaned against the wall and talked. "By the time James and Colin came along, there wasn't much money left. My husband said the accounts were very low and the whole estate was in dreadful shape."

"Who does the accounting now?"

"I have no idea," Grace said. "James was never one to sit at a desk for long. He's more of a physical person. You should see him on a horse! He's almost as good as young Ramsey who rides in the races. Anyway, when he was a child, James used to visit McCairn, and he loved it, and since his father died, it's been his life goal to take this place back to what it once was. He wants McCairn wool to become known for its quality. His uncle Angus introduces him to buyers."

As Temperance pushed on the hinge, the poker slid off and scraped her finger. Putting the injured digit into her mouth, she leaned against the door and looked at Grace. "What about McCairn's wife?"

"Oh, her. Poor thing, she cried for the whole two years they were married. She hated anything with the McCairn name attached to it: him and the land."

"That's easy to understand," Temperance said as she turned back to the door.

"She saw the state of this house and didn't have the gumption to clean it up or to do much of anything except whine."

"Didn't do her duty as the laird's wife, right?" Temperance said as she gouged the hinge with the poker.

"She didn't do anything. Did you see that key?"

"What key?" Temperance asked, then saw that Grace was pointing to the top of the door.

Temperance grabbed a rickety chair from the hallway, pulled it to the front of the door, balanced on it, then grabbed the key. It fit the lock perfectly, and after a few tries in the rusty old lock, it turned.

Inside was a ballroom. It was a huge, empty room, with a wooden floor made for dancing. At the end were tall windows with curved tops. The walls had been painted with scenes of sunlit gardens, complete with flowers and birds.

"It's beautiful," Temperance breathed as she batted at a cobweb hanging from the ceiling. Overhead was a huge crystal chandelier that, when filled with lighted candles, would no doubt make the room look heavenly.

As Temperance walked across the floor, she left footprints in the dust. The huge windows were so dirty that they let in little light.

"Ah, yes, the ballroom," Grace said, looking about her. "I'd forgotten this place existed."

"But you've seen it before?"

"No, only heard of it. My husband used to tell me about the parties he went to in here when he was a child."

"Ah, yes, society," Temperance said with a bit of contempt in her voice.

"Oh, no. James's grandmother used to give parties for all of McCairn. I know the place doesn't look like much now, but fifty years ago McCairn was prosperous. There was a lot of money from the sheep and the fish and—" She broke off, embarrassed.

"But everything was spent," Temperance said as she touched what had once been a red velvet curtain. The fabric came away in her hands.

"I guess," Grace said, looking at one of the murals on the wall. "My husband told me that James's grandfather went to his grave saying that his wife had spent more than he gambled. He used to say that she bought things and hid them."

"Like the dishes and the candlesticks."

"Yes, but on a larger scale. Gavie, that was my husband's name, said an old stableman used to tell him that the two of them fought horribly. They'd scream that each was spending all the money. Whatever, when they died, there wasn't much left."

Temperance was looking up at the chandelier and trying to count the number of candles it would hold. "I think the man won on that count, because if his wife had bought a lot, maybe some of it could have been sold later."

"That's just it," Grace said, and there was an urgency in her voice. "What happened to all that she bought?"

Temperance looked at Grace. "What do you mean?"

Walking toward her, Grace lowered her voice. "Gavie took care of all the accounts from the time he was a young man. He had a good head for numbers. If James's grandmother bought as much as her husband accused her of, and if she spent the McCairn fortune as she is still accused of, what happened to all the things that she bought?"

"Were they sold to pay gambling debts?"

"No. The old man gambled what he had, but he didn't die in debt. He died in relative poverty, but he owed no one. When my Gavie stepped in, there were years of receipts that had been thrown into drawers, and he began to sort through them. He used to come home at night and tell me about what he'd found. She bought silver and lots of it. There were punch bowls and vases. And she bought things like gold statues made by a man named Cel... I forgot the name. It was something foreign."

Temperance lifted one eyebrow. "Cellini?"

"That's it."

"My goodness," Temperance said. "I could see that someone of taste had bought some of the furniture, but even I have heard of Cellini." She was quiet for a moment. "Did your husband think that maybe the two of them were in a war? Maybe she was buying things to keep him from gambling it all away. *Investment* things?"

"That's what Gavie thought," Grace said quietly. "He used to say…"

"What?" Temperance said sharply.

"—that all the things that James's grandmother bought were still somewhere in this house. She had to hide them from her husband to keep him from selling them and gambling the money away."

"If that were true and neither of her sons were gamblers, wouldn't she have told them what she'd done and where she'd hidden the loot?"

Grace hesitated before speaking, as though she were trying to decide *if* she should speak. "Maybe she meant to tell, but he killed her before she could tell anyone anything."

"What?" Temperance asked, eyes wide.

Grace lowered her voice even more, then looked around as though to make sure that no one was listening. "Only my Gavie knew the truth, and he only told me on his deathbed. The old man had a terrible fight with his wife, worse than usual. He said he was going to kill her if she didn't tell him what she'd done with all the things she'd bought."

Grace took a breath and calmed herself. "No one knows this," she said.

"I won't tell, if that's what you mean," Temperance reassured her.

"The old man was a dreadful person, and he used to frighten my husband a lot. He said Gavie was a little snoop and if he ever again caught him where he shouldn't be, he was going to horsewhip him. So on that day when Gavie was only seven years old and had sneaked into the master's bedroom to snitch a chocolate, he hid in the wardrobe when he heard voices."

"And he saw the murder?" Temperance asked.

"Not murder, an accidental killing. They wrestled over a pistol, and it went off, killing her instantly. But the horrible part was that the old man told people that she'd committed suicide."

"Not exactly honorable of him, was it?"

"Worse than you know. He allowed his wife to be buried in unconsecrated ground, and later he tore her down to her own sons, and they in turn, told their sons until…"

"Until today James sneers at the mention of her name and hates her beautiful house so much that he lets it go to ruin."

"Exactly."

For a while Temperance was silent as she looked about the dirty room and saw the beauty hidden under the filth. To Temperance it seemed that all her life she'd heard one horror story after another of women who had been unfairly accused, innocently blamed, and, in general, persecuted by men. From the splendor of the ballroom, Temperance could see that the woman had loved beauty. But what had happened to this woman who had given parties for the villagers? She had been killed by her own husband, then had had her reputation taken from her.

After a while, Temperance said, "Shall we go?" Then, as they were leaving the room, Temperance said, "Tell me about this man Hamish. Surely James couldn't like him, so why does he allow him to stay?"

"Hamish was a McCairn on his mother's side, which means that James can't get rid of the man, that he has a right to a home here. Any McCairn can return to this land and he'll always be given a home."

"That could produce a lot of people who don't want to work for a living," Temperance said as they started down the hall.

"Not around James," Grace said. "No one lives near James and doesn't work."

"But I wonder if they work as hard as he does," Temperance said softly as she opened the door into the bedroom that she'd taken as her own.

And standing in front of the mirror was Grace's young daughter, Alys, a sea of Temperance's hats at her feet. And on her head was a hat that was nearly as wide as the girl was tall.

To Temperance it was an amusing picture, but Grace was very upset as she grabbed her daughter's upper arm.

"How dare you do this!" Grace said. "I'll—"

"There's no harm done," Temperance said.

141

"Here, why don't you keep that hat if you like it so much?"

Grace took the hat before her daughter touched it again. "You have done enough for us. We'll not accept charity."

For a moment Temperance was taken aback at Grace's change from friend and confidant to this prideful woman standing before her. But Temperance knew about pride.

"All right," Temperance said good-naturedly, looking at the girl, "how would you like to have this one?" Reaching into a wardrobe, she withdrew the hat she'd worn on the night she'd walked to McCairn's house. It had no shape now and was still covered with mud. Most of the flowers that had been on it were gone, but what remained were torn and dirty. "Would this make a nice play hat?"

"Oh, yes," the girl breathed as she reached for the forlorn-looking hat, but she looked askance at her mother first.

"All right," Grace said, then gave a small smile to Temperance. "We owe you too much," she whispered.

"True," Temperance said. "So maybe you could repay me by making me a nice lunch that I could take up the mountain."

Grace didn't move but stood there looking at Temperance. "You're going to the McCairn again today?"

At that Temperance laughed. "If you think there's going to be a romance, you can forget the idea. I need to find out what he wants in a wife. Although...he is a fine-looking man..."

Temperance had hoped to make Grace smile, but she didn't. Instead she was looking at Temperance as though trying to figure out something. And she looked at her so long that Temperance began to wonder if Grace was jealous. *Did* she have some feelings for James McCairn that she was hiding?

After a while, Grace said, "There's no lamb, but I do have a bit of salmon left. Will that do?"

Temperance laughed. There were three lambs in the kitchen now, all of them sent down the mountain by James to be slaughtered, but Temperance had adopted each of them. Young Ramsey had a full-time job looking after them.

"Salmon is fine," she said, and the women exchanged smiles.

Eleven

"And who does your accounts now?" Temperance asked James. They were sitting in the sunshine outside the little cave.

"What kind of woman are you that you can't enjoy the day?" James snapped.

"And what has put you into such a bad

143

mood?" she snapped back. "Missing your regular visits to Grace?"

"Who said they were regular? And you and your inquisition would put any man off his food."

"You don't seem to be off yours. You've eaten yours and mine."

"That's because you have your mind on something besides food. You want to tell me what it is?"

"I was wondering..." Temperance pulled her knees to her chest. What could she say? That she was wondering about his ancestors? About his village? About his brother the gambler?

When she said nothing, he said, "I do the accounts, and I hate every minute of it. You want to take them over?"

"Me? A mere woman? Don't you think your Hamish would say that a woman doing accounts was going against God?"

When he was silent, she turned around to look at him and he was staring at her.

"What's got into you today, woman?" he asked quietly.

She wasn't going to tell him the truth, that all the way up the mountain she'd thought about the dreadful life of his grandmother, with her gambler husband, and how she was now buried in unconsecrated ground. A restless soul, no doubt. Temperance wouldn't have been surprised if she had been told that the woman haunted the house where she'd been so very unhappy.

"Are there any ghosts in your house?"

"I'm sure there are, and maybe they'd be more pleasant company than what's here now."

Temperance laughed, stretched out her legs, and leaned back on her hands, putting her face up to the sun. "I think I would like to look at your accounts, actually. You wouldn't mind?"

"I'd kiss your feet if you did that for me." His voice lowered. "Or any other part of you that you would care to make bare."

Temperance knew how she was presenting her body to him now, and she knew that she should sit in a more ladylike position, but she didn't move. For all that they were alone, she felt safe near him, and she knew that he wasn't going to make a move without her permission.

On the other hand, she was already beginning to think of giving him permission. She was nearly thirty years old and she was a virgin. This was by choice, since she'd certainly had many offers to give up her virginity, but until now she'd never met a man who had made her consider doing so.

Today, in these first years of the new twentieth century, women were talking about "free love." After all, there was birth control now, and—

"There you are," said a voice that startled both of them, and a woman's head popped up over the side of the mountain not a foot from Temperance's shoe. The head was soon followed by a neck; then the woman put her palms on the ground and, with a great heave, she projected her whole body upward until she was standing on the very edge of the mountain and looking down at Temperance and James.

"They told me that if I'd follow the path, I'd find you here, but why bother with a path when there's a mountain to climb, is what I always say." She stopped talking for a moment as she looked down at Temperance as though she were something she was thinking about purchasing.

Temperance, with her hand shielding her eyes, looked up at her. The woman wasn't very tall, but she was certainly muscular looking. She stood with her back rigid, her bosom thrust out, her hands on her hips; her face was brown from the sun, making it impossible to tell her age, but had Temperance tried to guess she'd have said the woman had to be at least forty-five years old. Did James know her?

"Soft, aren't you?" she said to Temperance.

"I beg your pardon?"

Turning, the woman looked at James, apparently dismissing Temperance as of no consequence. "I hear you need a wife," she said.

At that Temperance made a bit of a gasp that she tried to cover with a little cough.

"Tubercular," the woman said with a look of contempt down at Temperance. "No oxygen to your lungs."

"I think I get enough ox—"

The woman turned away. "I'm Penelope

Beecher, and I am fit for the job of wife. I am a follower of Sandow and Macfadden, and I can lift a full-grown ram. I have climbed four of the ten highest mountains in the world, and I plan to climb the other six before I die."

"Which will be soon if you don't get off my mountain," James said quietly.

The woman didn't seem to hear him. "I have a thirteen-inch neck, my upper arm, flexed, is twelve and three quarters; my expanded chest is thirty-eight; deflated it's thirty-four. My waist is twenty-five, and that's without a corset." At that she looked down at Temperance with a bit of a sneer. "My—"

James recovered himself enough to stand up and look down at the woman. "I couldn't care less what the bloody hell your—"

At that Temperance got to her feet. Would he toss the woman down the side of the mountain? It was one thing to throw someone out the window into the rain, but it was another to throw a person down a mountain.

"Mr. McCairn wants children," Temperance said loudly as she physically put herself between James and the woman. "I think that perhaps you're a little old to—"

"I'm twenty-seven," the woman snapped, looking hard at Temperance. "It is *you* who are too old to bear children."

"Twenty-seven?" Temperance whispered, then gave a little prayer of thanks that she'd never climbed mountains or did whatever this woman had done to so age her. But, then again, maybe she was lying about her age.

147

"Would you like to see the size of my arm?" the woman said to James.

"I don't want to see anything you have," he said through clenched teeth. "I want you off McCairn land this moment."

"But I was told that you wanted a wife," she said. "A strong wife who could lift sheep and work beside you all day. I thought I had found a man, a true man, but here I see you sitting with this...this..." She looked Temperance up and down. "She doesn't have a muscle on her body. I can tell that she's soft."

When James took a step toward the woman, Temperance grabbed her upper arm. Maybe it was fear that gave Temperance extra strength, but, whatever it was, the woman gave a yelp of pain when Temperance clamped down on her. "I think you'd better leave now."

"I've dealt with women like you," Penelope said. "You're jealous of— Ow! You pinched me. I don't think that's fair. You—"

"If you don't leave now, he's going to pick you up and throw you down that mountain," Temperance hissed into her ear.

But the woman didn't seem to take this as a warning. "Oh?" she said, and there was interest in her voice as she tried to pull away from Temperance and return to James.

But Temperance squeezed the woman's arm again, then shoved her toward the path by the tree. "Go up there, take a right, and get out of here," she whispered to the woman. "Didn't they tell you that's he's insane? I'm his nurse. I have to keep him sedated. If I didn't,

148

he'd... Well, I can't tell you what he's done to women in the past. If you married him, you'd be his eighth wife."

"Really?" the woman said, her face full of interest as she looked over Temperance's shoulder at James, who was still standing by the entrance to the cave. "But I was told—"

"Let me guess. You met a woman, a nice, plump little woman, and she told you of this man's need for a wife. Did she have reddish gold hair and a little mole to the left of her right eye?"

"Yes! Have you met her?"

"Oh, yes," Temperance said as she visualized her mother for a moment before returning to her elaborate lie. "She recruits women for him. He..." Temperance couldn't think of another lie quick enough because her head was full of thinking of ways to murder her mother. What in the world had Melanie O'Neil been thinking when she chose this dreadful woman? Temperance had seen specimens in bottles that were better preserved than this creature.

"What does he do to them? To all those wives, I mean?" Penelope asked, eyes wide, obviously still interested.

"You don't want to know, but it's horrible. Now go. I'll try to hold him off as long as possible."

But the woman was not frightened and she hesitated.

Temperance gave a sigh of disgust. "He's broke," she said flatly. "Not a penny to his name. He won't be able to fund any of your expeditions to any mountains anywhere."

At that the woman scurried up the side of the cliff. "I'll tell that woman, Mrs. McCairn," she said over her shoulder as she began to run down the path. "I won't let her send any more unsuspecting girls up here."

Temperance looked at her long enough to snort, "Girls!" Then she went back toward the cave and James. "There," she said, "that's done."

Turning away, James looked out over the village; his fists were clenched at his side. "I'm going to kill my uncle," he said softly. "What would make him think to send me a... a...something like that?"

"Maybe someone told him you wanted help with the sheep and he just assumed..."

"That I wanted a bull?" He turned back to her. "What has happened that he's sent these last two? First there was the narcissist girl, then this Amazon. What has put these ideas into his head?"

Temperance looked down at her nails. They really did need a trim. "I can't imagine," she said, but knew she couldn't look at him, for she had been the one to tell her mother to send her someone brainless. Then she'd told her mother to send her an "athletic" sort. On the other hand, did her mother have to take her so very literally?

When Temperance looked back up at him, he seemed to be expecting an answer from her, but she didn't dare open her mouth to try to explain for fear that she'd reveal her part in all this.

"I'll, uh... Maybe I'll write your uncle a letter and try to explain," she said at last.

"And what do you plan to explain?" he asked, looking at her with one eyebrow lifted.

"That you don't want him to send you any more idiots?" she asked, smiling.

He didn't smile back. Instead, he stepped closer to her and reached out a big hand to touch her hair. "He did well in choosing a housekeeper for me," James said softly.

For all of Temperance's thoughts of maybe giving in to the man, now, when he touched her, she drew back. The truth was she was beginning to *like* James McCairn. And since she was only here temporarily, maybe it would be better if she didn't get too involved with him.

Stepping back, she gave him a devil-may-care grin. "Shall I tell your uncle that you've fallen in love with the housekeeper he sent? Maybe he'll shorten my sentence and I can go back to civilization, where people don't live in grass-roofed huts."

She'd meant to make him smile, but instead, he stepped back abruptly and his face lost all expression.

"I forgot how horrible we are to outsiders," he said coldly, "so go now and count your days until you can get away from us."

"I didn't mean—" she began, but stopped. "You're right. I can't wait until I get out of here. So I'll be going now," she said, then turned toward the path that led up. But when he said nothing, she stopped walking, looked back, and said louder, "I have things to do at the house, so I must get back there." He still didn't say anything, so she turned back around and again started walking. But it was as though weights were strapped to her feet. All that awaited her at the house was cleaning. And helping with the cooking and—

"Do you think you can count?" he said from behind her.

She turned around quickly. "What?" He was still scowling, but now she saw a twinkle in his eye.

"Do you think you can count sheep? Old Fergus falls asleep and—"

"Yes!" she said with too much enthusiasm.

His expression didn't change. "But maybe you should go down. I talked to Hamish about you, and he was thinking of asking you to teach a Bible class on Sundays, so he said he was going to call on you this afternoon to discuss the matter."

Temperance cast a fearful glance toward the village below them. "Why does he think *I* can teach a Bible class?"

"You rescue doomed maidens, don't you? At least that's what I told him. And isn't it true? I needed to tell him a great deal about your good works to make him overlook your more obvious sinful ways." He glanced down at her skirt that exposed her ankles. "I was telling the truth, wasn't I?"

"Well..." Temperance said, smiling at him. He was teasing her and she found that she liked it. In her life men had told her she was "formidable." "Beautiful but formidable," is what they'd said. So being teased was not something that had happened to Temperance very often.

Suddenly, she looked up at him in speculation. "You were a diplomat, weren't you? You smoothed out what could have become a war between that man and me, didn't you?"

At that James gave a tiny smile. "We're a small community, and it's better if people get along."

"*Hmmm,*" she said. "If that's so, why don't *you* go to church?"

James grinned broader. "I'll work myself to death to support them, but I don't have to listen to them."

"But that's—" Temperance began, frowning.

"You want to stay and help count, or do you want to go meet with Hamish?"

"Do I have to use a quill pen?"

"Big rock. Big chisel."

"Just so I don't have to write with a feather," she said, smiling. "So bring on the sheep."

❧❧❧

Dearest Mother,
Temperance bit on the end of her pen, trying to think how to phrase what she wanted to write. How could she tell her mother that she was doing an abysmal job of finding James a wife without offending her mother? Could she say, Let's put it this way, if you were employed by me, I'd have fired you a week ago? No, that wasn't the way.

153

I am sure the misunderstanding is all my fault, but the two prospective brides you have sent, so far, have not been women I or James would consider. Perhaps if I tell you some about him you could help me better.

Even though he is the laird of a clan and it might be assumed that he lives in luxury and comfort, nothing could be further from the truth. Actually, he is little more than a sheep-herder—and a farmer and a fisherman. Whatever he is, he is certainly a worker! I rarely see him because he is always overseeing the village he owns. Whereas another man might just collect rents, James lives and works with his people.

For example,

Temperance again put the pen into her mouth and thought about this afternoon up on the mountain. The process of counting sheep had been a long one, so she'd had plenty of time to observe. She hadn't met many of the villagers, but today there were six children on the mountain, all running after the sheep and helping the men with the counting.

She remembered once looking up and seeing James grab two children, one under each arm and swing them about; their laughter split the air. It was a lovely sight.

At one point Temperance asked a little girl why they weren't in school today.

"The master let us off," the child said before she went scampering off.

"And who is 'the master'?" Temperance

shot at James the first time he came near her, to grab a sheepskin of water and tip it up. But she didn't give him time to answer. "It's that man, Hamish, isn't it?"

"Yes, he's also the schoolmaster, if that's what you mean," James said. "And before you start on him again, unless you want to find yourself with the job of teaching seventeen children, you'd better stay out of it." There was warning and truth in his voice, so Temperance clamped her lips shut and wrote down the numbers that one of the men shouted at her.

But her silence didn't last long. "If you had a wife..." she said softly.

"But I don't have a wife, do I? I just have a snoop of a housekeeper who sticks her nose into everyone's business. If you want to help the brats, why don't you teach them something on Sunday afternoons?"

"Bible studies aren't really my area of expertise. I mean, I know a few stories, but—"

She broke off because he was looking down at her with one eyebrow raised. Clearly she was missing some point. He was trying to tell her something that was just between the two of them, but he couldn't say it outright because there were four men and three children near them.

Finally, it dawned on her. This was her chance to bring the twentieth century to McCairn. "Yes, I see. Maybe we *could* have Bible classes inside your house. Just me and the children."

"I think that could be arranged," James

said softly; then, as he raised the flask to his mouth again, he winked at her, and she had to duck her head to hide her red face—and her smile, for that wink had made her feel quite good.

For the rest of the afternoon, Temperance recorded numbers, but she thought of what she'd like to teach the children when she got them alone. That women were entitled to the right to vote? That little girls shouldn't let little boys seduce and abandon them? Not quite.

But no matter how hard she thought, she still hadn't come up with an appropriate topic for this Sunday's private lesson with all the children of the village. Children she'd never even met.

Now, she looked back at her mother's letter.

For example, he loves the children and he plays with them. From what I can see, between Sunday morning lectures and school days spent with a man who is a throwback to Cotton Mather, it may be the only play they ever have in their lives.

For a moment Temperance stopped and thought about how different her own childhood had been, with rides in the park with her parents, ice-skating, and—

"Skating!" she said aloud, then looked down at the paper again.

Mother! You must send me twenty-one pairs of roller skates, as I have found the perfect skating rink. And send them in a crate marked as something else so no adult here will know what's inside. Oh, yes, and send me seventeen white Bibles, each marked in gold with an angel, if possible. It looks like I'm going to start teaching Sunday school.

Temperance sat back, looked at the letter, and smiled. She'd send it off with Ramsey first thing in the morning, she thought as she slipped the letter into the drawer of the old desk in her bedroom.

⌒◯⌒

It wasn't until late the next day that Temperance got to finish the letter to her mother, and by then she had a great deal to add, for Grace's daughter had a secret to show Temperance.

"What is it?" Temperance asked when the little girl whispered that she had something wonderful to show her.

Alys put her finger to her lips to signal silence, then started up the stairs, pausing once for Temperance to follow her. The child led Temperance to the bedroom she shared with her mother.

Temperance had not been inside the room since Grace had taken it over, and now she frowned, feeling as though she were invading the woman's privacy. But Alys pulled on Temperance's skirt and led her inside.

It was amazing what Grace had done to

157

the room; it was clean and patched as well as possible. A person could actually see the room's former splendor.

Even though they were alone in the room, the child tiptoed over to a wardrobe that stood opposite the bed, then carefully opened the doors. She jumped once when the door creaked, and looked around, as though she expected her mother to jump out from behind the curtains.

The girl leaned into the wardrobe, bent, and then when she straightened and stepped from behind the door, she held in her hands a beautiful hat. Carrying it as though it were the Royal Jewels, the girl held it out to Temperance.

"Where did you get this?" Temperance asked, looking at the handmade flowers that circled the brim. She'd never seen anything like them. There were tiny rosebuds, lilacs, and sweet peas on the brim, but what made the flowers unique was that the colors were like nothing she'd ever seen before. Actually, the flowers weren't colored so much as they were tinted, as though they were from a distant time and place. The hat looked as though it had been taken from a romantic painting of a hundred years earlier.

"Did you find this somewhere?" Temperance asked as she took the hat from the girl. She couldn't resist putting it on and wasn't surprised to see that it fit her perfectly. There was an old stand mirror in the room, and she looked at herself in it. The hat, with its gentle flowers, the bit of veiling that softened the edges, made her look like...

"A romantic heroine," she breathed, then made herself stop being so silly. Reluctantly, she took the hat off. "We have to put this back," she said to the girl. "This belongs to some woman from long ago, and—"

"It's *your* hat," the girl said, obviously frustrated that Temperance wasn't understanding.

"But you can't give me something that doesn't belong to you."

The child looked at Temperance as though she were stupid. "You gave it to me, and Mother fixed it."

"Fixed...?" Temperance said, then abruptly turned the hat over. Inside was the label of her hatmaker in New York. It took her a few moments to digest the fact that the gorgeous creation she held was the same as that muddy, sodden old hat that she'd handed to Grace just the day before.

"How?" was all she could say to the girl. Now that the child had found her voice, she certainly seemed articulate enough.

"Mother took the backs off the curtains you wanted thrown out and made the flowers. She used to make flowers for the orphanage where she grew up. Do you like it?"

"Yes. Very much. It's beautiful," Temperance said, looking at the hat in wonder. The flowers looked old because the silk used to make them was many years old.

She looked around at the bedroom she was standing in. There wasn't a piece of fabric in the house that wasn't in danger of falling apart. There were curtains and bed hangings and upholstery. But Temperance knew that in every piece there was some good fabric, fabric that could be saved to make trimmings for hats.

"Alys, are you in here?" came a voice as the door opened and Grace entered; then her eyes widened as she saw that Temperance was holding the hat she'd refurbished.

"Alys shouldn't have bothered you with that," Grace said. "I apologize for taking your time," she said as she reached out to take the hat from Temperance.

But Temperance drew her hand and the hat back. "This is the most beautiful hat I've ever seen," she said softly. "The truth is that I've never seen anything like it. And, trust me, I'm an expert on hats. If you were in New York, and making these, they would sell…"

At that thought Temperance looked up, wide-eyed, at Grace.

"What is it?" Grace said, for even though she didn't know Temperance very well, she could see that she was thinking hard about something.

"We need a label, something big that can be seen. Is there anyone in the village who can embroider? I need someone who can do really fine work."

Grace had no idea what Temperance was talking about. "My mother-in-law was once a lady's maid, but now her eyes are too bad to do much. But even if she could see to sew, where would she get the threads? Do you want your clothes embroidered?"

"No," Temperance said, her smile growing wider with each second. "You and I are going into *business!*"

"We're what? But how—?"

But Temperance had no time to explain anything. "What do you want most in the world?" she asked.

"My own home," Grace shot back instantly.

"That's it! We'll call it House of Grace," she said as she gripped the brim of the hat, then started out the bedroom door.

"*What* are you talking about?"

Temperance paused with her hand on the door. "Start cutting silks that you can use for hat trims. I'll get feathers and the rest of what you need. Alys, go tell Ramsey to saddle his fastest horse. Tell him he's going to be riding into Edinburgh today and he's to stay there until he can bring back what I need." She started out the door again but turned and paused. "Grace, you said that your husband was good with numbers. Your daughter didn't by chance inherit that ability, did she?"

Grace put her arm around her daughter in pride. "She's the best in the village. The McCairn has her add his accounts for him."

"Does he, now? Well, dear," she said to the girl, "you can help me later, after I finish the letter to my mother."

In her room, Temperance pulled out the half finished letter to her mother and added to it.

Mother, I don't have time to explain now, but it looks as though I'm going to help a woman here start a business, but I can't do it without your help. Following is a list of supplies and services that I need.

1. *Hat blanks—Saratoga, Fairfax, Portland, Dresden, Raleigh*
2. *Feathers—ostrich and bird of paradise, plus some stuffed birds*
3. *Aigrettes of jet; rhinestone buckles; various beads and hat-decorating supplies that aren't made of fabric, as that I have*
4. *I need a selection of reading glasses of various strengths and embroidery supplies such as hoops, colored silks, and at least four yards of a fine, stiff cotton*
5. *Please send me the name of the premier hat shop in Edinburgh and where the most fashionable ladies lunch*

I need all this as soon as possible. Please send it all back with Ramsey.
Yours in love and in need,
Temperance

Minutes later, young Ramsey was speeding away on one of James's prize horses, heading toward Edinburgh, and he'd been told not to return until he came back with a wagonload of supplies.

And Temperance forgave her mother everything when, a mere two days later, Ramsey returned with a wagonload of goods for Miss Temperance O'Neil.

"She wouldn't tell me anything," an obviously tired Ramsey said, "but she asked me thousands of questions and she nearly worked me to death."

"Be the first time for you," one of the stablemen said.

Ignoring the man, Ramsey smiled at Temperance. "She's a nice lady."

"She is, isn't she?" Temperance said, as she rummaged through the boxes in the back of the wagon. There were three boxes of hat supplies, a crate labeled "Books of Good Works" that was full of roller skates, a box of embroidery supplies, a dozen pair of reading glasses, and a box of white Bibles with golden angels on the cover. Another box contained oranges and a huge box of chocolates.

There was also a letter from her mother saying that The Golden Dove restaurant in Edinburgh had been notified that Temperance and a guest would be having lunch there in three days and the meal was to be charged to Angus's account. Her mother also said how sorry she was that she had failed so miserably with the first two women, but it was difficult trying to find the right woman.

Scotswomen know of McCairn, her mother wrote, *so they want no part of it; therefore I must try to persuade foreigners, mostly Americans, and that isn't easy. Please bear with me. However, it might help if you tell me more about James so I can match him with the perfect woman.*

163

I am trying to find out the truth about why Angus is so desperate for James to marry, and I agree with you that there is a secret. Leave it to me, I'll find out what it is.

Since I assume that the skates are for children I took the liberty of including a few other things.

Included in the letter was a card from a hat store in Edinburgh. On the back, her mother had written, *The only place where fashionable women would buy their hats.*

"Hooray!" Temperance said, holding the letter aloft; then she grabbed Ramsey's shoulders and, much to his embarrassment, heartily kissed his cheek.

"I'd like to help celebrate whatever's made you so happy," one of the watching stablemen said, eyes twinkling.

"I'm sure you would," Temperance said as she turned away. It was her experience that the less you told men about the possibility of a woman being able to earn money, the better. Men liked women to be dependent upon them.

By six that evening, Alys, Grace, and Temperance were hard at work using tiny embroidery scissors to cut out patterns for flowers and leaves. Temperance was introduced to Grace's widowed mother-in-law, Sheenagh, and, with her new glasses perched on her nose, she began to embroider four large labels that would be sewn inside the hats that Temperance planned to have ready to show Edinburgh society when she and Grace went to lunch there.

164

At three A.M., Temperance leaned back on her chair, exhausted. "I am going to sleep for a week," she said. "Don't wake me until Tuesday."

"Did you forget that today is Sunday," Grace said, yawning.

"Great. A day of rest."

"Not in McCairn," Grace said softly. Alys and her mother-in-law were asleep on the bed, while she and Temperance were sitting at the table surrounded by the accoutrements of hat making.

"It will be a day of rest for *me*," Temperance said, standing, her hand at her back. On the table were four hats, finished at last. She'd worn hats for years, but she'd never had any idea of the amount of work involved in making one of the things.

"You're to teach a Bible class in just a few hours," Grace said.

"A...? Oh, that. I'll just cancel it. I'll do it next week," Temperance said as she started toward the door, her mind on nothing but getting into her bed.

"Yes, of course. I'll tell the children," Grace said flatly.

At the tone, Temperance paused with her hand on the doorknob. She didn't want to turn around because she knew that if she did she'd see a long face on Grace and she'd feel guilty. Temperance wanted to go to bed; she wanted to sleep. She did *not* want do one thing more for this village than she had to. She was trying to find the laird a wife, and now she was exhausted from trying to create a business for the laird's mistress, and that was *enough!*

She opened the door and took a step into the hallway. But she could feel Grace's eyes on her back.

Temperance gave a sigh that had tears in it, but she didn't turn around to see Grace's long face. "Wake me," she said, then closed the door behind her.

Twelve

"Don't these children ever have any *fun?*" Temperance said as she looked about the ballroom at the children standing stiffly against the walls. In the center of the room was a pile of roller skates.

"Yes, of course they do. But they've never been inside a ballroom and you're a *lady,*" Grace whispered. She said the last word as though Temperance were so refined she wouldn't drink tea out of a mug but must have only the finest china.

Temperance gave a sigh. "Alys, you and Ramsey—" She stopped when she saw the horror on the faces of these, the two oldest children. If they could have, they would have disappeared into the wooden paneling.

"And this is what I missed sleep for," Temperance said as she stifled a yawn. So much for her brilliant idea of giving the children of McCairn a secret day of fun. Maybe when the food arrived, they'd perk up. She'd had Eppie and her younger sister baking since four A.M., and there were the oranges and chocolate that her mother had sent, so maybe…

But Temperance couldn't help feeling great disappointment. Two days before, she'd had to actually meet—face-to-face—with that dreadful man, Hamish, and she'd had to be *nice* to him. She'd asked him to forgive her for her rude behavior of the first day and she'd quietly and demurely asked him to allow her to teach a Bible class on Sunday. She'd then shown him the Bibles that she planned to present to the children during her class.

Of course the odious man had made her grovel. He'd demanded to know what text she planned to teach the children. With a mind full of nothing but hat shapes and thoughts of what dreadful woman her mother would dredge up next, Temperance couldn't think of a single Bible story. Stalling for time, she opened one of the white Bibles and saw the word, "Esther."

"The story of Esther and King… And the king. I've always loved that story, and I think it has a good moral to it."

"That depends on how you interpret it," he said suspiciously.

"How would *you* interpret it?" Temperance said, then gave him the smile she reserved for men she was trying to persuade to donate money to her foundation.

After that she'd had to listen to a forty-five-minute lecture about the morality of the story of Esther.

"And all for nothing," Temperance said now.

"What?" Grace asked.

"I said that I went through all of this for nothing. I could have fed the children in the open, but I wanted to give them something that was more fun than just eating." But for all her persuasive powers, she'd not been able to coax the children into so much as touching the skates.

"But they do look dangerous," Grace said, looking at the pile on the floor.

"No they aren't," Temperance said in disgust. "I spent half my childhood racing along the sidewalks of New York. I was a terror on skates, and my mother constantly received complaints about me. There wasn't a kid in the neighborhood who could outrace me, or do more tricks."

"But these children don't know you, and they've never even seen skates, so of course they're a bit shy."

At that, Temperance had strapped a pair of skates to her shoe soles, and she'd taken a few turns around the ballroom floor, nothing fancy, just rolling about, and telling the children how easy and fun skating was. But still, the children refused to so much as try on the strange-looking contraptions.

Temperance would have sworn that Ramsey would have jumped at the chance to do something adventurous; after all, he rode dangerous horses on a daily basis. But Ramsey had looked at her as though she were crazy and said, "A body could get hurt on them things," and had stepped away from her. "When will the food get here?" he asked.

So now, here she was with over a dozen children all lined up against the wall, all looking sleepy and grumpy from the boring old church service, and she could get them to do nothing.

"Maybe if I—" she began, but at that moment the door to the ballroom flew open and in the doorway stood James.

Everyone in the room, including Temperance, drew in their breath sharply. Even if they weren't touching the skates, they all knew that what they weren't doing was having a Bible class.

"What's going on here?" James demanded with a scowl, looking about the room. "I thought you were teaching Sunday school?"

Temperance wasn't absolutely, positively *sure,* but she thought she saw a twinkle in his eye. Was he teasing or was he serious?

Temperance decided to take a chance. Skating to the middle of the ballroom (and the silence was so deafening a feather hitting the floor would have sounded like a crash), she picked up a pair of skates and held them out toward him.

"Bet you can't do it," she said, then held her breath.

The twinkle in James McCairn's eyes brightened until there was a galaxy of stars in there. "Want to put money on that, woman?" he said as he took the skates from her, then sat down on a chair and started to strap the skates onto his shoes.

But he didn't know how to use the key Temperance handed him to widen the front piece so his big shoes would fit. Instead, he tried to twist the skate and when that didn't work, he tried to wedge his shoe sole into the hooks.

When Temperance heard a tiny snigger, she thought she'd better help him. He might not take kindly to having the children laugh at him. "Like this," she said, then inserted the key and turned. Within minutes, she had the skates adjusted and strapped to his heavy work boots.

"Now, hold my arm," she said as she stepped back, "and I'll help you."

"Ha!" James said as he stood up. "I'm the Laird of Clan McCairn, and I don't need a woman to— Oh! *Oooooooohhhhhh,*" he said as he stood and the skates began to roll. James's long arms spread out, and he began to turn them in circles as he tried to keep his balance.

A child sniggered; then one laughed.

James's movements grew more exaggerated as he rolled across the floor. His legs spread wide, and when he started to roll faster, his arms turned in such big circles that he looked as though he were trying to fly.

Two more children laughed. Not loudly, and Temperance saw that they covered their mouths with their hands, but they were laughing. Most of the others were smiling.

James moved forward, toward Temperance, and when he reached her, he fell.

But how he fell! His face hit her smack in the bosom, and his hands grabbed her rear end.

Involuntarily, she gave a little squeal and started to push him off of her. But his feet kept slipping and he kept grabbing on to her for support. And each time, his hands latched on to a "forbidden" part of her. His hands held on to her thighs, her buttocks. At one point she pushed him away, but his feet flew out from under him and he would have landed on top of her with his hands clutching her breasts, but she did a quick about-face and skated away from him.

With sounds of *"Ooooooooohhhhhhh"* escaping from him, he tried to keep his feet under control as he slipped and rolled toward her.

As though the Hounds of Hell were after her, Temperance skated to the other side of the huge ballroom. But James was right behind her, and his hands were outstretched toward her. If he fell, he was going to take her down with him.

Frantically, Temperance fled from him, but his strength and ineptitude were too much for her; wherever she went, he was right behind her.

It was in front of the windows that he caught her. She was trapped in front of the glass and he was coming fast toward her! His legs were wide open, his arms twirling rapidly, and he was going to crash into her. There was nothing she could do to escape.

Putting her arms over her head for protection, she waited for the coming blow; she just hoped that he didn't propel both of them through the windows to the ground below.

But when he reached her, James's arms encircled her, pulled her forward, and only then did she hit the wooden floor—and the landing was softened by his arms around her waist. It wasn't so much that she fell as it was that he'd picked her up and set her on the floor. And in the next minute, he had flipped himself over and the back of his head was against her stomach and he was raising his arms as though to an audience.

It was only then that Temperance looked up. For the last several minutes she'd been fighting for her life as this crazy man had chased her about the room, but now she saw that everyone in the room was laughing hilariously. Grace had her arms around her stomach as she bent over in laughter. Ramsey's face was red from laughing so hard. All the children were screaming with laughter; some of them had even fallen to the floor, their legs unable to hold them up.

"You great fake," Temperance hissed into James McCairn's ear. "You *can* skate."

"Never said I couldn't," he whispered back, smiling at the children. "I didn't grow up in McCairn so I learned a little about the outside world. But you'd think, what with all those sidewalks in New York, that you'd be a little better than this."

She looked down at him, his head on her stomach, lounging on her as though he meant to spend the rest of the day there; then she looked up at the children. They had their laughter under control now and were beginning to talk to each other. But all she could hear was McCairn this and McCairn that.

Temperance would never have admitted to herself that what she was feeling was jealousy, but she was used to being the center of attention. After all, she gave speeches that hundreds of people paid to hear. But now she was just the buffoon in a skating melodrama, and... Well, maybe she wanted to have the children think highly of her. On the other hand, it was McCairn's land and his people and Temperance would be leaving soon, so maybe she should allow him to make such a laughingstock of her that the children would remember this for the rest of their lives.

"Like hell I will," she said under her breath, then pushed him off of her and came to her feet.

"How dare you treat me like that," she said loudly, and everyone in the room instantly stopped laughing and stared at her.

Then, with her eyes solely on James, Temperance began to skate backwards. "You think you can make a fool of me and get away with it?" she half shouted as she put up her fists as though she meant to fight him.

There was silence in the ballroom.

Slowly, James got to his feet. "I don't have to make you into what you already are," he said quietly, his dark eyes hard and angry.

For a moment Temperance hesitated. Was he serious? But then she saw those sparkles in his eyes, and she almost smiled in relief. But she didn't smile.

"You think you're man enough to take *me* on?" As though she were a clown in a circus, she began to make exaggerated gestures of anger, all the while backing up, her legs wide apart, her feet weaving in and out to give her momentum.

When James stood, at first he acted as though he were doing all he could to keep his balance and his dignity. No more churning arms, but he wove about unsteadily.

He was good. Temperance could see that now. He was good enough that he could purposefully throw himself off balance yet never lose control. As a kid, no one had ever been able to keep up with Temperance, but she could see that if she'd met an eleven-year-old James McCairn, he would have given her a run for the money.

Now they were at opposite ends of the ballroom, and around them the children were watching in wide-eyed silence. She could feel that they were afraid. Was this a real argument? Or were these two adults pretending again?

When Temperance looked up at James, she saw him move his chin downward in a quick gesture. It took only a second to know what he had in mind.

174

"I'm going to murder you," she yelled, then gave a couple of powerful strokes and went flying toward him. Could she pull it off? she wondered as she neared him. Had she understood his gesture correctly? Would he catch her, or would she go flying through the windows at the end of the room?

But she trusted him.

Seconds before she was about to run into him full force, she crouched down, tucked her head into her chest, stuck one leg out, then put her arms straight up in the air, and she was moving fast between his legs. James caught her by the wrists, and in one lightning-fast powerful movement, he then turned quickly, and instantly, they were both facing in the opposite direction and James was skating backwards, holding Temperance's uplifted hands, her compressed body balanced on her one skate, between his legs.

When James finally stopped against the opposite wall, Temperance didn't move. Her head was down, her leg was still up, and her thigh muscles were screaming with pain. But she didn't hear a sound from the children.

"Are they still there?" she whispered up to James.

"Scared," he whispered back.

But in the next second Temperance heard the sound of a single pair of hands clapping, and in the next, the room erupted in laughter and applause.

After several minutes, when the sounds began to die down, hands grabbed her under the arms and she was pulled out from between James's legs. When she tried to stand, she was stiff, both from the unaccustomed exertion and from her fear that the trick wasn't going to work.

It was Ramsey who'd helped her up, and Grace was beside him. "I've never seen anything like that in my life," she breathed, looking at Temperance with eyes full of astonishment. "Did you two practice that?"

"No," Temperance said, her hand to her back. "We just—" Breaking off, she looked up at James. He was surrounded by children, each with a pair of skates in hand and wanting him to help put them on. Grace was still waiting for an answer. "We just—" What? Have a natural rapport so we can communicate with just tiny gestures given between us?

Temperance was saved from answering by the door opening and Eppie and her younger sister bringing in the first of four trays full of food. With a collective squeal, the children ran toward the food, Grace behind them, so Temperance and James were alone at the far end of the ballroom.

Temperance didn't know what to say to him. In a way, what they had just done had been very intimate.

"And what are you planning to teach *next* Sunday?" he asked; then they both laughed and the awkward moment was gone.

"You have any horse liniment?" she asked, putting her hand on her hip where she was sure she was bruised.

"Never need it myself," James said. "Since I climb mountains and herd sheep and—"

At that moment one of the older children lost control of his skates and slammed into the back of James. This time he went down in earnest, grabbing Temperance as he fell, so that she landed on top of him.

Of course all the children thought this was more of the show, and with their mouths full, they laughed at the two of them.

Temperance pulled herself off James, then looked at him as he stayed where he was, in a crumpled heap on the floor.

"So?" she said, looking down at him, her eyes full of laughter.

"In the tack room, third shelf down, on the right. But, first, get these things off of me."

Smiling, Temperance bent down, and using the key that was on a string about her neck, she removed his skates; then he sat there while she took hers off as well. By now the floor was full of children, all wearing skates and pulling each other about the room. Frequent thuds of children falling were followed by screams of laughter.

Standing, James put his arm around Temperance's shoulders. "Think anyone will miss us?" he asked, standing on one foot.

She looked at the activity around them, with kids screaming, laughing, some eating, some scooting about on the skates. "Somehow, I don't think so," she said, then she caught Grace's eye and Grace nodded, meaning that Temperance had done well.

"Come on," James said. "I know where there's a bottle of wine and some cheese and something soft for our backsides."

"All right," Temperance said, smiling up at him. His arm was about her shoulders, and one of hers was around his waist. Her other hand was on his hard, flat stomach muscles. Usually when a man offered her wine and "a soft place," she ran the other way, and if he followed, she'd been known to use the steel point of her umbrella as a means to stop him. "Sounds wonderful," she said, then helped him limp out the door.

❦

The "something soft" was a pile of straw that wasn't too clean, and the wine and cheese was just that: a bottle of wine and a chunk of cheese. No glasses, no pretty porcelain plates, no candles; just sustenance.

However, as soon as they were in the dirty tack room that smelled of horses and old leather, James sat down on a bale of straw and pulled his shirt off over his head. "Right there," he said as he held out a bottle of wine to her, then pointed to the back of his left shoulder.

It took Temperance a moment to realize that he wanted her to rub liniment into that area.

All her life, she'd prided herself on being a "free spirit," an enlightened person. So what was she to do now? Say to him that her sense of propriety didn't allow her to pass a bottle of wine back and forth with a man? That she couldn't be alone with a half-dressed man? And, besides, wouldn't that sound absurd when, just ten minutes before, she'd been rolling between his legs?

"What are you waiting for?" he asked impatiently.

"For my mother to come storming in and tell me I'm doomed," Temperance said.

The look he gave her over his bare shoulder told her that he knew exactly her dilemma. His eyes turned soft and seductive. "You're not going to turn coward on me now, are you?"

Ignoring the bottle of wine, as she needed her senses to remain clear, she took the bottle of liniment down from a shelf, poured it on her hands, then began to massage his shoulder. His big, thick, muscular shoulder. On his warm, smooth, dark skin.

Well, she thought as she tried to override her senses with her brain, she was once again experiencing lust and, as before, she was going to be able to say that she had overcome it. She had not given in to her baser needs and—

"Care for a tumble in the hay?" James said with a lowered-lashes look up at her.

That broke the spell by making her laugh. "So tell me about your late wife. If you never liked her, why did you marry her?"

He grimaced, the invitation gone from his eyes. "For a housekeeper, you certainly are interested in things that aren't any of your business."

"It's none of my business to entertain the children of your village, either, but I did it, didn't I?"

"Oh? When I got there, it didn't look as though you were being very entertaining. It looked to me like you wanted to run away and hide. Oh! Watch those nails of yours."

"Sorry," Temperance said with no sincerity in her voice. "If you want to rub this on by yourself, just tell me."

"No, that's all right. Lower, yes, yes, that's the right place."

When she saw him close his eyes in what appeared to be ecstasy caused by her touch, she knew she had to either leave or talk very fast.

"Wife, remember? You were telling me about your wife."

"No, you were snooping into my business again, but I wasn't telling you anything."

At that Temperance took her hands off his bare back.

James started talking immediately, and Temperance went back to rubbing. "I was in love with a village girl, but my father took me to London and dangled beautiful women in front of me, so I gave in and married one of them. The one *he* chose. Then I brought her back here to McCairn to live. There's nothing else to tell except that she cried for the whole two years we were married."

"What happened to her?"

James was quiet for a moment; then he looked at the row of horse harnesses hanging on the wall. "One moonless night she tried to run away. She jumped on one of my nervous racehorses, and I guess she meant to go to Midleigh, but she must have become disoriented." His voice lowered. "She rode the horse over the cliff, and they both went into the sea."

Temperance didn't want to ask, but she couldn't help herself. "Do you think it was suicide?"

"No!" James said sharply. "I don't want another suicide in the family. With what my grandmother did, we have enough sins on us."

"But your grandmother didn't commit suicide," Temperance said, then put her liniment-coated hand over her mouth in horror at what she'd said. She'd just betrayed a confidence!

For a moment James just looked straight ahead, saying nothing. "All right, out with it," he said softly. "What has that nosy nature of yours snooped out now?"

"If you're going to talk to me like that, I don't think I'll tell you anything," she said as she popped the cork back into the liniment.

This time when he spoke, his voice held command. It was soft, but she knew that he wasn't joking. "You will tell me what you know about my grandmother."

But Temperance refused to be intimidated by him. "I thought you didn't like her. Didn't you call her The Great Spender?"

Standing, James picked up his shirt. "Because

the woman had faults didn't stop me from loving her. She was a good woman to me. Now tell me what you know."

Temperance didn't want to tell him anything and wished with all her might that she'd kept her mouth shut. But she could see from his face that he wasn't going to let her get away with saying nothing.

"Sit," he said, nodding toward the bale of straw he'd just risen from.

Temperance obeyed him, then sat in silence as he untied the laces from one of her walking boots.

"You might have the opinion that this was not a happy house," he said as he pulled off her boot.

At that Temperance could only make a sound of disbelief. Gambling. Murder. Revenge. No, not exactly a happy household.

"I know that the villagers love to talk about my family and Grace is a big talker."

"You would know *that,*" Temperance said, then opened her eyes wide, for her voice sounded quite bitter. Why had she said that? But when he'd mentioned Grace, she'd instantly thought of the very intimate relationship that he'd once had with the woman. And now Grace was living in the same house with him. Were they still...sharing?

"You want to..." He nodded his head toward her stockinged foot.

"Oh," she said, then hesitated before pulling up her skirt and unfastening her garter in front of him. Should she tell him to look away? There was a wicked part of her that wanted to stretch out her leg and—

But James solved the problem by turning away long enough for her to quickly unfasten both stockings and roll them off her feet. She tucked them into her pockets. When she was finished, he knelt and his big hands held her small foot.

James didn't seem to have heard the tone of her voice. "I know that you've heard of gambling and feuds that lasted for generations, but—"

"No one told me of a feud," she said with interest.

At that James clamped down on her ankle with his big hand. "Are you going to listen or try to get even more information from me?"

"I'd like to see all the pieces of the puzzle."

At that James shook his head. "Damn it, woman! My grandmother is buried in unconsecrated ground, and it plagues me. If you know something about her death, I want to hear it."

"Your grandfather killed her," she said, then held her breath as she waited for the coming explosion.

But there was none. Instead, James opened the bottle of liniment and began to massage it into her sore ankle. "Yes, I can see that," he said after a while. "The old man had a ferocious temper."

"And how many girls did *he* throw out the window?" Temperance said, trying to lighten the mood. After all, this had happened many years ago.

James looked up at her with a one-sided grin. "A few. So now, tell me everything that you know and where you heard it."

Temperance started to say that she was under a bond of secrecy, but it was too late for that now, so she told him how Grace's husband had seen the accidental shooting, then later James's grandfather had claimed that his wife had committed suicide.

"Bastard!" James said under his breath as he picked up Temperance's other foot.

"It was an arranged marriage," he said as he rubbed her ankle. "And they hated each other."

"Like you and your wife," Temperance said softly.

"Yes," he said flatly. "Like my wife and me. But theirs was a loveless marriage from the start, and my grandparents wanted nothing in the world but to hurt each other. He gambled and she spent."

At that Temperance leaned toward him, her face eager. "But where is what she bought?"

When James looked up at her, there was amusement on his face. "Don't tell me you've believed that old legend? That somewhere in that house is Aladdin's treasure trove?"

"Oh," Temperance said, deflated, as she leaned back and he began to rub her ankle with liniment. "I thought maybe..."

He looked up at her with one eyebrow raised. "You thought what? That you and I could start tearing down walls and looking?

You don't think that my grandfather did that, as well as my father? Or that my brother and I didn't spend every moment we were in that house looking for the treasure?"

Negativity had never made Temperance give up anything. "But Grace said that her husband found receipts for things that your grandmother bought, things made of silver, and even gold statues by Cellini."

For a moment James was silent as he massaged her ankle, and as his silence lengthened, her heart began to beat faster. As a child she'd loved the book *Treasure Island*.

"What receipts?" James asked quietly.

Temperance wanted to whoop with triumph. But she took a deep breath and calmed herself. "I have no idea. What do they matter, anyway, since there is no treasure to be had? Just because your grandmother spent the family fortune to keep it out of the hands of your gambling grandfather but she died without telling anyone where she'd stored the—

She broke off because James had grabbed her shoulders and planted a kiss on her mouth. It was a hard kiss that soon turned soft and sweet, and she never wanted it to end.

After too short a time, he moved away and looked at her. There was amusement on his handsome face. "Whatever you've been doing all your life, it's not been kissing," he said.

At that Temperance lost her good mood and pushed his hands away. "That's because I don't want to kiss *you*."

"Sure about that?" he said as he bent forward again.

But there was nothing that could kill ardor more effectively than being told one was no good at something. Her mother would say that Temperance wasn't supposed to be good at kissing because Temperance wasn't married. Whatever, all Temperance's good feelings were gone.

James put his hand under her chin and lifted her to look at him. "I hurt your feelings?"

"Of course not!" she said with an insolence that she didn't feel. "But are you interested in anything at all besides sex?"

At that he blinked at her. Obviously he wasn't used to hearing women say that word. "No, it's all I think about. I can't get any work done for thinking about what I'd like to do to women in bed. I think about—"

She knew that he was teasing her, but she also knew that she didn't like the way this conversation was going. "Receipts, remember? This all started when I—Hey!"

James had grabbed her by the wrist and was pulling her out of the tack room toward the house. He didn't seem to notice that her shoes had been left behind, but as Temperance stepped on stones and something squishy, she was well aware of her bare feet. Please don't let it be horse manure, she said as he half dragged her into the house.

186

Temperance tucked her bare feet under her skirt and yawned. Last night she'd stayed up till early morning helping Grace make hats. She'd spent today in a rigorous bout of roller-skating, and now here it was late at night and she was going over account books with a man who had told her she didn't know how to kiss.

"Nothing," James said for at least the seventeenth time.

Around them were account books dating back to 1762. "If these books were in America, they'd be in a museum," Temperance said, yawning again.

"If you want to go to bed, do so," James said, but his tone let her know that he'd forever after consider her a wimp if she did.

She stretched out her feet in front of her and wiggled her bare toes. There were half a dozen candles lit in the room, but the old library was still so dark that they might as well have been in a cave. "What I want to know is why your grandmother didn't tell someone what she was doing. If she did buy and hide all these things, why didn't she tell someone?"

"She didn't expect to die when she did."

"No one expects to die ever, but we still make out wills. Accidents can take anyone at a moment's notice. And if your grandfather's temper was such that you weren't surprised to hear that he'd murdered her in a struggle, why didn't she prepare for that possibility?"

"Accidentally."

"What?"

"It was an accidental death, remember? Not murder. It wasn't as though he picked up the pistol and shot her."

"Sure. Right. But I wonder who it was who had the pistol in the first place? Did he threaten her with it? 'You tell me where the things you bought are or I'll blow your head off,' that sort of thing."

"Remind me never to go to America," he said absently as he flipped through an account book for the fifth time. "Do you think Grace knows what Gavie did with the accounts he found?"

"She didn't say. You should go ask her. I'm sure you know where her bedroom is." At that Temperance froze. Why had she said that?

James didn't look up. "That's the second time you've acted jealous of Grace. Are you *sure* you don't want to stay here in McCairn?"

"Jealous?" she said. "Don't be ridiculous. And there are people in New York who need me. Look, I'm going to bed. We can look for whatever you hope to find in the morning," she said as she stood up. "It's just too bad that your grandmother didn't return your love enough to entrust *you* with the knowledge of what she'd put where."

"Sweet Mother of—" James said under his breath.

When Temperance turned to look at him, his eyes were wide in shock. "What?!" she demanded when he just sat there saying nothing.

188

"She gave me a pack of cards."

"She was buying great works of art and all she shelled out for her beloved grandson was a pack of cards? Didn't she know you *weren't* the gambling brother?"

"That's just it," James said softly. "She told me to hide the cards from Colin and my grandfather or they'd take them from me and lose them and they were very, very important cards."

Temperance's mind was racing. "If she'd given you anything else, you would have played with it and worn it out, but you've kept the cards hidden and safe all these years?" Hope made her voice rise on the end.

"Yes," James said, and the sound was barely a whisper. "In a box in my bedroom."

At that Temperance made a leap for the door at the same time that James jumped up and started running. They reached the doorway at the same time, and both tried to go through it at once. Temperance was determined to win, so she pushed hard, her body slammed up against James's as they were wedged in the doorframe.

It was after several moments, when she wasn't making any progress, that she looked up at him. He was smiling down at her, with that one-sided smirk of his. The front of her body was wedged up against the front of his body, and he was toying with her, keeping her from getting through the doorway.

She narrowed her eyes in threat at him. He laughed, then stepped back to let her pass. "You may be bad at entertaining the children, but you're certainly keeping *me* amused," he said.

Temperance didn't bother answering him as she ran up the stairs to his bedroom. At the doorway she paused; he was right behind her. She looked into his bedroom, then back up at him. "You touch me and I'll put sand in your food all next week," she said.

"After what I found out from kissing you, I'm not even tempted," he said, then moved past her to enter the bedroom.

For a moment Temperance stood outside the room frowning. She'd never met a man who could make her as angry as he could. Part of her wanted to turn away, go to her own bedroom and get some sleep. Let him unravel his own family mysteries by himself!

But then she saw him digging inside a big old chest that she was sure some medieval ancestor had carried on the Crusades, and she went into the room to look over his shoulder.

"Here!" he said as he pulled out a little box, then carried it to the bed. "Get that candle, would you?"

One of the "girls," Eppie or her sister, had lit a single candle in his bedroom, so Temperance carried it across the room to set it on the table by the bed. "No, put it here," he said, frowning, meaning for her to sit on the bed beside him.

She was so interested in what he had in his hands that she didn't hesitate, but climbed up on the high bed, put the candle in its pewter holder down on the heavy velvet spread, and looked at what he held.

"I haven't looked at these in years," he said, leaning on one arm toward her. "My grandmother gave these to me when I was nine, only a year before she died."

His voice was soft, and the heavy hangings of the bed made them seem as though they were isolated. Suddenly, all her annoyance with him was gone. It was as though she could see the little boy who had grown up among gamblers and a grandfather with a "ferocious" temper.

As he opened the box, he spoke softly. "She told me these were very, very valuable and that I was to keep them always." He looked up at Temperance, their heads mere inches apart. "She said they were my future."

Temperance thought of about a dozen things she wanted to say to that, but she bit down on her tongue and kept quiet.

"I thought they were fortune-telling cards, but I couldn't figure out how to use them."

By the time James spread the cards out on the bed, Temperance's heart was pounding. He spread them out in a perfect fan, and from the formation she could tell that he wasn't a stranger to a deck of cards.

But as soon as she saw the cards, her heart steadied. There was nothing at all special about them. They were red-and-white on the back, one of those intricate patterns that card makers seemed to love. Nothing at all even interesting.

When she looked at James, her disappointment showed on her face.

James gave her a tiny smile, then looked down at the cards. Slowly, he turned one over.

On the face of the card was a picture of a diamond necklace. In the corners were the symbols for the ace of diamonds.

The next card he turned over was the three of hearts. It had a picture of a small golden cherub.

Slowly, Temperance picked up the card and held it to the candlelight. "Looks Italian to me," she said, then looked back at James. He was smiling at her as though he were waiting for her to figure out something.

Looking at him, trying to read his mind, she suddenly had a thought. Turning, she reached down and flipped the whole curved fan in one gesture. When the other side was exposed, she saw works of art and jewelry and silver serving dishes.

"Oh, dear," Temperance said. "Do you think that these are the things she bought?"

"I always thought so, but I could find no verification. And of course my grandfather wasn't telling. That's why the reciepts Gavie found interested me."

"But in all those years you found nothing?"

"Not really. A couple of times we found some things like dishes, like you found, but nothing else. The first time we showed the dishes to my grandfather and he smashed them. After that we had to keep anything we found secret and we had to keep our searching a secret. He didn't like any reminder of his wife."

"Can't imagine why. Guilt maybe?" She held up one of the cards and looked at it. There was a sapphire ring on the four of diamonds. "Except for some of the silver pieces, everything seems to be small, and all of it's nonperishable, no oil paintings that would rot. All of these things would hold up over long storage."

"Any idea *where* she stored them?" James asked.

"That's the question I should ask *you*. Remember, you're the laird and I'm the visitor."

"Right," he said, smiling, as he picked up another card. The six of spades showed a small bronze statue, probably Greek, probably ancient. "So now that we have an inventory, how do we find the goods?"

"Did she leave you anything else? A map maybe? Think hard."

He knew she was making fun of him, but he still laughed. The treasure was part of his childhood, and since he'd become laird, he hadn't had much time to think of anything but work. As he gathered the cards up and put them back into the box, he said, "I can't see that we're any closer to finding the treasure than we were before."

There was something about the way he said "we" that suddenly made her aware that they were alone in a house where the other occupants were sleeping. They were alone in his room on his bed.

Quickly, Temperance rolled to the other side of the bed and put her feet on the floor. "I think I've had it for one night." She gave a fake yawn as though she were dead tired. Truth was, she seemed to have lost her sleepiness.

Lazily, James rolled off the other side of the bed. "That's right. You have to go into Edinburgh tomorrow, so you'd better get your sleep."

"Edinburgh?" she said, not having any idea what he was talking about. "Why—"

"You said you and Grace had to buy something for the house, remember?"

"Oh, yes, of course," she said. She'd forgotten the lie she'd made up to explain why she and Grace were going to the city. Tomorrow was the day of the secret luncheon when they were to wear Grace's hats. "Shopping. I nearly forgot."

"I have a few things you can pick up for me. Tobacco. Sheep-dip. A couple of wolf traps. A bit of horse harness."

With each word, Temperance's face became more contorted. "Wolf traps?"

"Sure. You can take the wagon and a couple of the men. You'll need the wagon if you mean to pick up produce, so why not get the other things at the same time?"

"Are wolf traps part of the housekeeper's job?" she asked.

"Maybe you're right. Maybe I should go with you. It would do me good to get out of here. I'll see if I can find some trousers and—"

"No!" she said, trying to think of a reason

why he couldn't go. But she'd had too little sleep to be able to think clearly.

"No trousers? I can see why a woman would want me to have bare knees, and if you insist—"

She was just too, too tired to think of a lie of any sort. "I don't care what you wear, but you're not going with *me*. I want a day away from this place and from you. And no wolf traps. Or sheep harnesses. Or—"

"Dip. Sheep-dip. Horse harnesses."

She saw then that he was teasing her again, and she doubted that he'd ever meant to go with her into Edinburgh. From what she knew about him, he'd probably rather walk across barbed wire barefoot than spend a day in a city. And she doubted if he *ever* wore trousers. Or underwear, for that matter.

She walked to the door, opened it, but he stopped her before she could close it.

"Thank you for what you did for the children today," he said softly. "That was kind of you."

She tried to keep from blushing with pleasure at his praise. "You're welcome. They're nice children and I enjoyed it."

"Me too," he said, and he sounded so like an enthusiastic little boy that she laughed.

"Good night."

"Yes, good night, and if I don't see you before you leave tomorrow, happy shopping."

"Yes, thank you and good night." She started to close the door, but she opened it again. "James," she said.

"Yes?"

"What happened to your village girl? The one you said you were in love with?"

"My mother felt sorry for her, so she sent her to school in Glasgow. I heard she married some old man a few years later."

Temperance wasn't sure, but there still seemed to be some bitterness in his voice. But then, she'd heard a thousand women tell her that they never got over their first love. So maybe it was the same with men.

"Well, good night," she said again, then quietly closed the door behind her and went to her own room. She was asleep minutes later.

Thirteen

"We *did* it!" Temperance said as she leaned back against the hard seat of the old wagon.

"*You* did," Grace said softly as she held the reins of the horses. "I had nothing at all to do with it."

Temperance ignored her words. "Remember the smug look on that awful woman's face when she said good-bye to us? She thought she'd pulled something off, didn't she? The House of Grace. By tomorrow all of Edinburgh will have heard of you."

"Not me, you," Grace said insistently. "I did nothing."

"Only made the most beautiful hat I've ever seen, that's all."

"But what does that matter? Many people have talent. Brenda tells wonderful stories and Lilias makes liqueur from seaweed, but they aren't selling their talents in Edinburgh. They aren't making money from what they can do."

"Oh, well, it just takes a bit of conniving."

"No," Grace said solemnly. "It takes a belief that you can do anything in the entire world, something that we don't have here in McCairn." Her voice lowered. "And something I don't know how we're going to do without once you leave."

"Pish posh," Temperance said, embarrassed by Grace's praise. She just wanted to think of the triumph of the day and nothing else. "Right now we both need to think about how we're going to hide your business from the people of McCairn. Somehow, I can't see Hamish condoning a woman earning money, especially not the kind of money that I think you're going to make. I've seen it in New York a hundred times. I'll help a destitute woman with a do-nothing husband and kids to support find a way to earn a living; then, when she's on her feet, the man's ego will be crushed, so he'll stop her from earning. Hundreds of times I've seen it."

"Do you think James will want to stop me?" Grace asked as she held on to the reins. Even though it was dark, with only the moonlight to guide them, the horses certainly knew the way back to the stables.

"You know him better than I do," Temperance said, then frowned at herself because she didn't like the little pang that went through her when she said that. So she was attracted to the man. It wasn't the end of the world, was it?

"Not really," Grace said. "I know I've shared his bed, but I've never seen him talk to anyone the way he does to you."

"Really?" Temperance said, then turned away so Grace couldn't see the broadness of her smile. "He's a nice man. I mean, there are things he shouldn't do, like toss women out of windows and threaten to murder them, but, all in all, he takes care of a lot of people."

Grace was looking at her with her head cocked to one side. "Murder?"

"Oh, it was nothing, just something he said. You had to be there to understand. Look, are you *sure* you want to try to conduct your business here in McCairn? I know my mother could find you a nice little shop in Edinburgh."

"No, thank you!" Grace said firmly. "Do you forget that I grew up in that city? If I lived there and I were to die, there would be no one to take care of Alys. But here..."

"Yes," Temperance said softly, "I know. She was born here, so she will always have a home here." And that sentiment was something that Temperance was coming to truly *like* about McCairn: The people all seemed to be pulling for each other. No one was isolated or left out. Even Grace, who'd become the laird's mistress, was as much a part of them as anyone else was. Yes, Temperance thought, smiling, she liked that attitude very much.

"My goodness, but it's late," Temperance said loudly, breaking her reverie. "Once I hit that bed, I'm not going to get up for a week."

Just then they turned a bend in the road, and the old stone McCairn house came into view. On the first night Temperance had seen the place, there had been a single candle burning in one room. But tonight it looked as though the whole place was alight.

"Something's wrong," she said quietly, then louder, "something's wrong." With a jerk, she snatched the reins from Grace and yelled, *"Hiyah,"* to the two tired horses; then, when they wouldn't move fast enough to suit her, she stood up, grabbed the long whip from its holder by the seat, and cracked the thin leather over the heads of the horses.

Beside her, caught unawares, Grace flew backward over the seat and slammed into the wagonbed. Her side hit something hard and she groaned. But she didn't have time to think about pain because if she didn't catch hold of something, she was going to go flying out the back onto the road. Her hat fell down over her face, so she had to feel for the side of the wagon. When she found it, Grace pushed her hat up and looked up to see Temperance silhouetted in the moonlight. She was standing in the front of the wagon, looking like something Grace had once seen on a circus poster, swinging the whip over the horses, the sound splitting the air.

When Grace saw how fast they were approaching the house, she was sure they were going to hit it. To prepare for the coming blow, she rolled herself into a ball and tried to wedge herself between the side of the wagon and the bags of whatever Temperance had bought and put into the wagon.

But just before impact, Temperance used her entire body to pull back on the reins. Grace was sure the front feet of the horses came off the ground. Then, before they had fully stopped, Temperance jumped down and ran into the house.

Shaking from fear and the ride-through-hell, Grace got down from the wagon and went into the house.

⁓⊙⊙⊙⊱

Dearest Mother,

It is late at night and I am dead with exhaustion, but I must tell you about what happened tonight. I apologize that I didn't get to see you while Grace and I were in Edinburgh today, but we had so very much to do that there was no time.

First of all, Grace's hats were a great success. We were seen and noticed, and she now has a contract to produce twenty-five hats as soon as she can make them. I told the owner of the

200

shop that it will be extremely difficult to get enough of the old fabrics that Grace uses on the hats, so she raised the price she was offering by nearly half. Considering the acres of rotting curtains that James has in this old place, Grace will be able to make hats for the rest of the century.

When we returned to the house, every window was ablaze with light. If you knew how frugal all of McCairn was, you'd know how unusual this is. I was terrified that something horrible had happened, so, without thinking, I grabbed the reins of the horses and made them run. Remember how Daddy taught me to stand in the wagon and crack the whip? I remember that the one and only time I showed you what he'd taught me to do, we had to use smelling salts to revive you.

Anyway, all of McCairn was inside the house waiting for us.

Mother, you have to understand this. For three days, Grace and her mother-in-law and Alys, Grace's daughter, and I have been making hats in secret. Total secret. We've let no one know what we were doing. But, somehow, everyone in the village knew and they were all waiting for us when we returned to McCairn.

You should have seen it! All the children were there, even the newborn daughter of Grace's husband's second cousin was sleeping in her mother's arms. Everyone, even Horrible Hamish, the tyrannical pastor, was there, all waiting for us to return and tell them how it had gone with Grace's hats in Edinburgh.

So much for secrecy in McCairn! I'd like to think that the pastor didn't know the full details of the way I skated between James's legs on Sunday afternoon, but I bet he knows enough to draw pictures!

Anyway, you know what a ham I am when I have an audience. You always said, Like father, like daughter, and I guess I am. I was very tired from the long day, actually, I was tired from several long days of skating and looking for treasure with James, but as soon as I saw those faces so very eager for a story, I lost my tiredness and started spinning the tale.

And what a story it is!!

Grace and I told no one what we were doing or the real reason we were going into Edinburgh because we were so afraid we'd fail. Now, knowing that everyone knew what we were up to, I see that they must have had a great laugh at all our elaborate attempts at secrecy.

Since we'd told people we were going shopping for household essentials, we set off in our everyday clothes. But once we were within a mile of the city, we stopped and changed into my two best outfits. Grace is a bit thinner than I am, but the clothes fit well enough. And of course we were wearing hats trimmed so beautifully by Grace.

We had lunch at The Golden Dove, just as you had arranged for us, and within thirty minutes of our entry, a woman came up to me and asked where I'd bought my hat. I said, "I can't tell you. If I told, my milliner would be inundated with orders, then I'd never get my hats, would I?"

When the woman walked away in a huff, I thought Grace was going to die. It took me a while to calm her down, but she was still so jittery that she ate little of the exquisite luncheon.

But I knew what I was doing. That woman wasn't going to give up, and if she did, then she didn't deserve one of Grace's hats.

At the end of the luncheon, a waitress dropped a very messy batch of cakes onto my hat, and before I could say a word, she'd snatched it off my head. (Thankfully, I had thought to remove the pins earlier, which meant that I couldn't so much as bend my neck during the entire meal.) The waitress took the hat away, insisting that she had to clean it for me. Ten minutes later, she returned the hat with a thousand apologies.

Grace was more nervous than ever, but I told her to calm down and eat her eclair. Minutes later, we saw the waitress hand a piece of paper to the woman who'd asked me for the name of my hatmaker.

I knew it was the name and address from the label inside my hat. We had made the label big enough that the most nearsighted woman could read it without her glasses.

After we saw that exchange of information, Grace and I could hardly contain ourselves. We ran outside where we could release our laughter in a great explosion.

After luncheon, we spent an hour wandering about the city (I had some things to purchase for James), then we took a leisurely stroll by the hat shop whose name you had given us. Since the silly proprietor didn't come out to us, we had to go inside to "look around." Since three women had already been there to ask about hats from the House of Grace, it took only thirty minutes to reach an agreement with the woman to produce hats for her shop and hers alone.

During the entire negotiations, Grace didn't say a word, just sat there and looked at me and wrung her hands. The shop proprietor said, "All artists are like that," and I thought Grace was going to faint from the praise. An artist!

So now Grace is established as an exclusive designer of women's hats. I'm to do the accounting and establish the prices for the hats for as long as I'm here. After that... Well, we'll find someone who can do my job later.

So when we got home, the house was lit up and all the people of the village were waiting to hear what had happened. James said that any business in the village benefitted everyone, so Grace's hats were everyone's business.

This is certainly different from New York where people can live next door to each other for twenty years and never know each other's names!

Anyway, we ate and drank—all at James's expense—and I told them all about the day. And, yes, dear Mother, I did enjoy myself immensely. They were an attentive, appreciative audience, and I had a good story to tell.

Oh! But it was all so wonderful to watch! I got to see Grace become a woman of major importance! Something that I hadn't considered in all this was that Grace would get to choose her employees. I could have burst my buttons in pride when she stood up in front of the fire that James had lit to take the chill off the big stone dining room, and looked at all those eager eyes as she thought about whom she was going to choose.

Oh, Mother, I was so very, very proud of her. She chose four women from the village who have no men to support them. At the time I didn't know who the women were, but later James told me everything. And now Grace has changed the fortunes of four families in McCairn, and if her hats take off, as I think they will, I wouldn't be surprised if more than four families' fortunes were bettered.

After we told all about the day—oh, but this is hard to believe!—it was Horrible Hamish who made us all laugh the hardest. He said that the real House of Grace was a sorry place to house a business.

When he said this, everyone looked at James because he owns the house where Grace was living. He keeps it repaired, but, still, it is little more than a sheepherder's shack.

James said that there was room in his old house for a hat business, but when young Ramsey made a rude remark about James living with so many unmarried women, the village decided that James should pay for the renovation of what was once a warehouse for sheepskins. I'm told that it's huge but now it's derelict, so it's going to take some time and money to fix up, but James is going to pay for everything.

Of course James protested that he had no

money or time to do anything like that, but he was booed down by all the village. It looks as though they may know enough about his finances to know what he can and cannot afford. As James has asked me to start doing his accounting for him, I'll let you know what I find out about him. All I know for sure is that he couldn't possibly be as poor as he says he is.

We desperately need sewing machines and supplies for Grace's business, so James said that, this year, he'd donate all the prize money he won from some big horse race he goes to every year to the House of Grace. At this the cheers were so loud that I feared the roof might collapse, so I think the prize money must be significant.

James clapped Ramsey on the back and said he was going to make the boy run up and down the mountain every day to get him in shape as a jockey for the race. Then HH (Horrible Hamish) said that from the way I had driven the wagon home, **I** should be the jockey. He then further shocked me by saying that if there was a race for roller-skating, we could enter me and I'd win so much prize money that we could buy all the sewing machines in the world.

I was so shocked by these statements and by the general joviality of the man that I couldn't get my mouth closed. Grace whispered to me, "Lilias is his wife and he won't remember any of this tomorrow." It took me several minutes to figure out what she was talking about. Then I remembered that she'd told me that Lilias made a delicious liqueur out of seaweed. My goodness!

But it seems that the woman gets her husband drunk every night!

Mother, do you think you could find me some information on the bottling and selling of liqueur? I haven't tasted Lilias's product yet, but I'm sure there's a market for it. If it can turn HH into a man who makes jokes, I may have found the Elixir of Life. Elixir of Humor, anyway.

So, that's about it. I must go to bed, as there is a lot to do tomorrow. James is going to start me on his account books, and I want to look at James's cards to see what I can find out about the treasure. I'll tell you all about that in the next letter.

Oh, yes, could you send about a hundred pounds of sheep-dip? It seems that I picked up lime. James made some unpleasant remarks about how he could use the lime and said I was better with ladies' hats than with sheep. I told him I was better at anything in the world than he was, and one thing led to another and now it looks like there's a chance that I might actually be riding a horse in the coming race. If you saw the way James's fancy racehorses dance around even when they have a rider on their back, you'd start praying for me.

Now I really, really must *go to bed.*
Love and kisses,
Your daughter,
Temperance

Fourteen

"What an extraordinary letter," Melanie O'Neil said to her husband, Angus, as she finished reading it aloud.

"I think I'd better bring her back here," Angus said, scowling. "It sounds to me like she's turning my nephew's whole village upside down."

"It does, doesn't it? But then, Temperance is so much like her father. Neither of them could ever see an obstacle. Whole mountains used to get in his way, but he'd just walk right through them, and smile while he was doing it."

"Miss him, do you?" Angus said, looking at her over the top of his reading glasses.

"Oh, my, no. Living with him was like living in the middle of a hurricane. There was much too much energy for me." She looked at the letter again. "But what is odd about this letter is that she mentions James so often. Look at this. 'Skating with James.' 'Looking for treasure with James.' 'What James said about business.' 'How James paid for the food and drink.' And here she talks of the kindness of James and how he lit a fire to take off the chill."

"Damned waste of fuel and money, if you ask me," Angus said, the newspaper again before his face.

She looked back at the letter. "The last pages are nothing but about James, James and James. I've never heard her talk about a man like this." She looked up at her husband. "You don't think she's falling in love, do you?"

"Temperance?" Angus snorted. "Not likely. But maybe she's met a man she can respect."

"What's this treasure she's talking about?"

Angus gave another snort, this time of laughter. "A stupid, senseless legend, that's all it is. My father used to say that my mother was spending the McCairn fortune and hiding everything she'd bought somewhere inside the house. It was absurd, of course, but it amused the children to search for the treasure."

"And what's this about cards?"

Angus shifted his newspaper. "I have no idea," he said, but then he put his paper down to look at her. "He must mean the playing cards. My mother had four sets of them made and gave one each to... I don't remember who. The nongamblers, I guess."

"Then you received a set?"

"I did, actually. My mother swore us to secrecy and made us promise that we would keep the cards forever."

"I see," Melanie said softly. "And where would your pack of cards be now?"

Angus picked up his paper again. "I have no idea. In the attic probably. In one of the old trunks maybe."

"Who would know where the other decks are?"

"My sister. She knows everyone and everything. She was always interested in that sort of thing, not me."

"I see," Melanie said again, then got up to go to the little writing desk in the corner to start writing a note to Angus's sister, who lived nearby in Edinburgh. She asked if they could have tea together on Thursday, at the sister's house.

⁓◦◖◗◦⁓

"Oh, you are a wicked woman," Angus's sister Rowena said to Melanie. "I've met that vain, silly girl, Charmaine Edelsten, and her dreadful mother. How could you send that girl all the way out to McCairn to meet James of all people? James would eat her alive."

"Yes, I figured as much from Angus's description of him. But I wanted to give my daughter some time away from the rigors of New York. Temperance is such a studious young woman, and so very serious. I've spent years of my life begging her to take a holiday, but she never will. So when Angus told me he was going to get Temperance to find a wife for his nephew, it seemed the perfect opportunity to force her to take a holiday. But if I'd sent some lovely young woman the first week, Temperance would have left McCairn and not had the vacation she needs so much."

"From what you've told me, it doesn't

210

sound much like she's taking any time off from saving people."

Melanie put down her teacup. She had liked Angus's sister from the moment she'd first seen her. Angus had said that Rowena was too bossy for his taste, but Melanie liked bossy people. If she hadn't, she wouldn't have married Temperance's father or Angus.

"Oh, but Temperance *is* having a holiday. She hasn't skated since she was a girl, and what could possibly have ever happened on McCairn that could rival New York City?"

At that Rowena let out a snort of laughter. She was only a year or two older than Angus, but she looked a hundred. She wore an ancient dress of what Melanie was sure was handmade lace, but the face the lace surrounded was dark and wrinkled; it was the skin of a woman who had spent her life on the back of a horse in all weather. "Like setting an iron teacup on a lace doily," Angus had said about his sister, whom he rarely saw.

"The things I could tell you about that place would curl your hair," Rowena said.

"My maid would thank you," Melanie said softly.

It took Rowena a moment to understand her meaning; then she let out a hoot of laughter. "I like you better than the other two women Angus married. For all that you look like a plump little dumpling, you've got steel inside you. My guess is that there's more of you inside that hellion daughter of yours than either of you knows."

"Oh, please don't tell Angus," Melanie said, smiling. "He thinks he likes soft women."

Again Rowena laughed heartily. "So I take it you came here to hear the history of Clan McCairn."

"If you don't mind, that is. And there are two decks of cards missing."

"My, my, you have been snooping. I have two sets, mine and my sister's, may she rest in peace. Don't tell me you found Angus's set?"

"Yes," Melanie said tiredly. "It took three maids and I two days, but we found them."

"Yes, indeed. Steel in you." She leaned toward Melanie so she could see her better. Like many truly ugly women, she was very vain and refused to wear her glasses. "What are you after? *Really* after?"

"I'm not sure, but I think I might be matchmaking my daughter and your nephew."

"Well, well, well. Think your daughter can stand up to a ruffian like my James?"

"Can your nephew stand up to my freespirited daughter?"

Rowena didn't laugh, but she did smile. Then her smile grew broader. "You may know about the cards, but do you know about the will?"

At that Melanie's eyes widened. "The will?"

"My brother is an idiot! You don't think he sent your daughter all the way out to McCairn to find James a wife just because he wants his nephew to be married, do you?"

"Well, actually, I don't think I questioned his motives."

"Angus! Playing cupid? Ha! He wants to sell James's wool."

"But he *does* sell James's wool. I don't understand."

"Angus wants to continue selling McCairn wool, and—How about if I order some more tea and…" She looked Melanie up and down. "—and some cakes. You won't mind that, will you?"

Melanie smiled. "I am rather fond of cakes," she said.

Rowena smiled. "All right. Cakes for you and a bit of whiskey for myself. You don't mind, do you?"

"We all have our vices," Melanie said with a smile.

"Then settle down and make yourself comfortable, because I have a lot of territory to cover." At that she picked up a little bell and gave it a good, hard ring. Instantly a maid appeared.

"Yes, ma'am?"

"Tea, cakes, and whiskey. And lots of all three. And hand me that box over there."

Obediently and swiftly, the maid handed her mistress a small ebony box, then left the room. Rowena handed the box to Melanie.

Inside were two decks of cards. They seemed to be ordinary cards except for the pictures of the art objects and jewelry on the fronts.

"Angus never believed any of it, nor did my sister, but I think those are pictures of what my mother bought and hid somewhere in McCairn."

"My goodness," Melanie said, holding up one of the cards. It had a picture of a sapphire ring on it. "I hope the maid brings lots of cakes and lots of tea, because I want to hear every word of the story that you can tell me."

"Gladly," Rowena said. "It will be nice to talk to someone of the younger generation. All my friends keep dying on me."

Melanie couldn't help smiling. How kind the woman was to call her "the younger generation."

⌒⊙⊙⌒

It was three hours later that Melanie O'Neil McCairn left her sister-in-law's house. By that time Rowena was drunk and Melanie had eaten three platefuls of the most exquisite little cakes. She would have eaten more, but her corset stays wouldn't allow it.

So now, riding home in the carriage, she was thoughtful, for she'd been told an extraordinary story. If James McCairn didn't marry for love within the next six weeks, before his thirty-fifth birthday, he was going to lose his ownership of McCairn.

"He'll keep the title of laird, not that it's worth much, but he'll lose the property," Rowena had said.

"But from what my daughter tells me, he loves that place and those people. They're his life. Who would like the place better?"

"No one would *like* the place," Rowena said as she poured herself more whiskey. "But his younger brother, Colin, would love to have the land. He could sell it and gamble away the proceeds, small as they would be. He has the family illness. Too bad he isn't a drinker like me; it's much cheaper."

"Oh, my," Melanie said, her mouth full of cake. "But, truly, I'm confused. If James loves the village and wants to stay there, why is he resisting my husband's efforts to find him a wife?"

"Because James doesn't know of the will."

"Doesn't know...?"

Melanie had put down her empty plate while Rowena had picked up the whiskey bottle to pour herself more, but it was empty. Leaning back against the cushions of the couch, she looked at Melanie. "It was the worst argument that Angus and I ever had. Just prior to the time of his father's death, James was in a bad way, locked into a miserable marriage and, from where he stood, he had no immediate future, as his father was still a young man. James used to beg his father to be allowed to try some things with the sheep or whatever, but my brother always said no.

"Then Ivor died in an accident. He was attending a Friday-to-Monday house party at some great estate in England and fell off the roof to his death. Afterward no one would admit to having been on the roof with him, but, knowing my older brother as I did, I'm sure he was probably chasing a housemaid.

"Anyway, James couldn't be found for nearly three weeks after his father's death. He had gone stalking in the High-lands with just a gillie, and no one knew where he was, so Angus and I had that time to hear the reading of the will and attend to what we heard."

"That James was to marry for love before he was thirty-five," Melanie said thought-fully. "But James was already married at the time."

"Yes. The will had been written some years before." Here again, Rowena's eyes bored into Melanie's.

"I see," she said. "For love. That's the key. Everyone could see that there was no love between James and his wife, so that meant that when he was thirty-five, if he was still married to his current wife, the estates would auto-matically go to Colin."

"Yes, exactly. But Colin—for I'm sure that he knew every word of that will—didn't think that the young woman would die within a year and thereby give James a second chance to complete the will's requirements."

Melanie thought about that for a moment. "But the horror of his first marriage had no doubt soured James on marriage, so he's been a confirmed bachelor all these years."

"Yes, and Angus and I have tried everything we can think of to get him married again."

"Without telling him the reason," Melanie said. "I see. If he thought he had to marry 'for love,' he'd never be able to do it, would he? You can't set out to be in love, but you can..." Her voice lowered. "—you can lie," she fin-ished.

"Now you see the argument that Angus and I had. Angus said that James should be told everything so he could get himself some pretty little girl and act like he loved her, marry her, and keep what he wanted. How hard could that be?"

"But James isn't the ne'er-do-well that I've heard that Colin is, is he?" Melanie said. "Colin could act the part but not James. But then, who is to be the judge?"

"The reigning monarch."

"What?!" Melanie said in disbelief.

"At the time of Ivor's death, Victoria was queen, and she agreed to be the judge in the dispute. Ivor and Colin were frequent guests at her house in Balmoral, and as he did with everyone, Colin charmed her—she liked the idea of marrying 'for love' so much that she agreed to be the judge."

"She certainly did believe she was going to live forever, didn't she?" Melanie asked.

"Yes, but, as far as I know, her agreement is still binding on her son Edward."

"My goodness," Melanie said. "I wouldn't want the responsibility to judge whether or not someone was in love."

"The king has a great deal of experience in that area, if you know what I mean."

At that Melanie smiled, for King Edward VII's affairs with beautiful women were all the talk of society. The talk was discreet, but it was still rampant. "What a state of things," Melanie said. "And James knows nothing of this?"

"No. I won the argument over Angus, so we agreed not to tell James."

"No wonder Angus keeps sending young women to his nephew."

At that Rowena shook her head. "We've had ten years of it! You can't imagine the number of women we've sent to my nephew. And when James comes to town... Heaven help us, but we parade them in front of him."

"But he's not tempted."

"Not in the least." At that Rowena's eyes closed for a moment. "My goodness. I'm too tired to talk anymore. Come tomorrow and I'll have Cook bake you some seed cakes. You'll like them; they're half butter," Rowena said, then she put her head on her chest and instantly went to sleep.

Melanie took a moment to pull a hand-crocheted spread off the back of the hard little couch and tuck it around Rowena before she left the room. But her mind wasn't on where she was; instead, she was thinking about all that she'd been told.

Fifteen

"Is James in love with her?" Alys asked her mother as she struggled to sew the tiny stitches that were needed to make the delicate roses that went on the hats. She was secretly being allowed to miss school to help with the hats. The secret came because she wasn't allowed to let Miss Temperance know that she wasn't in school. "Why can't she know?" Alys had asked her mother before the first question was answered. "If it's all right with the master, why wouldn't it be all right with Miss Temperance?"

"You shouldn't ask so many questions," Grace said, her mouth full of pins as she struggled to attach the flowers to the hat brim.

"I'm just trying to understand who is actually the McCairn. Is it the master or Miss Temperance or the McCairn?"

Grace stopped pinning long enough to give her daughter a quelling look and opened her mouth to snap at her, but then she thought of the way the horrible old fabric kept tearing in their hands, and there had been sunshine outside today.

Grace dropped the hat onto the table. She'd been working since four A.M. and it was now nearly six in the evening, and if she tried to do any more, her eyes were going to cross. She looked at her daughter, who'd been helping her for six of those hours. "Let's go outside, shall we?"

"Oh, yes," Alys said and dropped the hat instantly. Minutes later she and her mother were walking along the beach, and the sand between her toes made Alys feel good. Since she and her mother had been living in the big house, she'd had to wear shoes all day. The house was nice, but sometimes she missed the freedom of running barefoot along the sand.

"What's going to happen to us if she leaves?" Alys said.

There was no need to clarify who "she" was. "I don't know," Grace answered softly, "and, honestly, it worries me."

"Is that why you're trying to make as many hats as you can now, because after she leaves you think you'll not be asked to make any more?"

"Yes," Grace said simply. She was no longer surprised at her daughter's insight into what most people would call "grown-up problems."

"Would she be angry if she knew that I wasn't in school?"

"Oh, yes. She's an American, and she believes that little girls can grow up to be president."

"What's a 'president'?"

"A cross between a king and a member of Parliament."

"Is the American president like our king with all his lady friends?"

"Of course not!" Grace said in shock. "If an American president were like that, the people would throw him out."

"Is he in love with her?" Alys asked after a moment. She and her mother had been alone for several years now, and Alys knew when her mother was deeply worried about something, and it was Alys's guess that her mother was afraid of the future. Grace was afraid of taking on this business of hatmaking all by herself, for that's what she'd be doing as soon as Miss Temperance left McCairn.

When Grace said nothing, Alys persisted. "*Is* she going to leave soon?"

"Why not? There's nothing to hold her here. She likes to try to make us think that she needs a job, but anyone can see that she's rich. Her clothes, the way she speaks, the way..."

Trailing off, Grace looked out at the sea. In a way, before Temperance had come to McCairn, Grace had been content with what she had. She knew what to expect from the future. But now she was afraid to want what she could see. When she was near Temperance, everything seemed possible. It seemed perfectly reasonable to think that she could run a hatmaking business and make enough money to send her daughter to a university in Edinburgh.

"Alys is smart," Temperance had said.

"She's very, very smart. I've never seen anyone as good with numbers as she is. And I think she has an aptitude for science. Maybe you should think of sending her to school in Edinburgh; you'll certainly be able to afford it."

So now Grace had gone from the joy of making pretty hats to thinking that if she failed, she'd be cheating her daughter out of a wonderful future. That is, if being a female doctor was any kind of life for a woman. And, too, if Alys left McCairn, Grace would be alone, even more alone than after Gavie died.

So, Grace thought in disgust at herself, I've taken my daughter out of school and made her sew flowers on hats, something that she's no good at and that she hates.

"...laugh," Alys was saying.

"What?" Grace said, returning to the present.

"Are you angry with me?"

"No, of course not," Grace said, smiling at her daughter. "I have things on my mind, adult things, that's all."

Alys turned back toward the ocean and threw three more stones. "I think he's in love with her," she said quietly. "I don't think she loves him, because she's seen more people than he has, so she's mixed up about who's good and who's bad. But if he told her he loved her, she might love him back; then they'd get married and she'd never leave McCairn. Then she could run your hat business instead of you, and *you* could go live with me in Edinburgh while I become a doctor; then when I'm a doctor, we could come back here and make people well."

By the time Alys finished, Grace was staring at her daughter in openmouthed astonishment. She'd had no idea that Alys had heard Temperance's ideas about where Alys should go to school and what she should study. And Grace had certainly never said aloud her worries about being away from her daughter for the years of study required to become a doctor.

For a few moments Grace stared at her daughter. She knew that she had a couple of choices now. One, she could pretend to know everything there was to know and that her daughter was just a child and knew nothing. That's what Gavie would have done.

But Gavie wasn't there, and maybe her entire life depended upon this moment.

And, two, Grace could be honest. She chose the latter.

"What do you think we ought to do?" Grace said after a while.

"Leave it to Ramsey and me," Alys said so quickly that Grace laughed.

"You and Ramsey?"

When Alys looked at her mother, her face was very serious.

"And what do you two children have in mind?" Grace asked, unable to keep the laughter out of her voice.

"I don't know yet. I need to do some research on the matter."

Alys was so serious that Grace had to struggle not to laugh out loud. "All right," she said at last, "you and Ramsey work on it. Why don't you go now and find him?"

At that Alys nodded solemnly, then took off running, leaving her mother alone on the beach. Grace picked up stones and started tossing them. Part of her wished that Miss Temperance O'Neil had never come to McCairn, had never interfered in their lives.

But the truth was, there was something that was haunting her. Her daughter had said that James McCairn was obviously in love with Temperance—and Grace had seen it. Was it jealousy she was feeling? Or was it worry that...

Her head came up. She didn't want her life to go back to what it was. The truth was that she wanted her daughter to go to school as much as Alys seemed to want it. Grace wanted all the things that she was seeing that could be possible, and she knew that they were obtainable only if Temperance stayed with them.

"What have you got to lose?" she seemed to hear Gavie say, and his words put steel in her spine. With a determined gesture, she grabbed her skirt and started back toward the house.

❦

James was at his desk in the library, and there were papers in front of him. He looked as happy as a ship's captain on dry land.

"Why don't you tell her you're in love with her?" Grace said, her back to the closed door.

224

"Don't be ridiculous."

That he hadn't asked, "Who?" made Grace know that she was right. "You can't lie to me; I've seen you with your clothes off."

Frowning, James kept his eyes on the papers in front of him. "You shouldn't say such things, especially now that you're..."

"What?" she asked, walking toward the desk. "A businesswoman? I can make pretty flowers out of your old curtains, but that's it. It's her with the ideas, and she has the..."

When Grace didn't seem to have the words, he looked up at her. "—the belief that she can make anything happen?"

"Yes, she does. And she's what we need here on McCairn, and what you need after that first wife your father forced on you and—"

"Don't say any more," James said in a threatening manner. "I don't need your charity. Look to yourself if you want someone to pity."

"I have no pity for myself. I loved my husband, and after he was gone, you were there to warm my bed."

"Was that all I was to you?" he asked softly.

"That's all," she said, and there was relief in her voice. She'd been afraid that what she'd been feeling lately was jealousy. "You and I have seen too many bad things to have any belief that the world's a good place. But her..."

"She's never been hurt. She believes that if you want something enough, you can get it, so she decides to set you up in a business making hats. And if she were pushed, I have no doubt that she could come up with businesses for all of McCairn."

"Probably," Grace said. "But business isn't love, is it?"

"Don't you have something to do? Don't you have hats to make and food to cook?"

"Yes, much, but I can't stand to see you brooding over her and doing nothing about it."

"Brooding? I'm doing the accounts."

"Yes, so I can see," she said as she nodded toward the paper in front of him. There was nothing on it but doodles.

With an angry gesture, he crumpled the paper, then threw it across the room. "I'm not in love with her."

"Oh? What other woman has ever made you laugh as she does? What other woman cares about this dying village and has tried to keep it from its inevitable end?"

"It's not... And I don't..."

"Don't what? Need a wife? Need someone to inject new blood into this place? Look around you. You might as well live inside a mausoleum as in this rotting house. The hatred of your grandfather rules this place so much that there's a stench about it—and it's the stench of death."

"Get out of here," James said softly; then, standing, he pointed toward the door. "Out."

Grace knew when he was angry, and this was it. With her mouth set in a rigid line, she turned and left the room. But she slammed the

heavy door behind her and there was a sat-
isfying crack as something inside the room fell
and broke. Smiling, she went back upstairs
to the table covered with half-completed
hats.

⌒⊙⌒

"What is wrong with everyone today?"
Temperance asked as she sat next to James at
dinner that night.

He didn't answer but kept looking down at
his plate. He was pushing his food around, but
then it was his third plateful, so whatever
was bothering him hadn't affected his appetite.

"Well, actually," Temperance said in a
falsetto voice when James didn't answer, "I'm
sulking because Grace has met another man
and I've discovered that I'm in love with her
myself."

"*I'm not in love with anyone!*" James shouted
as he stood up so abruptly that he knocked over
his chair. "And I don't want to *marry* anyone!"

Temperance looked up at him, blinking. "And
I'm sure that no one wants to marry you," she
said softly.

It took James a moment, but he gave her a
half smile; then he picked up his chair, sat back
down, and resumed eating.

Temperance again tried to make conversation. "So what did you do today?"

"Accounts," he mumbled.

"So that's what's put you in a bad mood."

"I'm *not* in a bad mood," he snapped, then

227

grimaced. "People not minding their own business always puts me in a bad mood."

"Oh? And who didn't mind his or her own business?"

James had a mouthful of chicken (killed by Eppie, out of sight of Temperance), and he looked at her. "Tell me again why you came here. And where is your husband?"

"My—? Oh, right, my husband."

"The one who didn't teach you about kissing. The one you were escaping, remember?"

"I know everything there is to know about kissing," she said with narrowed eyes. "And my husband is... Well, he's somewhere," she said with a wave of her hand, then glanced toward the sideboard. "Grace got someone else to do the cooking. What do you think? Maybe the chicken is a little tough."

"Why did my uncle send you here?"

"What do you care?" she snapped, then calmed herself. "Did you know that Alys can add as well as her father could? I quizzed the girl, and she is brilliant. Grace and I are planning to send her to school in Edinburgh. You didn't by chance look at those cards any more, did you?"

"You're not married, are you?" James said quietly. "Never have been, have you?"

"I, ah... You want any more chicken? Or would you like some pie? Ramsey picked blackberries all afternoon."

She stopped because James had leaned back in his chair and was smiling at her as though he knew something that she didn't.

"Would someone *pleeeeeeeeassssssse* tell me what's going on in this house?" she asked. "Every person in it is acting strangely. Alys has been whispering with Ramsey, and Grace looks like she's at a funeral. And you have been brooding so much that Heathcliff would envy you."

But James didn't answer her. Instead, he said that he would like to have some pie. And for all the world he seemed to have solved some mystery, and he was very pleased with himself for having done so.

Sixteen

Mad, Temperance thought. Everyone on the almost-island had gone crazy.

It was the evening of the day after that strange dinner with James and, if possible, the people on McCairn had *all* gone mad. Maybe they'd drunk something that had a poisonous herb in it, she thought.

She was now at the top of the mountain, and she had practically run up the steep, narrow trail. A few weeks ago she'd been terrified by that trail, but not now. Now it seemed like the least fearful thing in the entire village.

For the last day and a half she had been living with people who made no sense at all. It was as though they were in on some conspiracy that she knew nothing of.

This morning Horrible Hamish's wife had come running up to Temperance and whispered that Hamish had seen her naked in the pond.

Taken off guard, Temperance had said, "He saw me? No, wait, I wasn't naked in any pond. Do you mean the bathtub?"

Lilias looked at Temperance as though she were daft. "Not you. Me," she whispered. "That's how Hamish and I met. I was taking a bath in the pond by the bottom of the rock fall, and he saw me. Of course I knew he was there and that's why—" She broke off when she saw Sheenagh walk by, then Lilias put her finger to her lips in secrecy as she hurried away.

Temperance was sure that Lilias had just shared some great secret with her, but *why* had she shared such an intimate secret? And then there was the thought of stripping off so Hamish would see her naked. At that Temperance gave a shudder of revulsion. Why in the world had the woman *wanted* that odious little bull of a man?

Shrugging, Temperance had continued walking down the street that ran through the center of the village. At the end of it was the warehouse where Grace's hatmaking shop was going to be established, and Temperance wanted to see how the work was going.

But she was stopped by Moira, who was a cousin of Grace's late husband. Moira whis-

230

pered to Temperance that her husband had broken his arm and she had nursed him back to health. "We were left alone a lot, if you know what I mean."

All Temperance could do was give a weak smile, and after the woman went away, she continued walking. But two steps later, a woman she had never seen before told Temperance that she and her husband had been trapped together in a shed all night. "After that we *had* to get married," the woman said with a great cackle of laughter before hurrying away.

By the time Temperance got to the warehouse, she was sure that the people had gone insane. Grace was there with Alys, and Grace was telling the men that, yes, the windows had to be made larger. "*You* spend fourteen hours a day sewing without good light and see how *your* eyes stand up to it," she was snapping at Rory, the man James had put in charge of the rebuilding.

Temperance dropped the big bag that Eppie had filled with food for the workmen by the door. "Could someone please tell me what's going on?" she said. "Is there a festival in the planning?"

"Not unless someone else does the planning," Grace answered quickly. "Why?"

"Because every woman in this village is telling me how she met her husband. I must say that for so quiet a little place, there have been some risqué meetings. The women of McCairn—"

She broke off because Alys looked at Grace, and the girl's eyes were wide in horror.

"I *told* them to tell *us!*" Alys said in a whine; then she turned and ran out the doorway so fast that she nearly knocked Temperance over.

"What's going on?" Temperance asked, eyes narrowed at Grace.

"The children are planning a surprise for you," Grace said quickly. "They're writing a history of Clan McCairn for you to take back to New York with you."

"And the history tells who had to marry whom?" Temperance asked. "You wouldn't believe what these women are telling me. Hamish's wife..." She trailed off because she didn't want to betray a confidence, but if it were a secret, why was Lilias telling it to be put into a book about the history of the clan?

"I don't think that what I've been hearing is quite suitable for a history," Temperance said. "At least not if it's to be published. Haven't there been some battles near here or something bigger—in a historical sense? And, anyway, should the children be hearing what their parents got up to before they were married?"

She looked at Grace and Rory, but they just stood there staring at her without saying a word.

Finally Rory said in a voice louder than it needed to be, "I think you have enough light. It's going to cost too much to heat the place in winter if you have these huge windows."

Grace turned her back on Temperance to face Rory and said just as loudly, "You don't know what you're talking about. It's my business, and I'll have it as I want it."

Temperance stood there looking at the back of the two of them and knew that what she'd just been told was a lie. Not about how Mrs. Hamish had danced about in a pond naked in order to attract the ramrod-stiff Hamish, but about there being a book written on the history of Clan McCairn.

But whatever the secret was, Temperance wasn't part of it, and they weren't going to let her in on it.

Slowly, Temperance turned away and left the warehouse. For the first time in a long while, she felt like an outsider in the village. As she made her way back down the street, no one grabbed her arm and whispered intimate secrets about how she'd snared her husband. When she saw Lilias, the woman turned brilliant red before dashing inside McCairn's one and only store. Temperance thought about following her and seeing if she could get some answers from her, but she knew that the village had closed itself and she was on the outside.

In the end, Temperance decided to spend the day in her room writing about all that she'd observed since she'd arrived in McCairn. She told herself that it was good that the villagers had shut her out of their lives because she needed to remember why she was there in the first place. She wanted to discover new ways to help the people in New York, the people who really *needed* her.

But Temperance found that she had difficulty writing because she kept remembering her time in McCairn. She thought of roller-skating with the children.

And sliding through James's legs.

She thought of helping Grace with her hat business. And just yesterday when she'd quizzed Alys on numbers. "What's 367 times 481?" she'd asked the girl. Temperance had no idea if the number 176,527 was right, but it sounded good. And the girl had looked into Temperance's eyes and said that she wanted to be a doctor more than she wanted anything else in the whole wide world. Temperance agreed that it was good to have an education, but why would the girl think that she wanted to be a *doctor?*

And Temperance remembered the night James had thrown Charming Charmaine out the window. And the afternoon the muscular woman had appeared outside the cave. And how they had laughed over each incident.

And Temperance remembered delivering a sheep with James. And how she'd worn his shirt afterward. She thought about the times they'd shared lunch in his little cave. She wondered if he had ever taken other people to the cave. His wife, maybe? What had his wife been like? Other than unhappy, that is? As for that, *why* had she been so very unhappy? After all, there was so very much to *do* in McCairn. For all that Temperance had managed to get one business started, it wasn't enough to sustain the whole place. The men had their sheep, but most of the women had...

Temperance looked down at her paper. She was supposed to be writing about what she would do when she returned to New York, but instead she'd written a list of things that needed or could be done in McCairn. She'd heard that Blind Brenda had some stories to tell. Were they good enough to be published?

After four unsuccessful attempts to get her mind back on New York, Temperance threw down her pen and went downstairs to the kitchen. Old Eppie was hacking away at some meat on the wooden table, so Temperance looked away. She would not now or ever again eat lamb.

"Letter for you," Eppie said as she pointed a bloody hand toward the windowsill.

Was it from her mother saying that she'd found the most perfect of women for James to marry and soon Temperance could leave the place?

Hesitantly, Temperance took the letter, then smiled. It was from Agnes in New York. Now she'd be able to get her mind away from McCairn and back to her *real* work.

Temperance went outside, then leaned against the wall of the house to open the letter. It was short, as Agnes wasn't much for writing. Temperance scanned the single page, reading that everything and everyone was all right, and that Temperance didn't need to worry.

"She could have at least pretended to miss

me," Temperance whispered to herself. She had been away a long time, first the six months it had taken to make Angus McCairn come to his senses and now these many weeks here in McCairn.

"Thought you'd like to see this," Agnes wrote. "She's ever so nice."

Attached to the page was a newspaper article that Temperance had to read three times before she believed what she was reading.

The news reporter had written a comparison of the "infamous" Temperance O'Neil and a Miss Deborah Madison, who had taken over the work "abandoned" by Temperance after she'd departed the country.

By the second reading, Temperance's hands were trembling. The article talked about Temperance as though she had left the U.S. of her own free will, as though she'd grown bored with helping distressed women and had walked away from them, leaving them in a much worse state than they had been originally. Miss Madison had taken over the work Temperance had abandoned.

The article went on to compare the two women in a personal way. It said that Miss Deborah Madison was a much gentler, less abrasive woman than Temperance and, as such, she was able to accomplish so very much more.

Also, the article said, the woman was much, much younger than Temperance, and her ways were "more modern." The article made it sound as though Temperance were 105 years old and her methods were from the Dark Ages.

"'Younger,' 'more modern,' 'less abrasive,' 'easier to work with,'" Temperance whispered as she looked down at the article.

It was while she was in a state of shock over this letter that Ramsey came to her and handed her a folded piece of paper. The edge had been lapped over and a bit of red sealing wax poured onto it.

"What's this?" Temperance asked the boy as she shoved the newspaper article and Agnes's letter into her pocket.

"I don't know. I was told to give it to you. That's all I know."

Yesterday she wouldn't have been suspicious, but today she was sure that every word said to her was a lie. She glanced down at the paper. There was no writing on the outside, and the wax had not been stamped with a seal. She thought, I'm not going to open this, then looked up to tell Ramsey to return it to whoever had sent it.

But the boy was gone, and she was standing alone outside the house. How Temperance wished she were the type of person who could stamp down her curiosity and not open the letter!

But it was no use wishing. She broke open the page and looked at it. She hadn't seen James's handwriting but a couple of times, but that was enough to recognize it now. He'd written the note in a hurry.

Come at once. I need you immediately. Tell no one. The sheepherder's cottage near where we delivered the sheep. J.

The treasure! was the only thought in her mind. James must have found out something about the treasure.

Without another thought in her head, Temperance started hurrying toward the mountain. After what she'd been through all day, it was good to be needed somewhere, by anyone.

It was only when she was nearly at the top of the mountain that she began to think. It was growing dark, and it felt as if it was about to rain. But then it was Scotland and it always seemed to be raining or about to rain, so that wasn't unusual, but she didn't want to be caught in the dark in the midst of a downpour.

Looking about her, she expected James to pop out of the bushes. He had the uncanny ability to walk absolutely silently and to be in places she didn't expect him to be in.

"James?" she said out loud, but she didn't hear anything except sheep. She took a few steps and her footsteps seemed to be very loud.

There was something about this whole situation that she didn't like. James wasn't the type to send her a note. He might tell Ramsey to deliver her somewhere, but he wouldn't order her to climb a mountain alone. Certainly not at dusk.

Turning, she started back down the mountain, but then she heard a voice call her name.

She stopped and turned back. "James?" she said.

"Over here," came a voice that sounded like James's, but she wasn't sure.

Unfortunately, as she hesitated, the skies chose that moment to open up and within seconds she was soaked—and freezing. With her hands shielding her face from the pouring rain, she ran toward the little stone cottage that she knew was just ahead.

She saw the cottage just in front of her, and there was light coming from the door that was standing open. Through the deluge washing over her, she could see that inside was a fire burning in the fireplace. For a moment she had a sense of déjà vu, as it was what she'd dreamed of finding the first time she'd seen McCairn.

Running, she nearly leaped inside the cottage and slammed the door behind her. There was a table and two chairs on one side of the single room and a bed covered in sheepskins on the other. In the far wall in front of her was a fireplace and a stack of peat to keep the blaze going.

Temperance was so wet from her run in the rain that steam came off her clothes when she got near the fire, and she was shivering with cold. As she turned her back to the fire, it was then that she saw that there was a sheepskin flask hanging from a peg on the wall and on the table was a loaf of bread and a huge chunk of cheese, and when she lifted a crockery cover, she saw two chickens that had recently been roasted.

"What is going on?" Temperance said aloud, holding her arms across her chest as she shivered.

But she didn't get an answer because at the next moment, the door flew open and in stormed James, his face drawn into a rage.

But when he saw Temperance, relief flooded his face. Crossing the room in one long stride, he pulled her into his arms. "Ye're all right," he said, and there was nothing but relief in his voice. "I was out of my mind with worry. Everyone is searching for you, and when I got your note that said you'd meet me here, I thought that maybe you'd been kidnapped."

Temperance's cold face was pressed into his wet clothing, and a sane part of her knew that she should disentangle herself and tell him about the note she'd received. Then they could sit down and logically discuss what was going on in the village and who had sent them both these manipulative messages. And who had called out to her?

But Temperance didn't say anything. Maybe it was that odious newspaper article that she'd just read, but right now she needed to feel young and feminine. She'd never thought much about her age before, but since she'd first met Angus McCairn months ago, her age had been dangled in front of her until she was beginning to need something to prove to herself that she wasn't a dried-up old woman.

She was sure that she was doing the wrong thing, but instead of pulling away, she lifted her face to look up at James. More than anything in the world, she wanted him to kiss her.

And he obliged. After a second's hesitation, as though he wasn't sure he should, he brought his lips down to hers.

A woman had once told Temperance that she couldn't talk about resisting temptation until after she'd felt true ecstasy with a man. And Temperance thought that she'd felt that because she had kissed a few men before, had even kissed James, but then, she'd felt nothing like what she was feeling now.

One moment her body was freezing and the next she was warm. As James's lips moved over hers, she stood on tiptoe to reach him. When he opened his mouth over hers and she felt the tip of his tongue, for a second, she pulled back; then she flung her arms about his neck and pressed her closed lips hard against his.

At that James drew back and looked at her, his eyes opened wide in wonder. "Merciful heavens," he whispered. "You're a virgin."

For a second Temperance thought he was going to move away from her, but instead his arms tightened about her waist; then he twirled her around, her toes just touching the floor. Sheer happiness was on his face; then holding her aloft, he began to rain tiny little kisses on her neck, kisses that warmed her down to her wet shoes.

She thought she heard him say, "Not even my wife was a virgin," but she wasn't sure. Whatever he said, he wasn't going to stop, wasn't going to send her away.

In the next moment he stood her on the floor and began to unbutton her blouse. My goodness! but he was an expert at buttons. They came undone on the wet fabric much faster than she could ever have done them herself.

It was warm in the cottage, and the light from the fireplace made a lovely glow. She could smell the burning peat and the succulent food on the table. But most of all, she could smell him, the warm, delicious male smell of him.

"May I?" she whispered as she put her hands on his chest.

At that he gave a laugh that she could feel under her hands. Slowly at first and shyly, she moved her hands downward. But when he put his big warm hand inside her cold wet blouse and touched the tops of her breasts, she lost a lot of her shyness. She had an irresistible urge to feel her skin against his.

Quickly, with urgency, she tugged his shirt out of his kilt, then pushed upward on it. With another soft sound of pleasure, he lifted his arms and let her slide her hands under his shirt, up his big warm, muscular arms, as far as she could reach. When she could go no further, he pulled the big shirt off over his head and dropped it on the hearth.

Temperance stared at his bare chest for a moment, then slowly ran her hand over him. He was beautiful, with dark skin and black hair curling softly across his wide chest. Tentatively, she ran her hand from his neck down his rib cage to his waist; then she moved across to his warm, flat belly and held her hand there as she looked up at him.

No man had ever looked at her as he was doing now, not with the intensity that she saw in James McCairn's eyes, and if a man had looked at her like that before, she would have run the opposite way. But not now. Now she smiled at him, and she had an idea that she had the same intensity in her eyes that he had.

In the next moment James again swept her into his arms and twirled her about in sheer joy.

And Temperance's laughter mingled with his. She was old enough and experienced enough in the ways of the world to now be able to see that they had wanted each other from their first meeting. And their laughter was the release of a great deal of pent-up desire.

When James dropped her down onto the bed, Temperance laughed in delight. She bounced once when she hit the sheepskin straps that held up the mattress, and this caused more laughter. The next moment James was beside her, and she snuggled down beside him, her head on his one arm, allowing his other arm freedom to finish undressing her.

He took his time. He didn't tear her clothes or hurry the lovely process of undressing her. Instead he gently pulled her blouse out of her skirt and finished with the buttons. Gently, he removed her arms from the sleeves, then unfastened her skirt.

All the while Temperance lay still, looking

up at him, at his strong, chiseled profile, at his dark hair. He mostly kept his eyes on the undressing of her, but when he did look at her, the glint in those dark eyes made her heart leap to her throat and pound hard.

They didn't say a word to each other. But then they had done nothing but talk for the entire time of her stay in McCairn. And all that time, she thought, this is what we really wanted to do. Putting her hand up to his cheek, she caressed it. Every night at dinner she had seen that jawline and had wanted to know what it felt like.

He was an expert at undressing her, and it seemed that within just seconds she was down to her lace-and-cotton one-piece undergarment. Only this thin fabric covered her skin.

He slowly and gently slipped first one strap, then the other down over her shoulders, and his lips kissed the tops of her shoulders as he bared the skin. The tiny buttons down the front of the one-piece garment went next, and his face followed his hands, kissing all the way down. When he reached her belly, she drew in her breath at the pleasure of the sensation he was causing in her.

When he parted the garment and exposed her breasts, for a moment Temperance almost turned coward and fled.

He must have sensed her fear because he withdrew his hand and put his lips back on hers to calm her. Tiny kisses, feathery kisses, little butterfly kisses, he placed all over her face and down her neck.

The second time he parted her garment, she wasn't afraid. And when his hand touched her breast, she trembled.

"No idea," she whispered. "I had no idea at all."

She could feel him smiling, his lips against her breasts, and the thought that she was giving him pleasure made her feel even better.

He took the tip of her breast into his mouth and sucked gently, and it was when he was on the second breast that Temperance wanted less gentleness and more... She didn't have the experience to know what she wanted, but it was *more.*

She meant to lift his head to her face, but instead she grabbed his hair and brought his lips to hers, and when she kissed him, it was with an open mouth.

Later Temperance wasn't sure what she'd done, but something seemed to make James lose control. One minute all he seemed able to think of was giving her pleasure, but the next moment it seemed as though he could no longer control himself.

His wet kilt, the scratchy wool so exciting against her bare skin, came off with a quick, one-handed twist, and in a second he was totally nude.

"Now I see why you Scotsmen wear kilts," she said with a smile as he moved on top of her.

But James was not smiling. His senses were too on fire for him to be able to speak.

Because of her vast experience with such matters, Temperance had thought she knew exactly what the sex act was like. She'd certainly heard it described often enough. And her response to every description had been to give a lecture about birth control and "resistance."

But now she knew that she had never known anything about lovemaking. Right now she could no more have stopped herself than she could have stopped a runaway elephant.

When James entered her, she gasped, and for a moment the pain was all that occupied her mind. Looking up at him, she saw the strain on his face as he used every bit of control he had to halt himself and wait until her pain subsided. She knew it was going to hurt more, but she gave him a tiny nod and he entered her fully.

For a moment he lay still and she adjusted to him; then, after a few long moments, she began to move under him.

That was all the permission James needed to start making long, slow, deep strokes within her, and after a few awkward movements, Temperance understood what she needed to do and she began to move with him.

His hands were on her body, stroking her, caressing her skin, and they were working together in an age-old way. "As we always work together," she said softly, and felt James lips smile against her neck.

She wasn't prepared for the pressure building within her; she hadn't expected that. She had her head back and her eyes closed, but once she glanced up and saw that James was watching her. He was waiting for something, but she had no idea what. And her pleasure at his deep, slow strokes was too overpowering to be able to think clearly.

It was when the pressure started that she opened her eyes and looked at him in surprise. And, by the expression on his beautiful face, she knew that that's what he'd been waiting for.

His slow strokes became faster, then faster, then deeper and deeper. Temperance could hear her own small screams as he seemed to hit something deep within her.

When the explosion came, she opened her mouth to scream, but James collapsed on top of her, his neck covering her mouth as her body went into convulsions. Wave after wave of pleasure ran through her.

It was a long while before she became aware of her surroundings. James rolled off of her but still held her very close with one arm as he pulled a couple of big sheepskins over the two of them.

Their skin was sweaty, and Temperance had never felt so deliciously relaxed in her life. She snuggled against his shoulder and kissed him.

"Not yet," he said. "Give me a moment."

At first Temperance didn't know what he meant; then she laughed and quit kissing.

"I always wondered about this part," she said, looking across him to the fire.

"And what did you wonder?"

"I thought that afterward the two people would be terribly embarrassed. After all, they had just acted in what is, basically, an animalistic way."

"And what do you think now?" James asked softly as he stroked her damp hair back from her forehead.

"This is almost the best part," she said, and when he looked at her, she smiled and said, "Almost."

Feeling warm and happy and safe, Temperance drifted into that state that is neither awake nor asleep.

"All right," James said quietly, his hand on her hair. "I'm going to give you what you want."

Temperance smiled, her eyes closed. "I think you just did, but you can give me more if you'd like," she said, then smiled more broadly. She'd just made one of those little jokes that lovers share.

"I'm going to ask you to marry me."

"*Mmmm?*" she asked, moving her leg against his.

She felt James let out a sigh, as though he were admitting defeat. "I've decided that I'm going to give in to you and ask you to marry me."

Temperance lay still for several moments. She was too warm and felt too good to understand words. "What did you say?"

"I said I'm going to allow you to marry me. You win."

Temperance lifted her head to look at him. "Whatever are you saying? You're going to give in to me?"

"Yes. I've decided."

She drew back further. "To marry me? Is that what you've decided?"

Smiling, James lifted his head and kissed her nose.

Temperance was blinking at him. "You'll marry me? Is this the consolation prize?"

Putting his hand behind his head, James looked up at the ceiling. "I know you were sent here by my uncle to marry me, and although I've tried to resist, I'm now going to admit defeat and marry you."

For several moments Temperance said nothing. Had he known her better, James would have known what her silence meant. "You are, are you?" she said softly. "You're going to...what was it? Admit defeat and marry me?"

James looked at her in surprise. "Are you getting angry?"

"Ah, now there's a brilliant remark. Am I getting angry? No, I am getting furious," she said as she grabbed her blouse off the foot of the bed and held it over her bare breasts. "I am in a rage. Truthfully, I don't think there's a word to describe what I'm feeling," she said as she got off the bed, clutching a sheepskin as she stood.

"What in hell are you talking about?" James said, coming up on his elbow. "You came here to—"

"To find you a bride," she shouted, then clamped her mouth shut.

He sat there blinking at her. "You did what?"

"Nothing. I didn't say anything." Grabbing her skirt, she started trying to dress while keeping her body hidden.

For a moment, James looked at her hard. "My uncle sent you here to find a bride for me, didn't he?" he said at last. "That's who those two women were, weren't they? I see. The first one was beautiful but brainless. Is that what you assumed I'd want?"

"I didn't know you then, and—" Even to her own ears, Temperance's voice was full of guilt.

"The second woman said she thought I wanted help delivering sheep. Did you write my uncle after that first day when we delivered the lambs and tell him you wanted an athletic woman?"

Pausing in her dressing, Temperance opened her mouth to speak, but no words came out.

"So that's your big secret," he said at last as he lay back on the bed. "I knew there was one, but fool that I was, I thought that *you* were the one my uncle sent. No, all of us of Clan McCairn were just something to occupy you, a toy for you to play with, weren't we? So, what's your true story? What hold does my uncle have over you?"

When Temperance kept dressing and didn't answer him, he turned his head and glared at her. "Come on, there's no reason to be shy, not after what you and I've just shared. Maybe I can help you. Since you've taken away Grace from me and I doubt if you'll agree to becoming her replacement, maybe I *will* get married. But what's in it for you?"

Temperance didn't want to lie anymore. "Your uncle married my mother and he has control of the money my father left me," she said quickly.

"I see. So he told you that if you could find a wife for his lonely nephew, he'd give you back your money."

"An allowance," she said as she fastened her skirt. She was still angry at Angus McCairn for the position he'd put her in.

"I see," James said.

Suddenly, Temperance's head came up. "Wait a minute," she said, glaring at him, but he was staring at the ceiling and not looking at her. "If all this time you've thought that I was sent here to marry you, then you've thought that everything I did was toward that goal." She was staring at his profile as she thought about this. "All the lunches, the roller skates, and Grace! You must have thought that I gave Grace a job to take away my competition, so to speak."

Temperance's hands clenched into fists. "You are despicable! You're like all the other men in the world: you think that all women are after you. For what? What woman would want to take on you and your bad temper and this poverty-stricken near-island? Do you have any idea how hard my mother is working to find women who will even *visit* this place? She can't get a Scotswoman to come here because they've heard of it. Clan McCairn is a joke to this whole country!"

James turned his head to look at her, and his

251

eyes were a cold black that she'd never seen before. "I think you've said enough."

But Temperance had *never* backed down from an argument before and she wasn't going to now. "No, I haven't. When I think of what you've thought of me all these weeks, that I was doing everything to try to catch *you*. I could *never* say enough!"

At that James sat up on the bed, the sheepskins falling to his waist, exposing his bare chest. When he spoke, his voice was quiet, calm even. "No, instead, you were occupying yourself, weren't you? You were just keeping yourself from being bored. What do you think is going to happen to these children after you leave? They'll never again be content to live here and accept discipline. Already I've heard three children say that when they reach fourteen, they're going to run away to the mainland and get a job so they can buy skates and oranges and chocolates. And what happens to the hat business when you leave? You think Grace has the confidence to wheel and deal with those buyers? No, of course not. I think, Miss Temperance O'Neil, that you may have just murdered Clan McCairn more effectively than centuries of my family's gambling ever did."

Temperance opened her mouth to reply to his accusation, but at that moment the door flew open, as though someone had pushed it open. For a moment both she and James looked at the door in anticipation, expecting someone to enter, but no one did.

The retort that Temperance had been about to make died on her lips. "I think we both know where we now stand," she said softly. "I will leave McCairn in the morning."

"And go live with my uncle? And make *his* life hell?"

"I—" Temperance began but could think of nothing else to say. What should have been the most beautiful night of her life had turned into her worst nightmare.

Picking his kilt up off the floor, James fastened it about his waist before getting off the bed. He closed the door, then went to stand by the fireplace and stare into the flames for a moment. "Things have been said tonight that should not have been said." When Temperance did not respond, he continued. "And I think that things have happened tonight that shouldn't have happened. Do you agree?"

"Yes," she said, her voice hoarse as she said it. She'd never meant to hurt him. Why had she said such dreadful things about McCairn? She didn't feel that the place was horrible. In fact, she had been growing rather fond of it, at least until the last few days, that is.

"I'll not marry again," James said softly. "That I can guarantee you. Not after what has happened tonight. I shamed myself before you, and I apologize."

"You didn't..." she began, but when she saw his back stiffen, she closed her mouth.

After a while James turned to look at her. "I know my uncle. Once he makes a decree, he'll stand by it no matter what anyone says. He'll not give you your freedom unless you find me a wife, and since I won't marry, you seem to have a choice of living with him or here on McCairn. Which will it be?"

"I want..." Temperance began, but she honestly couldn't say what it was that she wanted. Part of her wanted to go back to New York and fight this usurper who was trying to take over the campaign that *she* had started. But the other part wanted to see if she could make a go of the House of Grace. And there was Lilias's liqueur and Brenda's stories and, of course, there were the children.

"Can't ye reach a decision?" James said impatiently. "Are we that repulsive to you? Or can you not abide working for someone who's the laughingstock of all Scotland?"

Already, Temperance regretted having said that. Her mother had always told her to think before she spoke, but she never seemed able to do that.

But the words had been said, and she couldn't take them back. The choices in her life didn't include returning to her work in New York. To live forever under Angus McCairn's rule or in McCairn itself?

"My uncle is an old man," James said through tight lips. "Perhaps he'll die soon and you'll be released from your devil's bargain."

"The man is my mother's husband," Temperance shot back at him. "And for all that I dislike him, she seems to..." She almost choked on the word. "My mother seems to care for him. I don't wish for his death."

"It's not up to you, is it? So which is it? Do you stay here or return?"

"Stay," she said, then found that there was relief inside her at the thought.

But as far as Temperance could see, there was no expression on James's face, and she wondered if he wished that she'd leave McCairn forever.

"All right, then I suggest that we get out of here. There'll be enough talk as it is," he said as he pulled his shirt over his head. After pouring a bucket of sand over the fire, he walked to the door, then stepped back so she could go before him. "I suggest that we forget this night," he said once they were outside the cottage. "Forget what was said, forget what was done."

"Yes," Temperance said, looking up at the moonlight. But *how* was she going to forget?

She didn't ask him that. Instead, she followed him down the steep hillside in the dark, and neither of them spoke a word all the way down.

Seventeen

Four Weeks Later

"I have it," Rowena said excitedly as she held aloft a thick stack of writing paper. "But I haven't read it yet. I waited for you."

Melanie smiled in gratitude at her sister-in-law, who had become her close friend. It had been four long weeks since she'd had a proper letter from her daughter. Oh, she'd had letters all right, but each was colder than the last, telling absolutely nothing that was going on in McCairn. The only real information that Temperance had divulged was imparted when she told her mother to stop sending prospective brides for James, as he was never going to marry anyone.

By the end of the third week, Melanie had gone to her sister-in-law and asked her advice. What had followed were daily visits with each other. And every day there were tiered trays full of delectable cakes for Melanie and a full bottle of single-malt whiskey for Rowena, all devoured while Melanie had read Temperance's past letters aloud to Rowena so they could compare then and now.

"Something is desperately wrong," Rowena

had said after just one letter had been read to her.

"Angus is planning to tell James about the will," Melanie had told her on the third visit. "Angus says that James *must* know what's in store for him. James must either find himself a pretty little wife or Colin gets the place."

"You don't know my nephew," Rowena said, as she emptied her glass. "James is so stubborn that he'd hand the keys to that horrid house to Angus and tell him Colin was welcome to the place."

"Sounds like Temperance," Melanie said with a sigh. "If she wanted to get married and have children, she'd not do it because it would give too much satisfaction to too many people. Every man in New York who had any dealings with her said that what she needed was a man in her life."

In the end, it was Rowena who came up with the idea of writing Grace to find out what they could. "I knew her husband. He was always into what he shouldn't be into, so let's hope his widow is the same way."

So this morning Grace's reply had arrived, and Melanie had been almost frantic as she tried to get Angus off to work so she could go to Rowena and hear what Grace had to say.

"Settled, dear?" Rowena asked when Melanie had a plate full of cakes, a cup full of tea, and Rowena had a water glass full of whiskey.

Melanie nodded as she took her first bite.

" 'A lovers' quarrel,' Grace wrote. 'That's all

I know how to describe it: a stupid, childish lovers' quarrel. No one knows what happened, but we all know how it started. It was the fault of my daughter and James McCairn's son.'"

"His *son!?*" Melanie said and nearly choked on the pink icing of a lemon cake.

"Ramsey is James's son," Rowena said in surprise. "Didn't you know?"

"No. And I don't think that Temperance knows either. She uses that boy for a lackey, to send messages back and forth."

"Good for him," Rowena snorted. "He shouldn't get ahead of himself. Now where was I? Oh, yes, James's son."

Alys and Ramsey decided to play Cupid. They thought to get James and Temperance in a, shall we say, compromising situation, with the result being a marriage, but, being children, they didn't know what to do to make the adults admit that they were in love. Note that I say, "Admit to love," because everyone used to think that James and Temperance were in love.

What the children did was Alys's idea. They "researched" love. They asked the villagers how they got their spouses to marry them. I must say that there were some amazing and, sometimes, rather shocking replies. I had no idea such things went on in McCairn. But, somehow, there was a mix-up and the village women were telling their lurid stories to Temperance.

"And she had no idea what they were talking about?" Melanie asked, amused.

For a moment both women thought about that, remembering things that had gone on in their own lives that had been done to snare the man they wanted.

"*Hmmm,*" Rowena said after a moment, then picked up the letter again.

It seems that what the children came up with was to send notes to James and Temperance as though each desperately needed the other. Life and death, that sort of thing. The notes seemed to work, as both of the adults went running up the side of the mountain to where the children had equipped an old sheepherder cottage with wine, chicken, and a fire. As far as I can get out of them, the children saw Temperance and James go into the cottage, close the door, then come out hours later.

Rowena put the letter down on her lap and poured herself more whiskey. "I think we can assume what went on inside the cabin during those hours."

"Not Temperance," Melanie said in disgust. "You don't know my daughter. Her high morals would put the pope to shame. She is upstanding and infallible."

"But she's never before been confronted with a Scotsman in a kilt on a moonlit night," Rowena said seriously, without a hint of humor in her voice.

Melanie paused with a forkful of cake halfway to her mouth and remembered twice when Angus had donned his clan's kilt. "Perhaps you're right. Read on."

...hours later. They haven't spoken to each other since except in monosyllables and then only when necessary.

"Yes," Rowena said, "only a man you've been to bed with can make you that angry."
Melanie nodded in agreement on that issue.
Rowena looked back at the letter. "Oh, no, listen to this!"

The next day James went to Edinburgh and talked to Angus. As far as I can find out (and please do not ask what unscrupulous methods I've had to use), Angus told James the truth about Temperance, that Angus never meant for James to marry her. She was just to find James a wife.

Rowena looked up at Melanie in question. "I knew nothing about this. My husband told me nothing of a meeting with James."
Rowena looked back at the letter.

So now James stays away from the house almost all the time, and Temperance has occupied herself in helping the village. She wrote a publisher about Brenda's stories and contacted a brewery about making Lilias's liqueur.
On the surface one could say that nothing has changed, but it doesn't take much to see that

everything has changed. My hats have become a business but nothing more. Temperance does the negotiating, but she doesn't laugh over the bargains she's made as she used to do.

I've tried to talk to James about what's going on, but if anything, he's worse than Temperance. He says that Temperance chose her punishment and now she must bear it. No one can figure out what he means by that.

Truthfully, no one on McCairn knows what happened or what was said the night the children decided to play matchmaker. But we all know the results. Both James and Temperance are two very stubborn people, and they are both doing their jobs, but neither is giving an inch.

As for the rest of us in McCairn, life goes on as before, but this argument between Temperance and James affects us all. We would appreciate any help or suggestions you have.

Yours very sincerely,
Grace Dougall

"So it looks like there's no hope of a marriage between those two," Rowena said as she looked across her glass at Melanie. "What do we do now? Do we let Colin have the place? Get rid of it once and for all?"

Melanie bit into a strawberry tart and pondered the question for a moment. "I'm not sure, but I think this may be my one—and probably only—chance for grandchildren. I think that my daughter may indeed be in love with your nephew."

261

"No doubt about it that James is in love with your daughter."

"But you can't force people to marry," Melanie said with regret in her voice. "But it will be a shame for James to lose McCairn. If he doesn't marry Temperance, maybe he could marry someone else. Isn't there anyone he has *ever* been in love with?"

"Actually, there was a girl long ago, but it was a perfectly unsuitable match."

"You mean, like his childhood sweetheart?" Melanie said, eyes wide.

Rowena thought for a few moments. "Kenna. That was her name. I don't remember much about her, except that she was an extraordinarily pretty girl, much too pretty for her own good. If that girl had had the right parents and the right backing, she could have made a match to royalty."

"But, instead, because she was born in a crofter's cottage, she wasn't allowed to marry the laird's eldest son." Melanie, as an American, had disgust in her voice.

But Rowena had no such feelings. "Exactly," she said firmly. "But James's mother sent her to school in Glasgow and I seem to remember that she found a good husband. James's mother was always too generous for her own good."

"Oh," Melanie said. "Married."

"No, I believe she was widowed long ago. In fact...yes, now I remember, Angus and I approached her years ago, but she turned us down." Rowena took a drink. "I told you that we'd been sending lots of women to James. But perhaps now that she's had a taste of widowhood... *Hmm,* perhaps I should write her a stronger letter. I'll emphasize that if she ends up married to James, it would be a giant step up in the world for her."

"But what about love? James must love the woman he marries, but I think he loves my daughter." There was a bit of a whine in Melanie's voice.

"Fiddle-faddle. Land and inheritance are involved. If James is too stupid to know that he's in love with that rapscallion daughter of yours, then he deserves anything he gets in the way of love. Whichever way it goes, at least I'll know that I've saved McCairn for future generations."

Rowena put down her whiskey glass. "But I'm confused. Why would you suggest bringing in another woman?"

"When Temperance was a child, the only way to get her to do anything was to tell her she *couldn't* do it. I would say, 'Temperance, dear, you cannot possibly wear your new pink dress today, and when your great aunt arrives today, you are to stay in your room. She thinks children are messy and noisy.' Of course the result of this was that Temperance would sit in the parlor in her pretty dress in absolute silence, and my husband's old aunt would say what a darling, polite, obedient daughter I had raised."

"I see," Rowena said, but she was frowning in puzzlement; then she smiled. "Oh, yes. I

263

do see. Why don't you stay and help me compose the letter to Kenna? I'm afraid my hand isn't as steady as it used to be."

Melanie smiled demurely and said she'd be glad to help.

⁓◉◐◎⁓

Kenna Lockwood was in bed when her maid brought the letter to her. The sheets were silk and perfumed, and she was wearing the same. She well knew that when she was surrounded by yards of champagne-colored satin, she looked her best. The heavy damask curtains at the windows were closed even though it was bright noon outside. In Kenna's bedroom it was always night; candlelight was much more flattering than the sun.

Beside the bed Artie was undressing. He was one of Kenna's younger lovers, nearly ten years younger than she was, but he didn't know that. One of her older "friends" as she preferred to call them, had teased Kenna, saying that with each year her bedroom grew darker and, as a result, Kenna never aged. That was the last time that Kenna saw that man.

Now, lounging on the bed, turning her head so her best side faced this boy, she was curious about the letter. It had the McCairn crest on it.

When Artie took forever unfastening his trousers, then sat down on a satin-covered chair to untie his shoes, Kenna gave a sigh. What had happened to romance? What had happened to urgency? To that mad passion that she used to feel? And that men used to feel for her?

Hearing her sigh, Artie looked up at her with a smile, so she turned away so he couldn't see her frown; then she picked up the letter off the table, slit it with one long nail, and opened it. She scanned it quickly.

It the next second, she sat up in bed, forgetting all about keeping her sultry, provocative pose.

"Lord in heaven!" she said in astonishment. "They want me to return to *marry* him. Or at least they want me to pretend to marry him. Heavens, but I think the old biddy believes I *owe* her."

When she looked up at Artie, she saw the most interest on his face that she'd seen in weeks. Was she losing her touch?

"Who wants you to get married?" he asked, at last getting off the chair and walking to the side of the bed.

"No one," Kenna said, as she put the letter aside, then stretched up her arms to him.

"But that's good paper. Who wrote you on that?"

Kenna dropped her arms and turned her face away for a moment. It didn't matter that she'd married well and her late husband had left her a small fortune (all of which she'd spent instantly). Nor did it matter that she'd spent two years in Glasgow University. These young snobs always seemed to know where Kenna had come from. And it wasn't because she gave them favors in return for a few "gifts." There were a few down-on-their-luck countesses she knew doing the very same thing, but boys like Artie always knew who was what class.

Kenna gritted her teeth. "No one," she repeated. When Artie tried to reach around her, she drew back; then she saw that he was more interested in the letter than he was in her, and, well, interest was interest. "It's two old women. I met one of them years ago, and now they want me to marry a man I used to know. Or at least they want me to pretend to want to marry him. Truthfully, the letter doesn't make a lot of sense."

"They want to use you?" There was sympathy in Artie's voice, and Kenna hated it.

"I think they want to, but I'm not going back there."

"Why do they think you would go?"

"They seem to have the absurd idea that I owe them something. James—that's the man's name—his mother paid for my education, so they think I should repay the family by doing this favor for them now." As she thought of what was in the letter, her voice began to rise in anger. That woman Rowena McCairn wouldn't have so much as walked her horse around the likes of Kenna.

"But you owe them nothing, right?" Artie said as he lifted Kenna's arm and began kissing the back of her wrist.

"Bloody right I don't. James's mother knew I didn't love her son, and she threatened to expose my..."

"Indiscretions?" Artie asked, his lips moving upward.

"Yes, my indiscretions to her James. James was always blind to women."

"So what did you say to his mother to get an education out of her?"

Kenna smiled at the memory. "I told her that if she didn't send me away—in style—I was going to persuade her son to elope with me."

"So she sent you to school and now they think you owe them."

At that Kenna moved her arm out of his grasp. There was amusement in the boy's voice, and she remembered that he was one of "them." "Not now," she snapped as she threw back the coverlet and got out of bed.

The boy leaned back on the pillows and watched her walk across room.

Kenna went to the dressing table against the far wall. With each year the number of pots of oils and creams on top of the table increased. "There was only one man who interested me in that godforsaken place. Gavie Dougall," she said as she rummaged about in the drawers.

Moments later she got back into the bed, sat by Artie, and opened a little red leather box, then gently emptied the contents on top of the silk duvet. "I haven't looked at these things for years," she said softly as she picked up a necklace of dried heather. It started to crumble in her hand, so she carefully put it back into the box. There was a little book with a tiny pencil attached, the kind that girls have at dances to record their partners' names. There was a little rock made smooth by water.

Kenna's hand closed over the rock, and her eyes became dreamy. "Gavie gave me this rock on the first night we made love," she said softly. "We were both fourteen, and I can still smell the heather."

"And he didn't marry you? The cad." Artie's voice was teasing.

Kenna put the rock back into the box. "No, he wanted to marry me, but I was ambitious. I decided I was going to marry the chieftain of the clan's eldest son because he had more money, so Gavie ran away to work in Edinburgh. Later I heard that he married some orphan and returned home years later. But by that time I'd been sent off to school and James was married to someone else."

"What's this?" Artie asked, holding up a thin piece of brass and ending Kenna's reminiscences. The brass ornament had holes cut in it so that it was as lacy as a paper doily.

"A trinket from my first lover," Kenna said, smiling at the lovely memories that all the objects brought back.

"He wasn't a gambler, was he?"

At that Kenna's head came up sharply, and her mind left its reverie. "Why?"

"I saw one of these things when I was a child, and my father explained it to me. A famous gambler had one of these in a fan. It looked like decoration, but when he held the fan in front of his face and looked at the other players' cards, he saw a pattern that told what cards the other players held. Of course being able to use the template depended on the cards. They had to all come from the same printer, but the man had paid the printer to adjust the design on the back of the cards."

Kenna's heart was pounding so hard that she could hardly speak. "You wouldn't remember the name of that gambler, would you?"

Artie smiled as he held the thin piece of brass. "I can't remember the family name, but would you believe me if I told you that it was some old family? Mile-long lineage, that sort of thing. The family fought with kings. My father used to say the most amusing thing. He said the men in that family either died in honor or were killed in—"

"Dishonor. McCairn," Kenna whispered. "Clan McCairn."

"Yes, that's it. How did you know?"

"So that's what they fought over," she said softly. "One of the old man's templates for cheating." Slowly, she took the piece of brass from Artie, then held it as though it were something evil. "A woman died because of this little piece of brass," she said, then tossed it back onto the bed near his hand.

Artie didn't seem to have any qualms about touching it. Picking it up, he held it to the light. "Name of Edweena?"

"Yes," Kenna said. "How did you know?"

"The name's engraved on the edge."

"The *woman's* name is engraved on it?" Kenna asked in astonishment. "But that doesn't make sense. She found it, and her husband—" Kenna put her fingertips to her temples. "No, wait. What did Gavie say when he gave it to me? He said that he saw the thing on *her* desk. He was snooping in *her* bedroom, not the old man's. Gavie picked the thing up, but when he heard someone coming, he hid in the closet. He didn't realize that he still had the ornament in his hand. He said..."

She paused for a moment. "Yes, Gavie said that she was looking for it, frantically searching through drawers, and he felt bad that he had it because he'd always liked the woman. Gavie said he was planning to drop the thing on the floor after she left so she'd think it'd been there all along."

"But she was killed?"

"Yes. Her husband came into the room, and she accused him of stealing it. Gavie said there was a horrible fight and they got very angry, both of them shouting and screaming and accusing each other of dreadful things. Gavie was just a kid at the time, so he never thought to step out of the closet and give the thing back. But then the next thing that happened was that the old man shot her. Gavie said it was an accident. It was her gun. She screamed that she was sick of him and his snooping into everything she owned, so she drew out her gun, a tiny derringer. But when the old man tried to take the little gun from her, it went off."

Pausing, Kenna looked at Artie. "After that everyone in the house came running, and in the chaos Gavie sneaked out of the closet. He didn't even realize that he still had the brass ornament in his hand until he was outside, and by then he was too afraid to tell anyone what he'd seen. In fact, he never told anyone about what he'd seen until years later when we were in bed together."

"Was she a gambler too?"

"No, only the old man gambled, and I heard that later, his grandson Colin did. Gambling is like a disease in that family and it skips a generation."

"So what do you think she was doing with this template? Was she altering it so he'd lose at the gaming tables? Maybe she was hoping he'd be shot when it was found out that he was cheating," Artie said, still looking at the template in interest.

"Maybe, but why is *her* name on the thing? It's as though that was her template, not his."

"Maybe she was planning to do some gambling herself, beat him at his own game. But whatever it was, this thing must have been important to her because she pulled a gun on the old man when she thought he'd stolen it. Didn't she gamble at all?"

"In a way, she did. She outspent him. What he didn't gamble away, she spent. Gavie used to say that—" Suddenly, Kenna sat up straight, her eyes wide.

"What is it?" Artie asked enthusiastically.

"Treasure. She left it all behind. Cards. A pack of cards to James. Not to Colin. He showed me. Pictures of the treasure on the cards."

"You're not making any sense," Artie said, obviously annoyed that he was being left out of whatever she was talking about.

Kenna suddenly grabbed the template, then leaped across the bed, and picked up the letter, all while pulling the bell to call her maid. "Get out."

"I beg your pardon."

"Get out. Now. Go away. Never come back."

"Whatever is wrong with you?"

"Nothing. I'm going to get married, that's all. I'm going to marry a man who doesn't know it, but he's fabulously wealthy."

For a moment Artie looked annoyed that he was being dismissed, then he gave a slow, seductive smile. "May I come and visit you?"

At that Kenna looked him up and down. "If I remember James correctly," she said softly, "he smells of sheep. Of course you may visit me. But not until after I'm married."

"Of course not," Artie said as he gathered his clothes across one arm, then walked past the shocked maid stark naked.

Eighteen

Temperance was in her bedroom, where she was often since she and James had had their quarrel. She busied herself with making notes on what she'd observed in McCairn and tried to make a plan of what she could use when she returned to New York.

When she heard a knock on her door, she looked up and said, "Come in."

An older woman stood there, and it took Temperance a moment to place her. She was the mother of Finola.

Temperance gave the woman a smile, but she wanted to get back to her papers and besides, she knew exactly what the woman wanted. "Oh," she said, "it was your daughter who made the sketches for the dresses. Yes, I'm going to get to them soon. I just haven't had time."

"No," the woman said. "I didn't come about that. We want to invite you to dinner."

"Dinner?" Temperance said distractedly. "Yes, dinner. See Eppie in the kitchen; she'll give you something to eat."

When the woman didn't move, Temperance could feel her staring. Annoyed, Temperance put down her pen. "I really will get

273

to the sketches," she said to the woman. "I won't forget."

The woman didn't lose her smile. "I'm sure that you will, and I'm sure that you'll do with my daughter what you did with Grace, but right now, how'd you like to have something to eat?"

For a few moments, Temperance just sat there blinking at the woman. In all her years of helping women, she couldn't remember even one occasion when someone had invited her to dinner. When she went to visit a person in need, Temperance always showed up with a basket full of food—and she had come to realize that such an offering was expected of her.

"Don't tell me you don't eat dinner?" the woman asked, looking at Temperance in disbelief.

"No, I do; it's just that..."

"If you're waitin' for James to show up, ye'll have a long wait, as he's up on the mountain, keepin' his pride company."

At that Temperance laughed. "You know, I *am* hungry. I'll just stop in the kitchen and get—"

"No you won't," the woman said, her jaw rigid. "You come empty-handed or you don't come at all."

"Well, then," Temperance said as she stood, "I guess I'll go empty-handed."

As Temperance walked behind the woman, out of the house, and down toward the village, they met half a dozen children on the way. In the weeks since they'd been skating, Temperance hadn't seen much of the children. In fact, lately her time had been so taken up with hats and writing her observations that she hadn't been outside often.

As they walked toward the village, the children chattering beside her, Temperance tried to suppress a smile. They were obviously planning a sort of celebration, and she was the guest of honor. She wondered what they had prepared: speeches and tributes of various sorts? Would she be embarrassed by their effusive thanks? Truthfully, she did hope that they didn't go on too long, as she had work to do.

The woman stopped at one of the whitewashed cottages, opened the door, and went inside, then stood there for a moment while she waited for Temperance to enter. For a moment Temperance hesitated. They couldn't get many people inside that small house, could they? Where was everyone going to sit?

But then Temperance decided that this particular party wasn't up to her to organize and she wasn't going to hurt this woman's feelings by pointing out the obvious. They'd all soon see the need for more space.

Inside the house a peat fire burned in the hearth, and two children, a boy and a girl, were seated at the table, the younger child, the boy, diligently making marks on a slate tablet, while the girl was reading a book. How quaint, Temperance thought.

"Sit and make yourself at home," the woman said.

The boy looked up at Temperance when she was sitting on a chair on the other side of the table. "Mam felt sorry for you bein' up at the big house all alone," the boy said.

"Hush!" his mother said as she bent over a big iron pot hung in the fireplace.

Sorry for me? Temperance thought but only smiled. Where were the other people? "What are you reading?" she asked the girl.

"Homer's *Iliad*," the girl said.

"Oh," Temperance said, surprised. "Isn't that a bit difficult reading?"

"Oh, no," the girl answered. "Master says that a person only learns when he strives for the best."

"I see," Temperance said, but she couldn't imagine old Hamish as anything except a pest—but then, maybe there was another side to him. "And what else does Hamish say?" Temperance asked the girl; then her eyes opened wide as she heard the answer.

❧⟲❧⟳❧

Melanie McCairn walked right past her daughter and didn't recognize her.

"Mother!" came a familiar voice, but when Melanie turned, what she saw was a scene out of the children's story of *Heidi*. Her sophisticated daughter had her long hair, not in its usual neat upswept style, but in braids that hung down over her shoulders. And in place of one of her beautiful dresses that had been made specifically for her, Temperance was

276

wearing a plaid skirt that looked as though it had been washed in a mountain stream for the last five years and a rough-textured linen blouse.

But for all that Temperance looked very different, Melanie had never seen her daughter look so full of health.

"Temperance?" Melanie asked, eyes wide.

"Don't look so shocked," Temperance said, laughing, as she handed a bowl of what looked like milk to a waiting child.

Melanie looked from Temperance to the goat tethered near her, then back to her daughter, then at the child holding the bowl of milk, then back at her daughter.

"Yes, Mother," Temperance said, laughing, "I have just finished milking a goat."

Since Melanie could think of no words to reply to that bit of news, she stood there and stared in openmouthed astonishment at her daughter.

"Would you like a drink of milk?" Temperance asked. "There's nothing quite like it fresh from the, ah, source."

"Not really," Melanie said, backing up. "James's aunt and I have come here to talk to you two about something important."

"Of course," Temperance said, then gave her mother a warm hug, and when she moved away, she kept her arm about her mother, and they started walking down the village road toward the house.

"I have a carriage," Melanie said, looking out of the corner of her eye at her daughter.

"No, let's walk, shall we?"

Melanie was further puzzled because her daughter didn't like to walk anywhere. Temperance said it was faster to go by carriage, and Temperance loved to do everything as quickly as possible. But this Temperance, the one with her hair worn the way she had it when she was twelve, was someone her mother didn't know.

"What have you been up to!?" Melanie said at last, her voice full of her curiosity.

Temperance laughed, her arm still around her mother's shoulders. "You held out longer than I thought you would. What do you think of this?" Temperance asked as she pulled away and twirled about in her long, faded skirt. There was a wide leather belt at her waist, fastened with a heavy pewter buckle.

Temperance turned to look at her mother; then, with her eyes on the village and her mother, she started walking backwards. "I've had the most extraordinary three days of my life, that's what's happened."

"Milking goats?" Melanie said, an eyebrow raised.

Turning, Temperance looked back up the trail, and she slowed down her walking, for which Melanie was grateful.

"Yes," Temperance said after a few moments. "I..." Trailing off, she looked toward the big house and thought about the last few days; then as they slowly walked along the path, she began to tell her mother about her last days, starting with when Finola's mother had invited Temperance to dinner.

"It was such a simple thing, but it was extraordinary to me," Temperance said. "I'm used to dinners and speeches and—"

"But this was ordinary," Melanie said, watching her daughter closely.

"Yes, it was," Temperance said with a sigh. "No one cared who I was or what I could do for them. Instead, they were doing things *for me.*"

"Tell me every detail," Melanie said eagerly. "Don't leave out one word."

At that, words began to tumble out of Temperance as she walked with her mother, sometimes slowly, sometimes backwards, sometimes stopping to look back at the village as she remembered something unusual of the last days.

"I guess that in my line of work it's easy to see that I could forget that there is happiness in the world," Temperance said. "I tend to see only the women who've had dreadful things happen to them. And the men..." She smiled. "I think that sometimes I forget that not all men on the earth are deadbeats or drunks."

"You told me that James works," Melanie said softly, but when her daughter's mouth tightened at that name, Melanie changed the subject. "So you were invited to dinner?"

"Yes," Temperance said, smiling again. "And I thought it was for a ceremony or something. That's usually why I'm invited to dinners. But this was just a family dinner, and when my skirt caught on fire, I—"

"What?!"

"I wasn't hurt, but my dress was ruined, so

Finola's mother pulled this from a trunk and it's, oh, so comfortable."

"And quite becoming too."

"Yes," Temperance said thoughtfully. "They're nice people," she said softly. "They care about anyone they accept as their own. Let me tell you about the children."

Melanie watched her daughter and listened as she launched into a lovely story of spending a day with the children of McCairn.

"The children said that I'd given them so much that it was their turn to give to me. They said this from their hearts. No adult prompted them to come up with this idea. Can you imagine such a thing?"

Melanie was afraid to reply to that question. From the time her daughter had been fourteen and her father had died, it was as though Temperance had taken a vow to give up all pleasure in life. Sometimes Melanie thought that her daughter believed that she had caused her father's death, that if she hadn't been so frivolous, or so concerned with the birthday party of her best friend that day, maybe her father wouldn't have died. But whatever the cause, since that awful day when Temperance's father had gasped, then slumped forward on his desk, dead, Temperance had devoted herself to good works and good works only. Melanie knew that her daughter had never attended any party ever again without there being a redeeming theme behind the party.

But now, here was Temperance, at nearly thirty years old, talking as though she were fourteen again and the last years hadn't happened. She was talking about how the children had shown her birds' nests and oddly shaped rock outcroppings and tiny hidden springs.

"I think I thought they were deprived because they'd never seen a pair of roller skates," Temperance said, "but..."

"But there are other things besides modern entertainments?"

"Yes," Temperance said, smiling. "The children are part of each family. They have jobs and responsibilities, and everyone knows about everyone else."

Temperance paused to take a breath. "And, also, there's Hamish."

"HH?" Melanie teased. "Horrible Hamish?"

"I think I misjudged him. He was—at first anyway—he was difficult to like. He's so pompous, but I've discovered that he had the idea that I'm a..."

"A big-city girl here to corrupt his charges?"

"Yes, exactly," Temperance said. "But he works hard for these people, very, very hard. He makes lessons for each child, and he knows exactly what a child is good at and what she or he can't do. And that's another thing, he makes no distinction between male or female. I thought his wife gave him a sleeping draft at night to keep him away from her, but now I think he needs it to make him stop working."

They were at the big house now, but Melanie wanted to go on listening to her daughter. She'd not seen Temperance so...so...happily excited, is the only way she could describe it, since…well, since before Temperance's father had died.

But Rowena was standing inside the entryway to the house, and she led them through to the dining room, where James was waiting for them. And the second that Temperance saw James, her good mood left her. Of course it didn't help that James looked Temperance up and down, his eyes wide in surprise to see her in braids and tartan, then gave a little sneer and said, "Mixing with the heathens?" and in the next second Melanie thought they were going to get into a fistfight.

With a great sigh, Melanie took a seat at the table and waited for Rowena to begin.

⚬◦⌇◦⚬

"That is the most ridiculous thing I have ever heard," Temperance said. "Who could write such a stupid will?"

"A man has a right to do whatever he wants with his own property," James said, glaring at Temperance, his lips in a tight line.

They were sitting at the dining table in James's house in McCairn, a fire glowing in the hearth. Across the table from them were James's aunt Rowena and Temperance's mother, Melanie. The two women had just told James and Temperance of the will that said that James must marry *for love* before his thirty-fifth birthday or he loses everything.

Temperance had sat there blinking in disbelief when she'd been told of the will, not really able to comprehend what her mother was saying.

"He can have it," James said, his arms crossed over his chest. "Let Colin have the bloody place. Welcome to it."

That brought Temperance out of her thoughts. "You have to be the most selfish man in the world," she said under her breath, glaring at him. She hadn't seen much of him in the last weeks, not since the night they had... That they had...

"It's not just you involved, is it?" she said to him, angrier than she meant to be, but she didn't want to remember that night they had spent together. "What about the other people here? Don't you have any idea what a wonderful place this village is? It's a perfect little jewel where people *care* about each other. But you want to give it away! If your wastrel of a brother gambles the place away, who takes care of the people of McCairn?"

"And when did McCairn become any of your business?" James shot back at her. "You can't wait to get out of here and go back to New York, to the people who really *need* you." Every word was a sneer. "And what do you know of my brother to call him names? It was *your* father who—"

Temperance came out of her chair. "How dare you use *my* father's name? My father was a saint, an absolute saint, especially when compared to yours. My whole family is—"

James stood, leaning toward Temperance, ready to shout her down.

"None of us is quite ready for sainthood," Melanie said loudly, making both of them turn toward her. Melanie looked at her daughter. "And, Temperance, perhaps before you start throwing stones, you should remember Aunt Isabella and Uncle Dugan."

Instantly, Temperance's face turned red; then she sat down, as did James.

"Hmmm," Rowena said, looking from James to Temperance, then back again. "I was hoping that we could settle this in a civilized manner, but it looks as though you children can't behave long enough to discuss anything. Melanie, dear, I think we should leave."

"Yes, of course," Melanie said as she prepared to stand.

"Wait!" James and Temperance said in unison, then glanced at each other, then away.

"I..." Temperance began, "I think we should discuss this. The will is stupid—" She put up her hand to ward off whatever James was about to say. "It is stupid, but it does exist, and even though I have no idea why a man would write such a thing, we need to deal with it, as you said, in a civilized manner. First of all, I think it is a given that Colin cannot have the place. I haven't met him, but I've certainly heard enough about him."

She turned to James, her face cold. "Is that agreeable to you? Or do you really want to turn all of your beloved sheep over to a gambler?"

"Better a gambler than an American do-gooder," James muttered.

"What was that?" Rowena asked loudly, her hand to her ear. "Speak up, James, you know I'm a bit hard-of-hearing."

"I know no such thing," James said quietly, narrowing his eyes at his old aunt. "You can hear the servants sipping your precious brandy from three floors away."

At that Rowena smiled and leaned back against her chair. "So what do you two want to do?"

"Save the place," Temperance said quickly. "A person must make sacrifices for others." Turning to James, she looked at him with her eyebrows raised in question.

He took a long while to look into her eyes; then after a while he gave a curt nod, and Temperance turned back to look across the table at her mother and Rowena.

"All right," she said softly, "we will marry. Not because we want to but to keep the village together. There are people involved who are more important than us."

At that Rowena and Melanie looked at the two of them with blank faces; then they turned to each other, then back to James and Temperance.

"But, dear," Melanie said after several moments, "we aren't asking you and James to get married."

"You aren't?" Temperance asked in surprise. "But I thought that's what you wanted."

"Heavens no!" Rowena said loudly. "You two would have a worse marriage than James's grandfather and his wife, and look what happened to them! She killed herself to get away from him."

"No, she didn't." James and Temperance again spoke in unison, then glanced at each other and away again.

"Well, whatever. You can tell me about that later," Rowena said. "We have more urgent business now. The key words in all this are 'in love.' I think, James, that you should know that I believe that that scoundrel brother of yours coerced your father into adding that—as Temperance so rightly says—*stupid* clause to his will. You know what Colin is like. He thought that you'd been married off to that awful girl and that when the time came, everyone would know that there was no love between the two of you. Colin just had to wait until you and he reached your thirty-fifth birthday, then all of McCairn would be his."

"Such as it is," James muttered.

"The land is worth something, I'm sure," Rowena said.

"All right," James snapped, "what is it that you want of me?"

"To marry Kenna, and for Temperance to plan the wedding," Melanie said sweetly.

"Who?" James asked while Temperance stared at her mother in wide-eyed silence.

"Kenna, you dolt!" Rowena shouted at her nephew. "Kenna. The girl you loved when you were a boy, the one you wanted to marry, but your father hauled you off to London. Remember?"

"Oh," James said after a moment. "Kenna." At that he smiled, then looked out of the corner of his eye at Temperance, but she jerked her head back around to stare at her mother.

"Kenna," Temperance said flatly.

"Yes," Melanie said, smiling at her daughter. "I must tell you the truth, that I had hoped that you and James would... Well, you can guess a mother's hopes, but I can see now that it didn't work out as I wanted. I never saw two people dislike each quite as much as you two do, and, Temperance, dear, your last letters have veritably reeked—begging your pardon, James—of your deep dislike of all things McCairn."

"You told your mother you hated McCairn?" James asked softly.

"I did not!" Temperance said quickly. "Mother, I said no such thing. I said that McCairn needed to be pulled into the twentieth century, but, truthfully, after my last few days, I—"

"Oh, I see," James said, cutting her off. "It's just *me* you hate."

"And why not?" Temperance shot at him. "After what you thought of *me!!*" She turned toward her mother. "He thought that I came here to *marry* him. When I helped the children or Grace, he thought I was doing it because I was after him, like some floozy who—"

"We're going to get nowhere at this rate!" Rowena shouted. "Now listen, you two, the last thing I care about at this moment is who thought what about whom. That doesn't matter to me at all. What does matter is saving McCairn so the next generation can take care of the place."

Leaning across the table, she glared at Temperance and James. "For all that you two seem to hate each other, I think you agree that you don't want the land sold and the people driven out of their homes. Am I right on this?"

"Yes," Temperance said softly. "To destroy this place would be a sin."

"Aye," James said as he looked at Temperance in speculation, again looking at the way she was dressed.

"James, it's good that you can overcome that hateful pride of yours to admit that," Rowena said. "Now the problem is that we have very little time before James's birthday and he must be married *for love* by then. Since all my brother Angus's tricks to find you a wife have failed, now the ox is in the ditch and it must be taken out."

She glared at James. "Do you understand me, boy? You must *do* something, or this precious land of yours is going to be gone. Then what will you do? Move into Edinburgh and get a job? I'm sure Angus would let you work for him. Something behind a big desk for fourteen hours a day?"

James didn't bother to respond to that but sat in stony silence.

"Any other questions?" Rowena asked, looking from James to Temperance.

When neither of them said a word, Rowena leaned back against her chair. "As Melanie said, we had hopes for the two of you, but since that is obviously an impossibility, and—" She stopped when both Temperance and James started to speak.

"If either of you again tries to make the sacrifice of marrying each other just to save this place, I shall *myself* testify to the king that you hate each other and therefore don't fulfill the terms of the will. I will not have more marriages in this family based on hatred. Do I make myself clear?"

James just sat there and looked at his old aunt, while Temperance nodded her head.

"Does this woman Kenna *want* to marry him?" Temperance asked after a moment.

"Heavens yes!" Rowena said. "She was deeply in love with him when they were children. Remember, James, how you two used to climb the cliff side of the mountain and look for birds' nests? You two were inseparable."

Temperance turned to look at James, but he had his eyes on Rowena. "I remember," he said softly.

"The girl's heart was broken when you left her behind to go to London. Your mother felt so sorry for her that she took on the responsibility of educating the girl in hopes that she'd make a good match."

"And she's going to, isn't she?" Temperance said. "Whatever little money the McCairn has, I'm sure it's more than what she had if she grew up here."

"Maybe she was ashamed of being from McCairn," James said, his voice low, menacing, sarcastic. "Perhaps—"

"Oh, no," Melanie said loudly. "That's not the case at all. Kenna married a widower who, unfortunately, died just a few years after their marriage, but he left Kenna well provided for. She has no need to marry anyone at all, but she's agreed to this because she says she loves James and always will."

"She doesn't know him!" Temperance said. "She hasn't seen him in what? Twenty years? She must be old by now."

"Not quite twenty years. She's two years older than you are, dear," Melanie said calmly, smiling at her daughter. "And she is quite lovely. Beautiful actually. Wouldn't you say that she is beautiful, Rowena?"

"Quite the most beautiful young woman I've ever seen. I was telling your dear mother that Kenna should have been painted. Do you think that Gainsborough could have done her beauty justice?"

"If she's so damned gorgeous, why does she want to marry a man she hasn't seen in half a lifetime?" Temperance asked, her teeth clenched shut.

"She loves me," James said brightly. "Always has. Always will. True love never dies. Doesn't even fade, from what I've heard."

"And what would *you* know of love?" Temperance snapped at him. "If it's not furry and four-legged, you don't even know what it is."

James arched one eyebrow and lowered his voice. "You seemed to think I knew something about love, didn't you?"

"Has something happened between you two that I should be told of?" Rowena asked loudly.

"Temperance, dear, you *do* want to go back to New York, don't you? They need you there so much," Melanie said.

Temperance looked away from James's eyes and into her mother's. "Yes," she said, "I want to go back to New York." Unfortunately, Temperance's voice broke in the last half of the sentence—but she was glad to see that no one but she heard it.

"That's good," Rowena said. "Everything is going to work out perfectly." She looked at Temperance. "Your mother has told me of what you've done here in McCairn, and I commend you. You'll explain everything to Kenna so she can take over. I'm sure that she'll do a marvelous job, since she was born and raised here."

"And she's had a lovely education," Melanie added.

"Not to mention her great beauty," Temperance put in.

"Oh, that's for James alone," Melanie said sweetly.

Could a daughter hit her mother over the head with a cast-iron firedog and still get into heaven? Temperance wondered. But she kept the smile plastered onto her face.

"So? Is everything settled?" Rowena asked,

looking from James to Temperance, then back again.

"I'm not sure I understand everything," James said slowly, frowning as he looked at his aunt.

Temperance turned on him with a face full of fury. "What's to understand? You have to marry for love, or you lose McCairn to your gambling brother. So these women, my mother included, have dug up an ancient love for you to walk down the aisle with. This woman is educated, beautiful enough to start wars, and she will do a great deal better job at managing the businesses *I* started than I have. What part don't you understand?"

James's eyes were glittering in anger, and the smile he gave to Temperance was cold enough to freeze fire. "I like *all* of it," he said. "I like every bit of it. There isn't one small part of it that I don't like. I especially like that *you* have to make all the arrangements for the wedding. I want my..." He looked Temperance up and down. "I want my *bride* to have the best of everything. See to it, housekeeper."

With that he got up from the table and left the room.

Nineteen

Temperance shut the door behind her, put her head back, and closed her eyes for a moment. It was such a relief to have some peace at last.

"Are they getting to you?" Grace asked softly as she looked up from the hat she was attaching flowers to. The warehouse wasn't yet completed, so she was still working in a bedroom in the McCairn's house. Alys had gone back to school, and Grace still blushed when she thought of what her daughter had told her, that she and Ramsey had hidden in the bushes on top of the mountain and Ramsey had called out to Temperance in an excellent imitation of James's voice.

Temperance sat down on a chair across from Grace and gave a sigh. "Can one's own mother become the enemy?"

"I think that's a question for Alys," Grace said, smiling, as she picked up half a dozen pins and put them in her mouth. "What has your mother done? Other than what the entire village knows about, that is?"

Temperance grimaced. Was it just yesterday that her mother and James's ancient aunt had come to McCairn and turned everything upside down?

"That's just it," Temperance said in exasperation. "This village has taken a bit of information the size of a grain of rice and turned it into a fifty-pound book. If I hear the name 'Kenna' one more time, I think I'll scream. This woman's arrival is being heralded as the Second Coming. Actually, I think the Second Coming would be given less press." She gave a challenging look at Grace. "And if *you* insinuate that I'm jealous, so help me I'll... Well, I don't know what I'll do, but I'll think of something."

"*Are* you jealous?" Grace asked softly.

Temperance didn't hesitate. "You were his lover; are *you* jealous?"

Grace smiled, for Temperance hadn't answered her question. "If you aren't jealous, then what do you care what the villagers think of—" She broke off before she said the name. "—what they think of his future wife?"

Temperance got up from the chair and walked to the window. There were many holes cut in the old lining of the curtain where Grace had cut out pieces in the shape of rose petals. It wasn't going to be she who raided Angus's warehouses full of fabric and chose new curtains for the old house. "Maybe I am jealous, but not in the way anyone thinks. I thought people here *liked* me. I thought I'd done some good." Even to her own ears, her voice sounded as whiney as a child's.

Grace wasn't going to give a talk about all

the good Temperance had done because she had her own reasons to dread Kenna's arrival, but she wasn't going to tell anyone about those reasons. "What are they saying?"

Temperance sat back down on the chair. "Nothing bad, just that they remember so much good about this woman. I think she left here when she was quite young, but she seems to have helped everyone in the village in some way. And there's a rumor that I have reason to believe that my own mother started that James and this woman have been courting for years, and that now, at last, she's agreed to marry him."

"When the contents of the will become known, that information should help," Grace said quietly.

"And Kenna won't leave them! *She* will stay in the village *forever!*" Temperance said in an outburst that surprised herself. Looking at Grace, she grimaced. "I have no right to be angry or upset in any way. One of their own is coming home. Of course they should be happy and excited. And James at last gets to marry a woman he truly loves. Today I've heard at least eleven stories about their deep, deep love for each other. Tristan and Isolde never had such a love. Romeo and Juliet never loved so well. No one has ever—"

Breaking off, Temperance narrowed her eyes and looked at Grace. "What's wrong with you? Why aren't you celebrating with the others?"

"I, uh..." Grace said as she moved the pins

about in her mouth and avoided Temperance's eyes. "It's the McCairn," she said after a while, and seemed pleased with herself for having come up with this.

"What about him?" Temperance asked, tight-lipped. "He's getting the most beautiful, most saintly woman on earth for a wife. What else could he want?"

"You know, don't you, that he's frightened out of his mind?"

"McCairn? Since when is he afraid of anything? And don't tell me he's afraid of women. Remember that I had to keep him from throwing one of them down a mountain."

"And *you* must remember that his first wife was so unhappy that she was killed while trying to run away from him."

Temperance picked up a spool of silk thread and played with it. "Why do I get the feeling that you're making this up as you go along? You're upset about something, really upset, and I don't think it has to do with James McCairn."

Grace looked up at her friend, locking eyes with her. "The villagers might be idiots, but I'm not. I don't want you to leave. I wish *you* were marrying the McCairn and..." Feeling that she'd said enough, she looked back down at the hat she was working on.

"No..." Temperance said slowly, "that's not to be. I don't belong here. I was beginning to think that I did. I was beginning to truly *love* this place, but—But these last twenty-four hours have shown me that I don't belong here. You should see how excited the village is that one of their own is coming back."

"They've always known that their new-found prosperity was linked to you but that you were going to leave soon."

Temperance toyed with the spool of thread. "I see. And James too, I guess," she said softly. "You know, I think I've been acting like a selfish two-year-old. It can't be pleasant to think that you must marry someone you haven't seen in many years just so you can save a village."

Temperance looked at Grace. "Is it just me, or is it odd that the villagers all assume that James will do this? Not one person has uttered a word of doubt that he'll actually say the words that will link him forever with this woman. But what if she's changed? According to everyone she was a lovely child and a self-less young woman, but people change. She's lived in London, she's been married, she's lived on her own for years. Maybe she doesn't want to return to this dilapidated old house." The house I cleaned, Temperance thought. The house *I* have put life back into. The house—

"Maybe James would appreciate someone talking to him about these things. Maybe you two could put aside your personal differences long enough to actually talk. If I remember correctly, you two once liked talking to each other."

Temperance didn't want Grace to see how her heart leaped at the idea of spending time with James. They had hardly spoken to each other for weeks now, and, well, truthfully, she missed him. Just plain ol'-fashioned, *missed* him.

But she hesitated. "Maybe *you* should talk to him. He hates me." Temperance kept her eyes on the thread and didn't look up at Grace.

"Everyone in McCairn knows what I was to him, but only a few know about the night you spent with him."

Temperance knew that her face turned brilliant red, and her extreme embarrassment made her throat close.

"Temperance," Grace said with a voice filled with weariness, "you don't have to be perfect. You are allowed to make mistakes in this world. You seem to forgive everyone everything, so once in a while, you should allow others to forgive you."

Temperance could only give a weak smile; then she looked away. Grace's words were wise and those of a true friend, but Temperance didn't like to be the recipient of forgiveness. Worse, she didn't like having done something that needed forgiving.

Without meeting Grace's eyes, she stood. "I think I will go talk to him. It's time that we cleared the air between us. After all, it's almost over."

"Yes," Grace said softly. "Soon we'll have a proper Lady McCairn, one who will oversee everything."

"Right," Temperance said and wondered why that thought made her feel so awful.

James was, as always, on top of the mountain, surrounded by sheep. When Temperance walked into the clearing, she ignored the startled looks the other men gave her. She didn't want to think that everyone in the village knew that she and James had been on the outs, but worse, she didn't want to think that they had any idea why.

"It's almost over," she whispered to herself, then straightened her spine and walked toward him.

He was bending over a big, curly-horned ram, looking inside its mouth. Temperance made herself look away from his heavy thighs, which were exposed by the kilt.

"I think we should talk," she said.

He didn't acknowledge that he knew she was there, and she knew he was ignoring her on purpose. "Talk!" she shouted so loudly that the sheep jerked and James had to throw an arm around its neck to keep it from running away.

"Oh?" James said calmly as he wrestled the big ram. "Would ye be speakin' to me?" he asked in an exaggerated Highland drawl.

Temperance put her hands on her hips, and turning full circle, she scowled at the men around them. They were all openly listening and watching.

With smiles, they turned and left her and James alone.

"Are you going to continue trying to murder

that animal, or are you going to stop and talk to me?"

Still holding the sheep, he looked at her, and when he did, she remembered their night together. They hadn't been alone since that night weeks ago—and now knowing the men were nearby made her feel safe. "It depends on what you want to talk about." He glanced down at her belly, and his voice lowered. "Have somethin' ye want to tell me?"

"You overrate your fertility," she shot back at him.

"Or maybe I overrated yours," he answered quickly.

Temperance had to work to keep from laughing. She really had missed his vain sense of humor.

"There's nothing wrong with my fertility," she said, then realized that she was starting to defend herself—which meant that *he* was controlling the direction this conversation was beginning to take. "I hope he eats your hand," she said, nodding toward the ram; then she turned on her heel and started down the mountainside.

Just as she figured he would, he stepped in front of her. "Come on, let's go in here away from the others."

Temperance started to follow him until she saw that he was leading her into *the* cabin. She dug in her heels and wouldn't move an inch.

"Ah, yes, I see what you mean," James said. "The cave?"

Temperance shook her head. She did not want to be *that* alone with him.

At her refusal, he motioned to a flat rock, and she sat down while he stretched out on the grass beside her.

"Now what has made you come all the way up here to talk to me, especially considering that you haven't spoken to me in weeks—except to shout at me, that is? And are you sure a dunderhead like me will *understand?*"

It was on the tip of her tongue to say that she'd missed him, but she didn't. "We need to plan your wedding," she said.

"Ah, that," James said as he picked up a piece of grass and put it in his mouth as he stared up at the sky. "Do whatever you want. Weddings are women's business."

"I think—I mean… Oh, damnation! Do you *want* to marry this woman?"

Slowly, James turned his head to look up at her. "Do you see another way I can protect this insignificant place? This place that people laugh at?"

Temperance took a deep breath and counted to ten. "I think that you and I should forget what was said…and done…between us. What we've heard since then overrides our own personal problems."

James looked down at her ankle, and Temperance could remember his kissing the little bone there and saying— No! she told herself, it was better to forget that night. How many times had she told women to forget what

301

they'd felt when a certain worthless man had held them?

"Perhaps I've overestimated you and you aren't capable of forgetting anything," she said as she put her nose in the air.

When James didn't respond, she looked down at him and his eyes were cold. "As long as you're not in the family way, I can forget anything," he said quietly. "From this moment on, that night didn't happen."

"Good!" Temperance said firmly. "We are agreed then?" She held out her hand to shake his.

The instant they touched, she knew it was a mistake. He held her small hand in his for a moment, and she knew that if he so much as tugged a hairbreadth, she'd be in his arms. She didn't dare look into his eyes.

But he didn't pull her. Instead, he released her hand, and Temperance let out her pent-up breath. "All right," she said, still not looking at him. "I think we should get started." She withdrew a pencil and a little notebook from her pocket. "I need to know all that you can tell me about her, about…Kenna," she said, "so I can plan the wedding. What kind of flowers does she like? What's her favorite color? Do you think she'll want something formal or not so formal? Who were her favorite friends in McCairn?"

Temperance paused for breath, then waited, pencil ready; but when James said nothing, she looked at him. He was lying back on the grass, the weed in his teeth, and staring up at the sky.

"I have no idea," he said.

"About which question?"

"Any and all. I don't seem to remember her very well."

"But according to the village, you two were madly in love. Passionately. With all your hearts. Separating you was like splitting two souls."

James gave a snort of laughter, then switched the weed to the other side of his mouth. "We were children together."

Temperance put down the notebook in frustration. "But I distinctly remember that you told me that you were in love with a village girl. 'In love'—that's what you said."

"So maybe I was. Who knows what being in love is?" Turning his head, he looked at her. "Do you know?"

"Not at all," she said quickly, then picked up her notebook again. "All right, tell me about the first lamb that you helped to birth."

James grinned up at the sky. "White with a black face, three black legs. I hid him here on the mountain so the cook wouldn't feed him to me for dinner."

"And what was the lamb's favorite food?"

"Daisies," James said before he thought, then looked at Temperance.

"You can remember a sheep but not your first love," she said, her eyes narrowed at him.

"All right, I remember that she had lovely long legs," he said, smiling. "Kenna, that is, not the lamb."

303

"I see," Temperance said, writing in her note-book. "Like your horses. That's under-standable."

"Not quite like the horses," James said softly. "Kenna was the prettiest girl that McCairn ever produced. Her father was an ugly little thing, and her mother died when she was young. He doted on his daughter. Anything she wanted the man got for her."

"I see," Temperance said, writing. "Spoiled only child."

"Are you jealous of the girl, that she gets to marry me and not you?"

"Don't be ridiculous," Temperance snapped. "I have no wish to marry anyone. I need to get back to New York as soon as possible. There are many people there who—"

"—need you; yes, so you've said. Now, where was I?"

"So far you haven't told me anything about her that would help plan a wedding. Did your aunt tell you when she'll be here?"

"Three or four days," James said with a shrug. "I don't remember. Whenever it is, it'll be soon enough."

At that Temperance again put down her note-book and looked at him. "James, it isn't any of my business, but marriage is a very serious undertaking, and maybe you should think about this before you do it."

When James turned to look at her, his face was serious. "And what choice do I have?" he asked quietly but with much feeling. "Do I put my wants over those of all those people down there?" he asked, motioning toward the village at the base of the mountain. "Do I say that, no, I don't want to marry a woman who I used to care about, then stand by while families that have lived here for hundreds of years are thrown off the land? What happens to someone like Blind Brenda if I don't marry?"

"She and her whole family will live off the proceeds of Brenda's books," Temperance said. "The books *I* have just recently found a publisher for."

"You have an answer for everything, don't you? You know how to solve all the problems in the world, don't you?" James said quietly.

At that Temperance stood up. "I used to know what to do about everything," she said, and to her horror there were tears in her voice. "My life used to be sane and sensible and it had *meaning*. Now I don't know anything anymore. I don't know who I am or what I want or...or anything about anything."

She was looking down at him with her fists clenched at her side, but James didn't move. He still lay on the grass, his hands behind his head, looking up at her calmly.

And when he said nothing at all, Temperance kicked the bottom of his foot, then turned and went down the mountain.

She had no idea that, behind her, James lay still, staring up at the sky and smiling. "Love does that to people," he said after a while; then, eventually, he got up and went back to the sheep, where he called Ramsey to him. "I want you to go into Edinburgh tonight and deliver a letter."

"It's not to *her,* is it?" Ramsey said with a sneer.

"Mind your manners!" James snapped at his son. "But no, it's not to Kenna. It's to your uncle Colin."

At that name, Ramsey perked up. His uncle Colin was a great deal of fun.

"I want him to send for someone in New York."

"New York!" Ramsey gasped. "But that's where she wants to go. That's where—"

The look James gave Ramsey silenced him. "Have I ever given you bad advice? Have I failed you yet?"

Ramsey gave his father a look that was identical to one of James's. "I think you should court her. You don't give her the attention that you do to one of your horses."

"When I need the advice of a boy, I'll ask for it. You aren't getting into trouble with Alys, are you? I'm not ready for grandchildren yet."

"I'm ready for a sister," Ramsey muttered, but his father heard him.

"I'll do my best to give you one," James said solemnly.

"But with what mother?" Ramsey snapped, tight-lipped.

"It's my choice, isn't it? Now go and get the letter. It's in my bedroom on my desk. Make sure you give it directly to Colin and no one else. He'll know what to do. Now, go, and if anyone asks you where you're going, lie."

"But—" Ramsey began, then stopped at the look from his father. With a sullen look, he started down the mountain. He didn't want Temperance to leave. With her here, he saw hope for all of McCairn, but if his father married a local girl, what hope had they? What would a local girl know of hatmaking businesses and the publishing world? Or about marketing alcoholic beverages? Temperance was a woman of the world. What did this woman Kenna have to offer?

As Ramsey neared the bottom of the mountain, he debated whether or not to go into Edinburgh, and he wondered what his father wanted with Uncle Colin. For all that the men were twins, they were very different, with his father being the serious one, the one who was all work and no play. But Uncle Colin loved to play. He said that he'd travel a thousand miles for a laugh.

When Ramsey reached the house, he went up to his father's bedroom and on his desk was a thick envelope with the word "Colin" written on the outside. Beside the letter was a torn piece of newspaper and a letter that looked as though it had been dropped and walked on. But Ramsey didn't notice these two items.

Instead, he put his father's letter into his pocket, shrugged, and thought that at least he'd get good food at his uncle's.

Twenty

"She's here," Grace said, out of breath from her run up the stairs.

Temperance looked up from the sea of papers around her. Her mother had written that Angus was so happy that James was at last marrying that he was going to foot the bill for the biggest wedding that McCairn had ever seen.

"Does he think that will be difficult?" Grace asked when Temperance told her of Angus's generosity. "Or maybe he plans to use the change in his pocket."

Since the announcement of the pending marriage, Grace had become a different person, Temperance thought. The calm Grace she'd first met was now sarcastic and nervous. And, try as she might, Temperance couldn't find out what was bothering her. However, Temperance liked to think that maybe Grace was upset at the thought that Temperance would soon be leaving them and returning to New York.

It had now been four days since Temperance had spoken to James on the mountain. She had been embarrassed by her outburst, and when she reached the house, she'd had a little talk with herself. She was behaving like a child with all her moods and petulance. She had to stop herself from trying to figure out *why* she was constantly either angry or wildly happy or melancholy, or whatever the mood of the moment was. Instead, Temperance made a vow to get on with this final task of preparing a wedding; then she was going to leave McCairn forever. She was going back to New York, the place where she belonged, where she didn't live in a world of constantly changing moods.

"Such a waste of time," she told herself, then looked at the list of merchants that her mother had sent her, all of whom were to be consulted before the wedding.

"I don't know why Kenna can't plan her own wedding," Grace said, her mouth drawn into a tight, prim little round shape.

"I guess she's busy," Temperance said, refusing to be drawn into whatever was bothering Grace. Temperance had her own problems; she didn't need more. With every day that passed she was thinking more about never seeing the people in McCairn again. Would Alys get into medical school if Temperance wasn't there to bully some hardnosed administrator into admitting her? What was Ramsey going to do with his life? Had anyone ever thought of that? Maybe she should talk to his parents, whoever they were.

Temperance halted her thinking because she'd yet again picked up the sketch for the wedding dress that Finola had drawn. Such talent! Temperance thought. Such a beautiful dress. "I hope mine looks just like this," she said under her breath.

"What?!" Grace snapped.

"Grace, I think we need to talk about—"

"She's here!" Alys said from the doorway. "Don't you want to meet her?"

Grace looked at Temperance; Temperance looked at Grace. Both women almost said, "No," but then they turned back to Alys and gave her weak smiles.

"Of course," Temperance said. "Of course we want to meet her."

"She's ever so lovely," Alys said dreamily. "Just like a storybook princess."

At that Temperance looked down at what she was wearing. Ever since the three wonderful days she'd spent in the village, she'd left her beautiful clothes in their trunks. After all, silk skirts snagged on brambles and silk stained easily. Her cotton blouse and heavy skirt with its wide belt seemed perfect considering that she had so much work to do. But right now she wished she'd thought of making a bit of effort this morning.

As she followed Alys and Grace out the door, Temperance paused for a moment to glance at herself in the mirror. Her hair was straggling about her face and there was a stain on her shirt collar. Suddenly, she remembered the charming Charmaine mentioning Temperance's wrinkles about her eyes. Leaning forward, she looked into the mirror. No wrinkles. Happy at that thought, she smiled— and there they were!!

"Are you coming?" Grace said from the doorway, her tone saying that she'd rather swallow the pins that were usually in her mouth than meet Kenna Lockwood.

The lines at the corners of her eyes had put Temperance into her own bad mood. "Why are you so bad-tempered lately?" she asked, frowning.

As they started down the stairs, Grace opened her mouth to speak, then closed it, then opened it. "I think you're going to see," she said after a moment. "You saw inside me, so I think you're going to see what I know."

With that cryptic bit of dialogue, Grace moved on down the stairs and left Temperance alone.

Most of the village was inside the dining room, spilling out into the big entrance hallway. For a moment Temperance stood at the bottom of the staircase and looked at all of them. In the weeks that she'd been in McCairn, she'd come to know nearly all of them. She knew their babies' names and their grandparents' names. She knew that if Nessie ate strawberries, she broke into hives. She knew that Mrs. Headrick secretly nipped at her husband's whiskey. And she knew that Mrs. Means embroidered all her underwear and that she and her husband...

Anyway, Temperance had come to know these people, and she had difficulty thinking of leaving the place.

But she was going to have to, she thought, so she'd better make the best of it. Taking a

311

deep breath, she put her shoulders back and began to make her way through the crowd. She was the housekeeper and, therefore, the unofficial hostess until James said "I do" to another woman and threw Temperance out on her—

Again, she stopped her train of thought and pasted a smile on her face. In front of her was the back of the renowned Kenna, the woman whose name had been on the lips of every man, woman, and child of McCairn for many days now. Soon to be the wife of James McCairn.

She was a small woman, Temperance thought, short and very slim. She was dressed in a divine little creation that Temperance was sure was by Paquin. She's not poor, Temperance thought. She had reddish hair, perfectly arranged, and not covered by a hat.

For a moment Temperance stood behind her and looked at the faces of the people who were seeing their beloved Kenna for the first time in years. If they had been looking into the eyes of an angel, they couldn't have looked more adoring.

Quietly, Temperance waited until Kenna turned around and acknowledged her, and when she did, Temperance drew in her breath quickly.

Yes, Kenna was beautiful. She had dark green eyes and that perfect skin that comes from incessant care. Her eyebrows were plucked so that they looked natural but arched perfectly. Her lips were perfect; her nose exquisite; the shape of her face was—

Oh, yes, Kenna Lockwood was indeed beautiful. And Temperance had seen that kind of beauty many times. And she'd seen what was deep, deep inside eyes like those many times.

"How do you do?" Temperance said cheerfully, suddenly feeling as though an enormous weight had been lifted off her shoulders. "I'm Temperance O'Neil, the housekeeper."

For a moment something flickered across Kenna's perfect green eyes, then they changed to warmth. "And I'm Kenna, here to marry the McCairn."

"Better you than one of us," Temperance said loudly, then smiled when the villagers around her laughed. She had gone from feeling as though her life were ending to feeling wonderful.

"Yes, better me," Kenna said softly, and again that expression crossed her eyes.

What a temper she has, Temperance thought, but kept smiling. "You must be tired. May I show you to your room? It's the best in the house. Of course later you'll be wanting to decorate. If you can get any money out of James, that is."

Again everyone laughed, and again Kenna gave Temperance a quelling look.

"I'm sure I'll manage," Kenna said softly. "I'll have my own people to help me, the people I grew up with and have always loved." Her eyes said to Temperance, See if you can top that one.

But Temperance didn't take the challenge. Instead, she just smiled and motioned for Kenna to follow her up the stairs.

Of course half the village followed the two of them, Kenna's many trunks and boxes on their backs or under their arms. And once they reached the room that was to be Kenna's, Temperance stepped back and quietly walked down the corridor to the back stairs, then raced down to the kitchen.

"Where is he?" she asked, breathless. She'd run down the stairs so fast that she'd lost her breath.

"He wasn't with the others?" a sullen Ramsey said as he bottle-fed a lamb.

Temperance could have kissed the boy. Only he and Grace seemed to have any regret that Temperance was leaving McCairn. Temperance shook her head no.

"He be in with the money," Eppie said—her way of saying that James was working on the account books in the library.

"He'll be in a bad mood then," Ramsey said.

"He's going to be in a worse one after what I tell him," Temperance said joyfully over her shoulder as she went running out of the room.

She ran into the library so fast that she skidded on the stones in the entryway. Without bothering to knock, she threw open the double doors to the room, shut them behind her, then leaned against them. James looked up from a desk piled high with papers.

"You can't marry her," Temperance said, still out of breath.

"*Hmph!*" James grunted, then looked back

at the papers. "I thought you had something new to say to me."

"No, I mean it: you can't marry her." Temperance started to walk forward, but her skirt was caught in between the two doors.

Putting down his pen, James looked up at her. "All right, I'll bite. What's the problem now? Why can't I marry Kenna?"

"She's—" Temperance had to stop for a moment as she got her skirt out from between the doors. "She's... She's..." How did she say this politely? she wondered.

"She's a woman who's seen hard times?" James asked, one eyebrow raised.

"Yes, but she's also—"

"Had some men other than her husband?" James asked without hesitation, then looked back down at the papers. "I thought you were going to help with the accounts. I hate paperwork."

Temperance walked to his desk and put her hands on it. "You know this? You're going to *marry* such a woman?"

He looked up at her in surprise. "You'd be the last one I thought was a snob," he said in surprise. "You're not the only one who can write letters, you know. Kenna and I have been corresponding ever since your mother and Aunt Rowena were here. I know a lot about her."

"You know that she...?"

"Yes, I know that she..." He was laughing at her. "Really, Miss O'Neil, I thought that with your background you would be more worldly-wise than this. You didn't really believe that romantic nonsense of my aunt's, did you? That Kenna and I were once in love?"

"But you said you were," Temperance said, looking at him in shock.

"I said no such thing!" he said in a voice of injury.

"You told me that you were in love with a village girl and that your father made you marry someone else."

"Oh," James said, smiling. "That." He picked up a couple of papers and looked at them. "I was probably trying to make you jealous, which would probably get you into bed with me. Did you give me the receipt for the sheep-dip you bought in Edinburgh? I can't find it anywhere."

Angrily, Temperance bent over, rummaged through the papers and withdrew the receipt. "Is that all you were after?"

Looking up at her, he raised one eyebrow. "Aren't you a little old to think that men are after anything else?"

At that Temperance threw up her hands, then turned her back on him. "If one more person mentions my age, I'm going to—" Taking a breath to calm herself, she turned back to look at him. "Have you thought about what you're doing? I think that Kenna may have had..." She lowered her voice. "Paying customers. I've seen what's in her eyes many times. I don't think she just 'fell on hard times.'"

James looked at her in silence. "Are you finished?" he asked after a while. "I *do* know about her. She was left a widow, some man stole all the money her husband left her, and she had to earn her living how she could. Can you tell me what's the difference between her and Grace?"

"I don't know," Temperance said honestly.

"Why do you champion one woman who was down on her luck and want another one thrown out on her fanny? Why are you telling me she's not good enough for marriage?"

"I don't know," Temperance said again, looking at him. Lately, she'd been saying that a lot. Truthfully, it seemed that she'd been confused since the day she met this man.

Standing, James moved to the other side of the desk and companionably put his arm around her shoulders. "You didn't really believe that she agreed to marry me out of love, did you? She can help me fulfill the terms of the will, and I can help her. It's quite simple, really."

He was walking her toward the door. "And after the marriage?" Temperance asked quietly.

"She'll probably go back to Edinburgh, and I'll send her an allowance. I'm sure both of us will be quite happy with the arrangement." At the door he halted and looked down at her.

"But it's so cold. What about the people of McCairn? They're expecting a lot from her."

"If they get to keep their homes, that's enough, isn't it?"

When Temperance didn't say anything, James put his fingertips under her chin and tipped her face up to him. "Thanks to you, we now have the hat business and Lilias is going to make her liqueur and Blind Brenda has her books, so McCairn is better off than it's been in many years. You can go back to New York and help other people. You've helped us all we need. Now go and plan the wedding. Give my people a party to tell their grandchildren about and make it cost Uncle Angus thousands."

Bending, he gave Temperance a fatherly kiss on the forehead. "Now go and do some work. And stop worrying about Kenna. She's my concern, not yours."

At that he opened the door and gently shoved her into the hallway. And once he closed the door behind her, James McCairn leaned against it and closed his eyes for a moment. It was difficult being that near her and not grabbing her to him and kissing her with all the desire that was inside him.

For a moment, he rolled his eyes skyward. "Please make this work," he prayed. "Please make her choose us." He glanced at the desk covered in papers, then decided that what he needed was a long, hard run on a fast horse.

⁂

Temperance avoided the crowd that was still downstairs and went to the peace of her bedroom. At the foot of her bed was a trunk full of clothes that she hadn't worn since she'd arrived in McCairn: beautiful clothes, but when she touched them, they seemed out of place here.

Tossing the clothes aside, she pulled out a scrapbook that her mother had made for her. In it were clippings of all the newspaper articles in which Temperance had appeared. Stretching out on the bed, she slowly turned the pages, reading every word of the articles. In New York she had done good work, she thought. She'd helped people, many, many people.

She looked at a photo of herself on the day she opened her first tenement that rented only to women in need. In the photo was a Temperance whom she hardly recognized now, wearing an elegant silk suit, an enormous hat on her head, laughing in a flirtatious way with the many reporters and politicians surrounding her. In the background were half a dozen women with children in their arms or hanging on to their skirts.

Temperance was smiling at the picture and about to turn it over, but then she lifted it and looked harder at the women in the background. She'd never thought of it before, but she knew the names of every newspaperman in the picture and all the politicians, but she didn't know anything about any of the women who were to live in the building that she owned. She had chosen the residents from life stories that were taken down by women who voluntarily worked for Temperance. Personally, Temperance hadn't met even one of the inhabitants of the building she owned.

Personal, she thought. Wasn't that the key word? In New York she'd helped people, but there had been nothing in it for her *personally*. Closing her eyes for a moment, she remembered the three days in the village. On the second day, one of the children had fallen down a rocky slope, and immediately Temperance had stepped forward; after all, she was used to taking charge of situations. But she'd been brushed aside as the whole village, as a unit—like one large, living organism—stepped in and took over. Ramsey carried the child back to the village and as he put the girl down on a bed in a cottage, someone said, "She's on her way." Temperance, in the back with the others, started to ask who "she" was, but moments later young Alys came into the cottage. Temperance had stood by, openmouthed, as she watched the girl demand boiled water, thread, and a needle that had been washed in carbolic acid. In openmouthed astonishment Temperance had watched Alys tell the worried mother what to do as Alys gently stitched the four-inch-long cut in the girl's leg. Temperance hadn't known that Alys had a talent for healing. She'd known the girl was intelligent and good with numbers but not that she was also a healer.

But now, Temperance looked back at the photo of herself of two years ago and she felt an emptiness inside her. Today she was still young enough and pretty enough to flirt with the politicians and the press and have them flirt back. But what would happen to her when she was forty? Fifty? And when she went home at night, what was going to be waiting for her?

Slowly, she closed the scrapbook and looked at the leather cover for a moment. Her mother had said to her many times, "Temperance, you take care of everyone but yourself, and always giving and never receiving can oftentimes be very lonely." Each time her mother had said something like that, Temperance had laughed, but now that she'd been here in McCairn, she'd been more involved with people than she had ever been before in her life. And she'd experienced moments of true, genuine happiness.

"If I had a child, I'd want her to grow up here in McCairn," she said softly, then told herself to quit being maudlin. She didn't have a child, and right now it looked as though the people of McCairn didn't *want* her.

"Work to do," she said, then got off the bed and put the scrapbook away.

Twenty-one

Three days, Temperance thought. It was only three days until James McCairn was to marry Kenna. In the days since she'd met Kenna, Temperance had never worked so hard in her life as she had to prepare for this wedding. There were flowers and food and guests to see to, plus a thousand other details.

And Temperance was doing it all on her own, for Kenna had no interest in any of the proceedings, not even in her own gown. Nor did she seem to have any interest in James. As far as Temperance could see, the two of them never spent any time together. James was always on top of his beloved mountain, and Kenna... Well, it seemed that Kenna mostly made messes.

"I don't want to have to clean up after her again," Eppie said with her old arms tight across her bony chest. "What's she lookin' for anyway?"

"I have no idea," Temperance said tiredly.

"Treasure," Alys said. "Everyone wants the treasure."

Temperance had thrown up her hands in despair. The last thing that she cared about was treasure.

In truth, Temperance was doing her best to

not care about anything in the entire world. She was, according to Grace, "hiding" inside the big McCairn house, not leaving to walk up the mountain, where she might see James, and not going into the village, where she'd have to hear about how happy they were that "one of their own" had returned to them.

"Don't think," Temperance told herself at least four times a day. "Don't think and don't feel." She tried to focus her mind on one thing and that was getting back to New York and to her real work. She tried to remember what she'd wanted to accomplish when she knew she was going to go to McCairn. She'd learned a lot here, and she could use what she'd learned in New York.

"I'll be able to help women get jobs rather than just charity. A way to support themselves will last longer than low rent," she had said to Grace as they were going over the guest list and trying to figure out where to put people. James had so very many relatives. "Now that I've seen what I can do when I make an effort, I won't rely so much on others."

"We'll miss you," Grace had said quietly.

Temperance wasn't going to think about that. She wasn't going to think about individual people in McCairn and the laughter she'd shared with them. She grabbed another list and looked at it, but her eyes blurred. She remembered one evening she'd gone to Blind Brenda's cottage and sat with half a dozen children and listened to a story about when giants ruled the earth. James had quietly come into the room halfway through the story, and he'd sat by the fire and smoked a long clay pipe. She'd never seen him smoke before.

While she was sitting there, a two-year-old asleep on her lap, Temperance had thought, I never want to leave this place and these people.

"Did you hear me?" Grace asked.

"No," Temperance said honestly. "I was thinking about something else. Do you think she's going to make a good wife for him?"

"No," Grace answered just as honestly, "but it's not really a love marriage, is it? It's to fulfill a will, and it's to make her respectable. They're both getting what they want. Are you?"

"Am I what?"

"Getting what you want?"

"Oh, yes," Temperance said quickly. "I want to return to New York and do what I was meant to do. It's just that right now I'm feeling a little...nostalgic, I guess, because I've enjoyed my time here and I've come to care about the people here, but once I'm back there, I'll be fine. But I..."

"You what?"

"I think I'll do things a bit differently," she said. "I might—"

"There's someone coming!" Alys yelled as she ran up the stairs, causing Temperance to break off her sentence. "And she's beautiful!"

"Tell her the McCairn already has a bride," Temperance shouted toward the door, making Grace smile.

"No," Alys said when she reached the doorway. "She's come to see *you.*"

"Me?" Temperance said. "I hope it isn't an early wedding guest," she said as she followed Alys down the stairs.

"Her name's Deborah Madison and she's from America."

At that Temperance stopped on the stairs. At first she wasn't sure where she'd heard the name before; then it hit her hard. The Contender, she thought, for that's what the woman's name had come to be inside her head. This was the woman who wanted to take away what Temperance had started and had built. This was the woman whom Temperance was going to have to fight as soon as she returned to New York and to her real work.

Deborah Madison wasn't beautiful; she was cute. She had lots of reddish hair, an upturned nose, freckles, and a little-girl mouth. As she stood on the stairs and looked down at her, Temperance knew that she was the kind of woman who'd always look twenty years younger than she actually was. And Temperance could also see why men adored her. She had no doubt that Miss Madison could look up at a man with those big green eyes, bat her lashes, and make the weakest man feel strong.

"There you are," she said, looking up. "I would have known you anywhere." Her voice was that of an excited child's.

"Won't you come in," Temperance said cautiously.

"So you *do* know who I am," the girl said,

for Temperance could only think of her as a "girl." Already, she was making Temperance feel quite old. However, the way she said "who," as in "who I am," made Temperance even more cautious.

"Yes, I've read about you. Perhaps we should go in here and sit down," Temperance said, opening a door on a rarely used drawing room. The room was quite shabby, and she hadn't bothered to do much with it, as it was so seldom used.

"I heard that you'd been exiled, but this is ridiculous," Deborah said, looking around her as she unpinned her hat and set it on a round table in the center of the room. "My hat's not as big as yours, but then, it's not *my* trademark," Deborah said, looking at Temperance as though they shared some secret.

Silently, Temperance motioned toward a deep sofa, and Deborah sat down. "Why are you here?" Temperance said once they were seated.

"I was sent for; didn't you know that?"

"No..." Temperance said slowly. "Who sent for you?"

"I thought *you* did." Before Temperance could answer, Deborah stood up and began to pace about the room. "You're my hero, did you know that? Of course I plan to surpass you, and now that you've given up everything—"

"I beg your pardon?"

"You *are* staying here in Scotland, aren't you?"

"No, actually—"

326

"Well, good then," Deborah interrupted. "I can stand the competition, but I warn you that I do indeed plan to give you a run for your money."

"Pardon me," Temperance said, "but I haven't the faintest idea what you're talking about. Compete with me about what?"

Deborah stopped pacing and looked at Temperance for a moment; then she picked up her bag off the sofa and opened it. "I do hope that you don't mind that I smoke. Willie—you remember him, don't you?— Willie says that smoking makes me look more sophisticated." At that she took out a short, fat cigarette and lit it with a match. However, she started coughing so hard that she had to stub it out, unfortunately on a Meissen plate.

"They take some getting used to. Now where was I? Oh, yes, competing. Dear," she said to Temperance, "you and I are competing for the history books. You know that, don't you?"

"No, I had no idea we were competing at all, so why don't you explain this to me?" Temperance sat still, her hands folded on her lap, and listened to this woman she'd never met before talk about famous women in history. Deborah Madison included Joan of Arc, Elizabeth I, and Catherine the Great in what was an obviously well-rehearsed speech. In conclusion, Deborah said that she planned to add herself to that illustrious list.

All in all, Temperance was feeling very stupid. First of all, she couldn't figure out who had summoned this woman and what she wanted from Temperance. That she wanted something was a sure bet, because already Temperance could see that Deborah Madison didn't do anything without receiving something in return. It was obvious that Miss Madison was one ambitious young lady.

"However, if you don't mind, I plan to borrow some ideas from you. You have your hats, and I'll... Actually I haven't come up with my trademark yet, but it'll be something like your hat, something that makes people notice and remember me."

"I used the hat to help call attention to the people I was trying to help," Temperance said softly, but her teeth were clenched. This girl was *not* going to make her angry!

"Yes, yes, of course you did," Deborah said quickly. "All those destitute women. I know. The prostitutes, the drug addicts, all those illegitimate children. But then we never really touch them, do we?"

"Yes," Temperance said firmly. "They are people, and they need—"

"A bath," Deborah said, then laughed at her own joke. "Yes, I know that at first you had a great deal to do with them, but then you were just starting out and couldn't help it, but later, you learned to deal with the mayor and the governor—the *important* people. Willie says that I should set my sights on the president, and that I should try to get him to create some position for me. He said—and you'll die at this—you do remember how funny Willie is, don't you? He said that I should have the president form a House of Prostitution and I'd be the director of it. Get it? House of Prostitution?" When Temperance didn't seem to understand, Deborah pushed. "Like the House of Representatives, but since we work with prostitutes and where they work are called houses..."

Temperance still didn't smile. She didn't remember Willie as being particularly funny. In fact, she couldn't seem to remember Willie as much of anything except a nuisance.

"So, anyway," Deborah said, "I was sent for, so I'm here."

"But why and by whom?" Temperance asked.

"I have no idea. A lawyer visited me and handed me tickets for the first ship out. He said I was to get to Edinburgh pronto. I had four long days on the voyage over to think about all this, and I decided that maybe, instead of competing, we should form a team. I could be the one in front of the cameras, and—"

"I could be the old cow in the background who does the work," Temperance said with a smile.

At that Deborah laughed. "Willie said that you had a great sense of humor, and he was right."

"Tell me, Miss Madison, what would you advise a young, unmarried woman who told you she was in the family way?"

"Well, first of all, I'd let Agnes handle her. You remember Agnes?"

"Yes," Temperance said, then thought with

embarrassment of the night that she'd thrown her hat into the audience and how she, Temperance, had enjoyed the adoring look Agnes gave her. That seemed so long ago. Had she needed worshippers?

"Well, Agnes handles all those women, but if *I* had to advise her, I'd tell her that she should have controlled herself. If you know what I mean."

"I see," Temperance said, then realized that she'd seen more than enough, so she stood up. "It has been so nice to meet you and I do hope you can stay for the wedding of the McCairn to Miss Kenna Lockwood. And although I'd like to invite you to stay here, I can't, as we will have a full house."

As Deborah stood, she looked about her. "That's all right. I'd be afraid of bedbugs anyway. No, the ticket included a good hotel in Edinburgh, so I'll be going back there tonight, then sailing home tomorrow. You know, I think I like you," Deborah said. "You don't say much, but I think maybe you're smart, and I think that together we can put ourselves into the history books."

"I'm sure we could," Temperance said softly as she opened the door to the drawing room for the young woman, then stood there and watched until she walked out the front door.

For several minutes Temperance stood where she was, her back against the doorframe, not moving. But suddenly her chest began to heave, and there were sobs inside her throat that she couldn't hold back. James, was all she thought. All her life she'd lived with women and Grace was upstairs, but Temperance didn't want to talk to her. No, right now, the person she needed most in life was James.

With tears blurring her eyes, she turned and ran down the hall, through the kitchen, then outside across the stable yard and toward the mountain. She was halfway up when she saw James coming down.

"I heard you had a visitor from America," he said, "and I wondered who— What's this?" he asked when she flung herself into his arms. "Ah, lass, you aren't crying, are you?" he said softly as he began to stroke her hair.

"Yes," she blurted. "I've just seen myself, and I hated me. Really, really hated myself."

"This isn't about those wrinkles, is it? Personally, I *like* them."

"No!" she said, pulling away from him; then when she looked up at him, she could see that he was teasing her. It was then that she began to cry in earnest. Maybe it was all the emotion that she'd been holding inside over the last weeks, but tears began to come out of her at a prodigious rate. When James saw that she was serious, he picked her up and carried her off the path. He knew every inch of the mountain, so now he took her to a private little glade, where a tree overhung them and a tiny stream formed a trickling fall of water.

Gently, James set her down on the ground, her back against a rock; then he pulled a handkerchief from his sporran, dipped it into the water, and began to wipe her face. But when she continued to sob, he sat beside her, and Temperance put her head in the hollow of his shoulder. For a while he just held her, but then gradually her sobs decreased and he pulled her head away to look at him.

"Now, tell me what's happened," he said softly.

"My mother," Temperance said, then hiccuped.

James bent to one side and scooped up water in his hand, then held it out for her to drink. Putting both her hands on his, she sipped water from his cupped hand, then tried her best to sit upright. Taking his handkerchief, she wiped at her eyes.

"I didn't mean to do this," she said. "I don't usually fall apart."

"But the wedding—"

"This has nothing to do with the wedding!" she snapped. "I'm sorry, it's just that..."

"Go on, tell me what's happened."

"My mother sent a woman here to visit me. At least I think my mother sent her. It's like something she'd do."

"Who was she?"

"She's the woman who wants to take my place in New York."

"But no one can take your place because you're going to go back there and take your own place, aren't you?"

"Yes. I..."

"But what is the problem?"

"Me," she said, looking up at him with red

eyes and a swollen nose. "It's me. I saw myself. She *is* me."

James smoothed a strand of hair back from her face and tucked it behind her ear. "That couldn't be too bad then, could it?"

"You don't understand," Temperance said, moving away from him. She dipped the handkerchief in the icy mountain stream and held the cloth to her face. Now that she was calmer, she was able to think better. Why had she run crying to him? Why not to Grace? Why run crying to anyone, for that matter? What happened to the rational woman she used to be? But then, the woman she used to be was just the problem, wasn't it?

Turning back to James, Temperance took a deep breath. "Her name is Deborah Madison, and she is exactly like what I used to be. Is that what I was? Is that how people saw me? She's awful. Terrible. She's so sure of herself, so full of herself. And I'm a snob just like she is."

At that, James reached out and pulled her back against his chest. "You're not a snob. You came here and cleaned the house with your own hands."

"But only because no one else would do it."

At that James laughed softly. "Because no one else will do it is no guarantee that someone else will," he said, smiling. "Did I ever tell you how lazy my wife was? She lived in squalor because she was too lazy to do anything. She was stupendously lazy. Others feel guilty for not doing something, but not my wife. When she dropped her hairpins, she used to call Eppie in to pick them up for her."

"You're making that up," Temperance said, but she smiled against his chest. She'd never before been comforted by a man, and it was...well, it was nice. And maybe she didn't want to leave McCairn. Maybe...

"That girl, that Deborah Madison, can do my job in New York," Temperance said softly. "I'm replaceable in New York but not in McCairn."

At these words, Temperance felt James stiffen, but he said nothing, and she had no idea what he was thinking. He certainly wasn't encouraging her, that's for sure. "Sometimes," she said tentatively, "I think it's more rewarding for me here in McCairn. I seem to have made some true friends here, but in New York I don't think I was a real person. I think I was like her, like that girl, Deborah, but I told myself that I was helping people. But now I'm not so sure that I was. And, anyway, my absence hasn't halted the work I was doing, so I'm not sure they *do* need me."

When James still didn't say anything, she pulled back to look up at him. He was ramrod stiff, and he was looking at some distant point over her head. Temperance knew that she'd said enough. She wasn't going to beg him to say something, to say anything. And her pride certainly wasn't going to allow her to beg him to ask her to stay in McCairn and forget about going back to New York!

For a while they sat there in silence, Temperance looking down at the damp handkerchief in her hands, James staring at nothing above her head. At long last he said, "What is Kenna doing now?"

At that Temperance's heart started pounding. Was he going to go to Kenna and tell her the wedding was off because he'd just realized that he was madly in love with Temperance? And was that what Temperance wanted?

She tried to lighten the moment. "We think that she's tearing the house apart looking for the treasure," she said with a smile.

But James didn't smile. Instead, he nodded. "Yes, I know," he said after a while. "So perhaps she knows something that we don't."

It took Temperance a while to realize that for all the understanding that was passing between them, they might as well have been on different planets. She was talking about life; she was hinting that if he asked her to stay, she would. But all that was on his mind was the treasure. That damned treasure that might not even exist.

"I am so sorry to have bothered you," she said coolly, then slowly stood up.

"Temperance, I..." he said, still sitting, looking up at her.

"Yes?" she asked. "You have something to say to me?"

"Just that— No, I can't say anything now. Not yet."

"I see," she said, but she was lying. She didn't see anything. "I'll be here," she said, trying to sound as though there were nothing wrong in the world, "until after your...wedding, then I'll be leaving for New York."

James looked at her, but he didn't speak again, so Temperance went down the mountain.

After she left, James hit his hand with his fist. What he'd just done had been nearly impossible for him, but it had to be done. He knew Kenna well enough to know that she'd come back for a reason, and he'd guessed that she had some information, something that would lead her to the McCairn wealth. If James did anything now to make Kenna think that she wasn't going to get her pretty little hands on the loot, she'd stop searching. And what would make her stop more than an announcement of marriage between the McCairn and Miss Temperance O'Neil?

"Three more days, sweetheart," James said aloud. "Just give me three more days."

Twenty-two

By the morning of the wedding, Temperance was sick with... She didn't know what it was that was making her sick, but something was. Part of her thought that she was in love with

James McCairn and that she wanted to stay in McCairn forever. But another part of her wanted to return to New York and prove that she could do a better job than she'd done before. This time she'd do a more *personal* job. This time she'd get to know the women she helped.

"I started out right," she told Grace as they carried flowers into the church. "I had all the right intentions. I wanted to do something for women who had no resources. But somewhere along the way I became—Oh, put it over there," she said to one of the florist's workmen. "But at some point I became a...a..."

"Holier-than-thou prig?"

"Well, yes, I think I did," Temperance said, pausing with her hands on a stalk of lilies.

"I disagree," Grace said. "Maybe you had some absurd ideas about men and women being able to control their baser urges, but I've never thought you were a prig."

"Thank you," Temperance said, then felt an impulse to continue talking. And talking and talking, until there were no more words to be said.

All her life she'd prided herself on knowing exactly what to do about every problem that faced her. Her mother had said that Temperance and her father had never had a moment of indecision in their lives. "It must be wonderful to know at all times exactly what to do about everything," Melanie O'Neil had said many times. "But, dear, unlike you and your father, I'm mortal and I can't even make up my mind about which dress to put on in the morning, much less about what I need to do with my life over the next ten years."

But Temperance was like her father, and she'd always had one-year goals and five-year and ten-year goals. And, what's more important, she'd stuck to them.

But now, in the short time she'd been in McCairn, it seemed that her very foundation had been shaken. For the first time in her life she didn't know what to do about anything.

Part of her wanted James to act like a hero in a novel and sweep her off her feet. She wanted him to declare undying love for her and tell her that she *had* to remain in McCairn forever and be his wife. Temperance could see herself living in that big stone house and producing babies, all of whom grew up to wear kilts and play bagpipes.

The other part of her wanted to run away from this place and never see it again. She remembered how she had been in New York, always sure that what she was doing was right, always moving toward a goal, a big goal, something that she was sure was going to change the earth.

"Do other women have this dichotomy inside them?" Temperance had asked Grace last night.

"No," Grace had said sleepily. "Most women know exactly what awaits them: a man and a lot of children. If they're lucky, the man is good and he supports all of you and he lives a long time. If the woman is unlucky, he drinks or beats her. Or he dies," she added softly.

"But that's just it," Temperance said with passion. "When I was in New York, I felt that I was giving women a choice."

"No, you gave them a place to stay when the men ran out on them," Grace said with a yawn. "You were a landlord."

At that Temperance had sat back on her chair and stared in openmouthed astonishment at Grace, for Grace had just reduced years of Temperance's do-gooder work to one word, "landlord."

"Is that all I was?" Temperance had whispered.

Grace gave her a weak smile. "What do I know? I wasn't there, so I can't be a judge. I only know what you've told me. It just seems to me that here on McCairn you've done more. You've given women a way to help themselves. I can buy my own house someday even though there's no man in my life, and Alys can go to school. Now, if you don't mind, I must get some sleep. Tomorrow's the big day."

"Yes," Temperance said softly, then got up and went to her own bedroom. Tomorrow was the big day, her last chance. Tomorrow she had to *do* something or she was going to lose... What? she asked herself. What was she going to lose? It wasn't as though the McCairn was begging *her* to marry him. She'd hinted to him three days ago that if he did ask, maybe she would remain here in McCairn. But

James hadn't taken the hint. In fact, he'd told her that he was going to marry Kenna, so that was the end of it.

For the three days before the wedding, Temperance had lost herself in work. James's relatives had started arriving, and it had been up to Temperance to welcome them. She'd started to apologize for the state of the rooms, but they had laughed at her. They well knew the state of the finances of the head of Clan McCairn.

Three times Temperance had tried to talk to Kenna about the coming nuptials, but she never had "time" to discuss anything. "Do what you want," she'd said over her shoulder, then run off to some other part of the house.

"Ain't found nothin' yet," Eppie would inform Temperance twice a day, meaning Kenna's quest for the treasure.

"Why doesn't she at least *try* to be discreet?" Temperance had asked in frustration after she'd had a fight with the butcher. Wasn't it Kenna's job to deal with her own wedding?

The kitchen had been full of people, but no one had answered her. Ramsey was, as always, holding a bottle for a lamb. He'd looked up at Temperance and said, "Maybe she hopes she'll find the treasure before the wedding so she won't have to marry my father."

For a few moments Temperance stood there blinking at him. "Father? James McCairn is your *father?*"

"Aye," he said. "No one told you?"

"No," she said softly. "No one told me."

Temperance found James at the top of the mountain. For once he wasn't doing something to a sheep but was sitting with his back against the stone wall of the cottage where they had...

Anyway, he was smoking a pipe.

"I saw you," he said. "Do you realize that when you first came here, you were out of breath at that climb, but now you can run all the way up?"

Putting her hands on her hips, she glared down at him. "Why didn't you tell me that Ramsey was your son?"

For a moment James blinked at her. "It's not a secret. Why didn't you know?"

"That's not an answer. Who is his mother?"

"A girl I met in London. Long time ago." He took the pipe out of his mouth, looked at it, then put it back between his lips. "What's that all over the front of you?"

Temperance didn't bother to glance down. "Flour and blood. I've been in the kitchen. Are you going to tell me about this or not?"

"There's nothing to tell."

"Have you provided for the boy? Is he to inherit the title, the land? What have you done to see to him? Not much, if his living accommodations are any indication of what you've done for him. I thought he was a stableboy!"

"An honorable position, if you ask me."

Temperance glared at him harder.

"All right," James said with a sigh. "What do they teach you women in America that you're always concerned with money? Did you know that the women in McCairn now earn more than the men? Last week Lilias told Hamish that he couldn't have his nightly draft because she was now selling all the tonic that she made. And Blind Brenda—"

"You are *not* answering me."

"I haven't done anything about anything, if that's what you want to know. The girl and I were together one night; I didn't even know her. Two years later her mother came to me and told me the girl had died of consumption, then shoved a scrawny boy at me. I brought him back here to live with me. As for the rest of it, I guess my legitimate son will inherit, if I have any, that is."

At that he looked at her waist.

"Tomorrow you're marrying Kenna, remember?"

"Yes. So where's she looking now? The attics?"

Temperance threw up her hands in disgust at him and his whole clan, then turned and walked down the mountain.

So today she was putting flowers in the church and trying not to think too hard about anything. This time tomorrow everything would be finished and she'd be free to return to New York and...and...

What? Fight Deborah Madison for the title of who would go into the history books? At the thought she gave a shudder.

"Are you all right?" Grace asked.

Temperance started to say that she was

fine, but instead, she straightened. "No," she said at last. "I'm not fine. I'm... Actually, I'm not sure what I am, but it's not fine."

At that she turned and left the church. If the flowers didn't get put in the right place, what did it matter to her? If it didn't matter to the bride or the groom, who was *she* to care?

Twenty-three

It was when she was introduced to Colin that everything began to whirl about in Temperance's head so fast that she thought she was going to faint.

With her hand to her forehead, she swayed back against the paneled wall of the entrance hall. Grace caught her before she fell.

"Is she all right?"asked a voice that was identical to James's. In fact, everything about Colin was identical to James.

Before Temperance could reply, Colin had picked her up and carried her into the drawing room. "Out!" he ordered the people who'd filed in behind him, and it was the same way that James ordered people about.

"Here," Grace said as she handed Temperance a glass of brandy.

"Wrong glass," Colin said with a frown. "You can't serve brandy in a water glass."

At that Temperance, lying on the sofa, her eyes closed, smiled. They might look alike, but they certainly weren't alike in personality, she thought. James drank brandy from a sheepskin flask. "I'm sorry to have caused such a fuss," Temperance said as she sat up. "But it was such a shock seeing you. I knew you were twins, but it was still a shock."

At that Colin looked down at her, one eyebrow raised in speculation. "You're not Kenna, but you're in love with my brother," he said, as a statement of fact, not a question.

"I most certainly am not!" she said quickly, then got off the couch. The contents of the will came to her mind, a mind that was already filled with too many other thoughts. She took the glass from Grace and drained it. Unfortunately, the brandy had the effect of making her feel sick, but she swallowed hard and regained her composure. "James is in love with Kenna, and Kenna is in love with him. This is a love match," she said while looking Colin hard in the eyes.

Now that she was over her initial shock, she could see many differences between the two men. Years of being outside had weathered James's skin, but Colin looked as though he'd lived in nothing but candlelight. Probably at the gambling tables, she thought.

"This *is* a love match," she said again, in case he hadn't heard her the first time.

"I see," Colin said, looking her up and

down in speculation. "And who, exactly, are you?"

"The housekeeper."

For a moment Colin stared at her, then he threw back his head exactly as James did and laughed. "Yes, and I'm the head gardener."

"She is," Grace said softly from behind them. "She does everything in McCairn. She gets jobs for the women, and she runs the house, and she's done everything for the wedding."

"I see," Colin said, again looking Temperance up and down. "But why? That's the question, isn't it? I can't believe that my brother pays you enough to buy a dress like that. And those shoes..."

"Your uncle Angus purchased my wardrobe," Temperance said stiffly. She didn't like this man, didn't like him at all. He looked like James but only superficially. There was a cold, calculating look in his eyes that she'd never seen in James's. Temperance had to hold herself back from running out of the room to find James to warn him. But he didn't need warning, did he? All of Clan McCairn knew about this man, knew of his gambling and how he was going to try to take McCairn away from James.

"I do think you've heard about me," Colin said, then gave Temperance a smile that she was sure was meant to make her like him. He put out his hand to shake hers, but she turned and acted as though she hadn't seen his gesture.

"I have so much work to do," she said,

then hurried out the door and nearly ran up the stairs. Only when she was in her bedroom did she breathe again. She shut the door, leaned against it, and let out her pent up breath. Whatever happened, someone must marry James today, she thought. Today was his thirty-fifth birthday, and if he didn't marry for love today, then everything would be turned over to that dreadful man. That they were twins made Temperance's flesh crawl. Were they the epitome of the old story of the good and bad twins? One evil, one good?

"And he thought I was in love with James," she said aloud. But Temperance knew that wasn't true. She couldn't possibly be in love with any man who wasn't in love with her in return, could she?

Suddenly, Temperance had an overwhelming urge to find Kenna. By now she should be in a room with some of the village women who had volunteered to "dress the bride." Temperance had excused herself from that. For some reason that she didn't want to think about, she didn't want to see Kenna in the beautiful dress that Finola had designed until she absolutely had to.

But after a search of the house, which took over an hour because Temperance was constantly stopped by one McCairn relative after another who wanted to ask her a question ("Where's the whiskey?" "Is there any soap in the house?" "Where's the whiskey?" "Will there be races this afternoon?" and "Where's the whiskey?") Temperance still hadn't found Kenna.

346

"Eppie," she said to herself, then went in search of the little old woman. Eppie was sitting on a bale of hay outside the stables, watching Aleck soap one of the McCairn's gorgeous racehorses. The man was wearing only his kilt, with his shirt, shoes, and tall socks off.

Already in a bad temper, Temperance couldn't resist snapping at Eppie. "There isn't enough for you to do inside the house?"

Eppie picked her teeth with a straw. "You haven't met the McCairn's branch of the family from over on the east, have you?" Eppie said as though that were an answer.

"No," Temperance said, then let out a sigh and sat down beside Eppie to enjoy the view of Aleck with his shirt off. "Take over, do they?" Temperance asked. She looked at the watch pinned to her shirt. Colin had specifically noticed that watch, and now Temperance remembered with a wince of regret how much she'd charged to Angus's account when she'd bought it. Perhaps she shouldn't have been quite so hard on him.

"I can't find the bride," Temperance said at last. The sun glistened off Aleck's skin, and the shadows played on muscles as he dipped a big sponge into a bucket of soapy water and washed the hindquarters of the horse.

"Back up in the attics, last I heard."

"But she's to get into her wedding dress," Temperance said.

"Did that. Right pretty it is too. They say that Finola drew up the pattern. You plannin' to put her into business?"

"Maybe Kenna can. I'm going back to New York, remember?" Aleck now had the horse's foot between his heavy thighs and was soaping the ankles. His kilt was hiked up so that the curve of his buttocks showed. Neither Eppie nor Temperance had taken their eyes off of him during their conversation.

Eppie gave a little snort of derision. "Kenna ain't doin' nothin' that ain't for Kenna."

It took Temperance a moment to understand what the old woman was saying; then slowly, she turned to look at her. "I thought that everyone in this village believed Kenna was an angel. All I've heard about is what a lovely child she was."

"And you believed it?" Eppie said, then nudged Temperance with her elbow to look back at Aleck. He'd bent over to wring out his sponge, and his kilt was folded on one edge in a way that exposed the side of him from waist to knee.

For a moment, Temperance forgot what she was saying. Right. Kenna. "I thought that all of you—"

"Ask Grace, if you want to hear the truth," Eppie said. "I bet she ain't said nothin' good about Kenna. And you ain't seen the McCairn with her much, have you?"

As Temperance was thinking about this, Aleck finished with the horse; then with twinkling eyes, he turned to the two women and gave them a bow, as though he were an actor who'd just finished a performance. Temperance turned red and wanted to pretend that she'd not been watching and admiring him, but Eppie began applauding; then Temperance thought, What the hell, and applauded too.

Smiling, Aleck went back into the stables with his bucket. Temperance got off the bale of hay. "You know which attic Kenna is in now?"

"Looks like that one," Eppie said, nodding upward toward a window where Temperance could see what looked like a candle flame flickering.

Temperance turned on her heel and went inside the house. She had to sneak up the back stairs before anyone saw her and started asking about the whiskey again, but as she reached the top floor and put her hand on the door into the attic, she drew back. What was she going to say to Kenna? Would it be news to Kenna that everyone in the house knew that she was looking for the McCairn treasure?

For a moment Temperance sat down on a chair outside the door and tried to think about what was going on, but the truth was, she couldn't figure out anything. McCairn wasn't in love with Kenna; Kenna was only after treasure. If everyone knew that, then how could they pull off a deception of the king? And what was this about Grace and Kenna, and about Saint Kenna *not* being loved by the village?

It was while she was sitting there that she heard voices. Right away she recognized the voice of James and knew that he was in the attic with Kenna. When a pang of what had to be jealousy shot through Temperance, she had to hold herself back from throwing open the door and demanding to know what they were doing in there together. Alone.

But as she put her hand on the doorknob, Temperance reminded herself that tonight James was going to be in bed with Kenna and that forever after...

She did open the door, but only slowly. Maybe if she saw that James was actually in love with Kenna, it would cure this indecision that was eating at Temperance's stomach.

"Once you find the treasure," came a voice that was like James's, but there was a smooth, slick quality to it that was not like his, "we can kill him."

Temperance froze in the doorway. Every muscle of her body was alert.

"You'll be his widow, so you'll own everything. It will all be yours."

"And yours," came Kenna's voice in reply.

Very slowly, so she made no sound at all, Temperance turned and left the attic and went downstairs.

James was in his bedroom getting dressed for his wedding; his only attendant, Ramsey. Fitting, Temperance thought, since Ramsey was the McCairn's son. There was bile in her throat as she thought of this and wondered how many other great secrets were being kept from her. But what she had to tell James, she wanted to say to him in private.

"I want to see you in the library immediately,"

she said to James, then turned to Ramsey. "In the attic are...two people." She couldn't bear to say their names. "I want them in the library *now,*" she said, then shut the door.

She found Alys on the stairs and told her to go get Grace and send her to the library. Downstairs in the library, Temperance had to shoo eight half-drunken relatives out of the room. She was able to do this by picking up the drinks tray and setting it on the buffet in the hallway. They followed docilely, still laughing and enjoying themselves, seemingly unaware of the change of room.

Within twenty minutes, they were all assembled in the room: Temperance, James, Colin, Kenna, and Grace. Temperance shut the door behind them, locked the door, then put the key in her pocket.

"Where's the whiskey?" was the first thing that Colin said.

"I think that all of us need to be sober for this," Temperance said solemnly.

"Ah, yes, puritanical Americans," Colin said, then sat down on the sofa. "So what do we owe this little meeting to? Have you been a bad boy, brother?" Colin asked in a lazy way that made Temperance want to hit him.

For a moment she hesitated. Maybe she should have told James everything in private, but she didn't like secrets, not horrible secrets like this one, anyway. She took a deep breath and turned to look at James. "Your brother and the woman you're to marry today are planning to murder you."

At that James turned laugh-filled eyes to his brother. "Are you, now?"

In that single moment Temperance knew that everyone knew everything—except for her. She sat down on a chair. "Not that I care anything at all about this family, but no one is leaving this room until I'm told what's going on."

"You bastard," Kenna said under her breath, her eyes narrowed at Colin. She was wearing the gown that had been designed for her, and except that there was a streak of dust along one edge, it was a stunning dress.

Temperance turned to look at James. He was wearing his wedding outfit, a black velvet jacket, a pristine white shirt with a lace jabot in the front. His kilt was clean, his sporran silver-edged. Beneath the kilt his heavily muscled legs showed that he didn't spend his life behind a desk.

It was Grace who broke the silence. "Whatever is going on, someone has to marry the McCairn in about an hour, or the will gives everything to Colin," she said softly.

"Ah, yes, the will," Colin said, great amusement in his voice. "Are you sure you put *all* the whiskey outside?"

"James," Temperance said in a low voice, "if you don't tell me what's going on, I shall leave here this moment and *you* will have to take care of all those houseguests by yourself."

At that James had real fear on his face. He looked at his brother. "All right, where do I begin? I've always known about the will," he said.

At that Temperance opened her mouth to speak, then closed it again.

James smiled at her. "I really did think that you'd come here to marry me, and I thought that at last my uncle was showing some sense. But that presumption turned out not to be true, as you so forcibly told me.

"But I knew that Aunt Rowena would come through. I was surprised that she didn't demand that you and I marry immediately, but when she said Kenna was willing to marry me, I knew that that meant Kenna knew something about the treasure. The only things in Kenna's heart were money and Gavie, in that order. She never loved me."

At this Temperance turned to look at Grace, who was staring at her hands on her lap. So now Temperance knew why Grace had been in a bad mood since Kenna's name was first mentioned. "I see," Temperance said slowly. "Everything has been a joke."

"Oh, the will is real enough," James said. "I'm to marry today, for love, or I lose everything to my wastrel of a brother."

From the way the men were looking at each other, it was plain there was no animosity between them.

"Do you gamble?" Temperance asked Colin quietly.

"Not much," Colin answered with a smile.

"But one of us was expected to, you see," James said, "and—"

"And when dear Aunt Rowena, the old gossip, saw me with a deck of cards after my father's death, she told everyone that she'd been right all along and that I *did* have the family sickness."

"The truth is that my brother is a hard-working barrister with a wife and three children to support."

"Not much time to play the gaming tables," he said cheerfully.

For a moment, Temperance sat still, trying to comprehend that what she'd been told about the family was actually nothing but a pack of lies. She looked at Kenna, sitting silently in her wedding dress. Her beautiful face was full of rage, and she seemed to understand everything that was going on.

"What about this?" Temperance asked, nodding toward Kenna.

"Like to hand it over, dear?" Colin said. "Might as well now that there's to be no murder."

At that Kenna stood and pulled a thin piece of brass from inside the front of her dress, and as she handed it over to James, she looked at Temperance. "Not that it matters, but murder was *his* suggestion and I refused to have any part of it. I draw the line at murder."

"True, she did," Colin said as he moved to stand beside his brother to look at the brass ornament.

"Shall we have a look?" James said, then reached into his sporran and withdrew all four packs of cards, the ones that his grandmother had had made for them.

Temperance knew that someone had searched

her room to find two of the decks, but she didn't mention that fact.

Kenna, Colin, and James spread the cards out on a long table that ran the length of the big leather sofa and began to twist and turn the ornament on top of the backs of the cards. Temperance and Grace stood to one side watching, silent, not speaking to each other or commenting on what the others were doing.

After about fifteen minutes, Kenna said, "I don't see anything. How does it work?"

"I have no idea," Colin answered. "I don't have the mind of a gambler. If the gambling spirit skipped us, do you think that maybe Ramsey inherited it?"

"Or one of your daughters," James shot back, annoyed that the whereabouts of the treasure hadn't been immediately revealed.

"Get one of your relatives in here!" Kenna said angrily. "Surely one of them must be a gambler."

"Gamblers, yes, but cheats seemed to have died with my grandfather."

"All this trouble and we've still found nothing," James said slowly as he looked at Kenna in accusation. "I gave you as much time as possible without actually marrying you, so I think you could have—"

It was Grace who remembered. "The wedding!" she said. "We have to go tell them the wedding is off. Everyone is waiting. They must all be at the church by now."

Colin gave a slow smile. "Well, brother, it looks like the place is about to become mine."

At that Temperance turned away and looked out the window.

Behind her, James said in a teasing way to Kenna, "I guess you still wouldn't want to marry me?"

"I'd rather be burned alive."

"You?" James said to Grace.

"No more men for me, thank you. It's much more fun to earn money."

Behind her, no one spoke for a few moments, so Temperance turned around to look at them. All eyes were on her.

James's eyes were hot and intense. "On a fast horse we could get there without being too late."

Temperance's heart was pounding. What could she say? All she could feel was joy that James had never intended to marry anyone except her, and now she wouldn't have to leave McCairn and go back to have a war with a girl who— "I'm a mess," she heard herself say.

With a jaw-splitting grin, James grabbed her hand. "Later, I'll buy you wardrobe from Paris."

Temperance's heart was pounding so hard that she couldn't think of anything to say. Married! She was about to get *married!* She swallowed. "Actually, Finola showed me a dress she'd made and I was thinking about expanding the House of Grace to include women's clothing. And Struan in the stables has made shoes and—"

It was Grace who shouted, "Go! Go! Go!"; then Colin gave his brother a push toward the door. There was a moment of throaty laughter as James fumbled in Temperance's breast pocket for the door key; then they were in the empty hallway. As Grace had said, everyone was now at the church.

"Ready?" James said, then Temperance laughed and he started running, never releasing her hand as they ran toward the stables. There was a saddled horse waiting as though they'd been expected. James leaped into the saddle, then pulled Temperance up behind him, and they were off and running.

Maybe it was the wind in her face, or just the now-familiar path to the village, but as she clasped his broad back in her arms, Temperance's confidence faded a bit. "They'd rather have Kenna. She's one of their own," she said to him.

"If they think that I'll *give* the place to Colin and he can run them all off!"

Smiling, Temperance hugged him closer, but questions started going through her mind. Why? Why? Why?

"Why did you push me away that day I was crying? You must have known that I almost asked you to marry me that day," she said, her face turned up to look at the back of his neck. After today she'd be allowed to touch him any time she wanted.

"I knew that Kenna would return only if she knew something about the treasure," he said over his shoulder. "I wanted to give her all the time I could."

What he said made sense, but Temperance

couldn't help frowning as she remembered her pain of that day. He'd done nothing to alleviate her pain. Why? Because he wanted his bloody treasure—which he didn't get anyway.

She could see the church at the end of the long street, but at that moment a large flock of James's beloved sheep decided to cross the road, so he halted and waited. He'd do nothing to make a sheep panic and maybe break a leg. There was something else bothering her. "Do you know anything about Deborah Madison?"

James threw a smile over his shoulder at her. "I found the newspaper article and the letter in the sheepherder's cottage after the night we spent there," he said. "I could see nail prints in the letter, so I knew you'd been upset by what you'd read. It was a hunch, but I had an idea that this Deborah Madison was like you were when you first came to McCairn. I wanted to show you that you were a much better person with us than you were in New York, so I contacted Colin and he telegraphed New York and Miss Madison took the first boat over."

"Oh," Temperance said, then put her head back down on his back. His hunch had been right, and she'd seen what he'd hoped she would. He was wise and perceptive, she'd give him that.

But there was something about this that still bothered her. Couldn't he have *talked* to her about what he'd read? Sat down with her and *told* her that she'd changed? Why did he have to do such a sneaky and elaborate thing as go behind Temperance's back and arrange for Deborah Madison to come to McCairn? It was the kind of thing that you'd do to teach a child. *Show* them. But grown-ups had reasoning power. Couldn't he have...?

Shaking her head, she tried to clear her thoughts. This was going to be her wedding day, and this was the man she loved. She knew him; he was a good man. She'd seen the way he took care of people. Later, they could iron out their differences. Later, after the requirements of the will had been fulfilled and McCairn was safe, she and James would talk.

But still, she remembered herself saying to women, "Didn't you think of that *before* you married him?" Usually this pertained to the man's love of whiskey. The answer the women gave was always the same: "No, I was in love and I didn't think of anything past 'I do.'"

When the sheep were clear of the road, James nudged the horse forward and Temperance tried to still her thoughts. James McCairn didn't have any bad vices like those of the men involved with the women she'd dealt with back in New York. James didn't drink to excess, certainly didn't gamble. Perhaps he was a little high-handed, but every man had flaws, didn't he?

In the next minute they were at the church, and the second they stepped inside, the place went wild with excitement, with everyone cheering and shouting. At the end of the aisle in the front row were her mother and Rowena, and they fell on each other, crying and laughing at the same time.

"Looks like they don't mind having you after all," James shouted down at her.

Temperance was smiling, but, inside, something was bothering her deeply. There had been no hesitation on anyone's part when *she* had appeared in the doorway with James. But hadn't they been expecting Kenna? "One of their own," as they'd said a thousand times.

Everyone was there, all of McCairn, plus scads of James's relatives from all over Scotland. And as she walked beside James up the aisle, nearly everyone slapped him on the back.

"You said you could do it, and you did," she kept hearing. Along the way, someone thrust a bouquet of flowers into her hands.

But she didn't understand what the words of the people meant. James had been able to do what? Get married and save McCairn from a gambling brother who doesn't actually gamble?

It was at the altar that everything became clear to her. Hamish, a man Temperance had once despised, smiled and said to her, "James said he wouldn't let you leave us, and he was right. Welcome home, lass."

Then Hamish put up his hand for silence, and when the church was quiet, he began the wedding service. "Dearly beloved, we are gathered here today..."

Turning, Temperance looked out at the congregation, all of them beaming in that way that people do when they've pulled off some great feat. It was difficult for Temperance to comprehend, but she suddenly realized that everyone in the village had been in on this. They hadn't hesitated when they'd seen Temperance at the entrance to the church because they had been expecting *her* to show up with James.

I don't like this, Temperance thought. I don't like it at all.

"Do you, James, take this woman..." Hamish was saying, but Temperance was still looking at the congregation. Her mother was sitting in the first row, crying softly into a handkerchief.

I thought he was serious about marrying Kenna, but he wasn't, went through Temperance's head. And she'd thought the people of the village were serious about wanting Kenna more than they could ever want an "outsider."

When James said, "I do," Temperance turned to look up at him, but she didn't smile.

Hamish said, "Do you, Temperance O'Neil, take this man—"

Temperance turned back to look at the people. She'd had a lot of experience giving speeches, and she knew how to project her voice so that she could be heard by the people in the last row. James was holding her hand, but she pulled away from him. "I helped you in a spirit of honesty," she said to the people, "but you didn't treat me with the same respect. You weren't honest with me."

To say that the people were stunned was an understatement. Only Grace, standing to one side, having arrived on a horse with Colin, had a look on her face of, I knew this was going to happen.

It was Lilias who spoke out. "We never wanted Kenna. She was always after young Gavie. The boy was mad about her, but she left him to go after the McCairn. She deserves what she gets. If we used her, then it was because she deserved it."

At that the people made noises of agreement.

"And what did *I* do to deserve to be tricked by all of you?" Temperance asked, then looked at her mother. "You were part of this, weren't you?"

Melanie didn't make any answer as she put the handkerchief up to her face and cried harder. Her silence was enough admission of guilt for Temperance.

"I don't like this," Temperance said softly, but everyone in the church heard her.

"Darling," James said from beside her. "I think that—"

When she turned to look at him, she felt as though everything in her life had been leading up to this moment. Her mind was crystal clear. "All you had to do was *ask* me to marry you," she said. "That's all. Not say to me, 'All right, I'll give you what you want; I'll marry you.' No, I wanted what it seems that most of the women in this church received: a proper marriage proposal on bended knee, preferably with a ring in a pretty box, the same things that all women want. But instead, I got tricked and manipulated."

As he'd always done, James tried to tease her out of her bad mood. "Isn't it all fair in love and war?" he asked, eyes sparkling.

"Yes, I believe it is," she said, then stopped. Everyone in the church was holding his or her breath; she could feel the tension. She knew that if she allowed the service to continue, there would be more cheering and great happiness. But Temperance couldn't do it.

She wanted more. She wanted more than trickery and things done behind her back. But, most of all, she wanted *love*.

She looked down at the bouquet of flowers that had been thrust into her hands. She wasn't wearing a wedding dress because this wedding had been planned for another woman. After Temperance had asked Kenna for the fourth time what kind of flowers she liked best, Kenna had reluctantly said, "Lilies." So now the church was full of white lilies. But Temperance hated lilies. Hated the shape; hated the smell of the things. But then, this wasn't *her* wedding, was it?

No, she wasn't going to marry a man who until an hour ago she'd thought was to marry someone else, a man who had yet to *ask* her to marry him. And he'd certainly never said those words every woman wanted to hear. He'd never said, "I love you."

She looked up at James. Truthfully, she was finally, at last, *sure* that she was in love with him. No one could look at a man and get all jittery inside as she did with him and not be in love. But she was going to take her own advice: she was going to think of problems *before* she married a man.

She thrust the bouquet of flowers into his hand, then turned and started down the aisle.

No one in the church said a word after the first gasps of disbelief.

James caught her arm halfway down the aisle. "You can't do this," he said quietly; his eyes were pleading with her. Don't embarrass me in front of my people, he was silently asking her.

"If you leave, I'll lose McCairn and people will be homeless," he said softly.

Looking into the eyes of the man you love and saying no had to be the hardest thing that Temperance had ever done in her life. And she knew that if, right now, he'd say those three little words, she would turn and go back to where Hamish was still standing, the prayer book in his hand, his mouth still open in astonishment.

But James said no more and the moment was lost.

And because she didn't hear those words, Temperance couldn't continue. She couldn't make herself marry a man for the sake of a village. "You should have thought of that before the last day," she said. "And maybe you should have paid as much attention to *me* as to your treasure." When he said nothing in reply, just stared at her, she turned and started walking again.

Outside were two of James's racehorses,

one ridden by Colin. Temperance wasn't much of a rider, but right now she knew that she could do anything in the world. Easily, she propelled herself into the saddle and urged the horse forward. There were three of James's sheep in the road, and when she came to them, she leaned down and shouted at them to move. For all that she might have just done the dumbest thing of her life, she suddenly felt very free.

At the crossroads, she didn't hesitate. She wasn't going to do the sensible thing and return to the house and pack her belongings. No, she was going to... Well, she didn't know where she was going or how she was going to get there, but she was *leaving* McCairn—*that* was for sure.

She pulled just a bit on the horse's reins, and the animal went right. On the road to Midleigh, with McCairn behind her, there was Kenna walking, her beautiful wedding dress now a muddy mess.

Temperance halted the horse.

"Did you come to laugh at me, *Mrs. McCairn?*" Kenna said nastily.

"I didn't marry him," Temperance said calmly. "Would you like a ride?"

Kenna opened her mouth a couple of times, then closed it. "Aye, I would," she said at last, then put her foot into the stirrup and climbed on the horse behind Temperance.

Twenty-four

Two Years Later
New York, New York

The sign on the brownstone house said
"Women's Employment Agency—*If you have
a talent, we have a job.*"

James McCairn stood before the front door
and raised his hand to knock, then lowered it.
Right now he'd rather face a line of men with
cannons than do what he'd come here to do.
Standing still for a moment, he reached down
to scratch his leg. Both of his legs were raw
from wearing the confounded trousers instead
of a kilt that allowed a man's skin to breathe.
And he was sick of the heat of the lowlands.

Running his hand around his collar, he felt a
trickle of sweat there, and for a moment he
almost turned and fled. But then he remembered Temperance and what his life had been
like for the last two years. She had only been
with him for a few months, but since she'd left,
his life had been...

Taking a deep, bracing breath, he raised the
brass knocker and let it fall. A maid opened
the door almost immediately.

"They only find jobs for women," the
woman said, looking him up and down. "And

366

you ain't one by a long shot," she said, and there was an invitation in her voice and eyes.

"Delly!" came a voice that James well knew, and when he heard it, he knew that he'd done the right thing.

When Temperance turned a corner, she saw him, and instantly, he was sure that she had been as miserable as he'd been these last years. This is going to be easy, he told himself, and his self-confidence returned. Putting his shoulders back, he walked toward her as proudly as though he were on his own land and wearing his kilt.

"Hello," he said, smiling. "Remember me?"

For a moment Temperance stared at him; then she smiled slowly. "James," she said. "You haven't changed a bit." But that wasn't true. He was, if anything, better looking than when she'd last seen him—and just the sight of him made her heart beat faster.

James smiled warmly. "I should have told you that I was going to be in New York, but I never got round to it," he said, trying his best to sound as casual as possible.

"No, of course not," she answered softly. "Won't you come in so we can visit? I'd like to hear all about what's been happening in McCairn. My mother writes me, but..." She trailed off as James moved closer to her. His nearness made words impossible, and it was as though the last two years hadn't happened.

There was still the old magnetism, he thought, and smiled again.

"Won't you come inside?" Temperance

said softly as she opened a door to a prettily decorated little parlor. "Delly, would you send in some tea and cakes?"

They didn't speak again until they were alone in the room. Temperance sat down on a small sofa, then indicated that James was to take the chair across from her. But he didn't sit. Instead, he stood by the fireplace, his arm resting on the mantel. She was prettier than he remembered, but there was something new about her, an air of maturity that he hadn't seen before, and it was becoming to her.

Once they were settled, James opened his mouth to tell her why he'd come. He planned to tell her that he was ready to forgive her for the way she'd humiliated him at the altar and take her back.

But just as he opened his mouth to speak, the door flew open and in ran a little boy. He had dirt all over his face and hands and down the front of his blue-and-white sailor suit. "Mom! Mom!" he yelled as he buried his face in Temperance's skirts. Behind him ran a young woman, her nanny uniform's hat askew.

"He got away from me, I'm sorry," the nanny said.

Lovingly, Temperance stroked the boy's dark blond hair. "What have you done this time?"

"He dug up every one of the new bulbs the gardener put in last week!" the nanny said in exasperation.

"Oh?" Temperance said, raising her eyes to

look at the woman. "And where were you? Meeting your boyfriend again?"

At that, tears sprang to the girl's eyes. "I'm sorry, miss, it won't happen again. I'm new at this. It's so much easier makin' a livin' on my back than doin'—"

"Mable!" Temperance said sharply as she looked down at the boy; then she lifted his head from her lap and held his little face in her hands. "There's someone I want you to meet," she said as she turned the boy to look at James. "This is James McCairn and he's from Scotland. Go and shake his hand."

The little boy left his mother, solemnly went forward, and held out his hand to James to shake. Just as solemnly, James shook the small hand. He was a handsome child. "It is a pleasure to meet you," James said quietly.

The maid brought in a large tray covered with a big pot of tea and three plates holding little cakes and cookies. With a squeal of delight, the boy grabbed three cakes at once, stuffing two into his mouth.

"Go and wash him," Temperance said to the nanny, "and stop sniveling. And, Delly, from now on you'll—" She broke off, instead, giving the girl a warning look. After a quick kiss to the boy's cheek, the two maids and the child left the room, closing the door behind them.

"I apologize for that," Temperance said, looking up at James.

He was doing all that he could to recover himself, for the bottom of his world had fallen out when the child had yelled, "Mom!" then run to Temperance. "I see that you're still saving your wayward women," he said, trying to sound lighthearted as he sat down. All the arrogance had left him in the last moments. Why hadn't he acted sooner? Why hadn't he—?

"Tea?" she asked as she picked up the pot.

"You're doing well," he said, looking about the room.

"Yes, I think so. I—" She cut herself off as she handed him his cup of tea. "You didn't come here to hear about me. What brings you to New York?"

You, he wanted to say, but his pride held him back. "Business for McCairn," he said, then put his cup down and reached inside his coat pocket and withdrew a small box. "I brought you something."

Temperance took the box from him and slipped the ribbon off of it. Inside, wrapped in tissue, was a golden shell on wheels. Atop it was a tiny man holding on to a rope as thin as hair that was attached to the front of the shell. Not only was it exquisite, it looked to be made of gold.

"Ah, yes, my mother wrote me that you'd found the treasure," she said, then set the beautiful object down on the tea table. That treasure had cost her a lot, she thought, and after she'd been told of its discovery, she'd written her mother that she never wanted to hear another word about McCairn. When she looked back up at James, she was smiling. "You figured out about the cards and the template, then?"

James gave her a one-sided grin. "No, not really. At least not until later, that is. I, uh, threw something through the big mirror over the fireplace in the library. When the glass fell away, there was a deep hollow back there and everything my grandmother had bought was in there."

"That must have been exciting for you," Temperance said, sipping her tea and looking at him. "And how did your grandmother put the treasure behind the mirror?"

"You always were clever," he said, smiling, but Temperance didn't smile back. "There was a trapdoor in my grandmother's bedroom. It was extremely well hidden, and we never would have found the door if we hadn't found the treasure first. And the template was a key, not something to be used on the back of the cards."

"What an interesting woman your grandmother must have been," Temperance said, then glanced at the clock on the mantelpiece. "I'm so happy that you found your treasure. And how is everyone in McCairn?"

"Well. Everyone is doing very well," James said, too aware that she was already wanting to get away from him. "Grace married the man who delivered hat blanks, and they moved to Edinburgh, and young Alys is already starting to take courses in medicine."

"That's wonderful," Temperance said, finishing her cup of tea.

"And I had my grandmother buried in consecrated ground."

"I'm glad. I know how much that meant to you."

"And you?" James said quietly.

"Your uncle honored our agreement in spite of the fact that I hadn't fulfilled my end of the bargain," she said. "I didn't find you a wife."

"It wasn't your fault," he said.

"That's what Angus said too. When I stopped hating him, I found that he was a very nice man. He's allowed me the use of my father's house and access to some of the money my father left my mother, all under supervision, of course."

"The girl at the door said, *'They* only find jobs for women.' Are you, by chance, in partnership with Miss Deborah Madison?"

"Heavens no! But I must say that that dreadful girl turned my life around. She made me see that, somewhere along the way, I'd sold out."

"You?"

The way he said it, made Temperance frown. It was as though he was insinuating that she was too perfect to be human. It was something she'd been accused of before. "Deborah Madison made me realize that I'd been feeding my pride rather than helping people who needed help. I'm ashamed to say that I used to love being a 'celebrity.' I liked having little girls ask for my autograph. I liked—" She waved her hand in dismissal.

"Anyway, after McCairn, I thought that maybe I had a talent for finding people work, so I returned to New York and opened an employment agency. I let others try for the history books," she said with a tiny smile.

"You said that your money is 'supervised.' By a husband?" he said, then wanted to bite his tongue off. He hadn't meant to ask that. Ever since he'd seen the boy and realized that he'd lost her, he'd meant to be cool, reserved, to keep his pride intact.

"No," Temperance said with real amusement. "Kenna is my partner and she keeps in contact with Angus's bank managers. Financially, we're well looked after."

"Kenna?" James said in disbelief. "Kenna Lockwood? From McCairn? The one who—"

"The very one. Mother talked Angus into allowing Kenna to be my guardian. 'A good McCairn girl down on her luck,' is what my mother called Kenna."

For the first time since he'd arrived, he saw a spark of the old Temperance he used to know. Did she hate him? He could have sworn that when he first saw her, there had been a spark in her eyes. But now he wondered if it was a spark of hatred. "So Kenna handles your money," he said. "I hope you have a trustworthy accountant overseeing the books."

For a second, Temperance's eyes flashed fire. "Kenna is my partner in this business," she said angrily. "She and I and my son live upstairs, and together we manage the employment agency." With a clank, she put down her teacup, then looked at him across the table. This time there was no mistaking the anger in her eyes. "You really haven't changed, have you, James McCairn? You know how my mother got your uncle to agree to Kenna's being given a job? My mother told Angus that he needed to bring back honor to the McCairn name after what you'd done to her, after what you and all of McCairn had done to her."

At that James stood. "I never did a damned thing to that girl. Years ago she tried to trick me into marrying her because she was after the McCairn money! She deserved what she got."

Temperance also stood, her face full of fury. "So I guess you're considered a clever man because *you* used trickery to try to find your beloved treasure, but if a woman uses trickery to try to get money, she's a thief and deserves punishment. And I guess I, too, deserved what I got, didn't I? After all, I'd done so many bad things to all of McCairn that I deserved to be tricked and manipulated, didn't I?"

"*You* were tricked?!" he said. "You were scheming to marry me off to—" Breaking off, he stepped away from her and lowered his voice. "I came here to tell you that I was willing to forgive you for the way you humiliated me, but now I—"

"Forgive *me*," she said under her breath. "Forgive *me?*"

"I can see that I wasted my time," he said, his back rigid; then he turned and walked out of the room, slamming the door behind him.

In the hallway he was so angry that he was shaking. He'd traveled all the way to the United States just to... To what?

It certainly wasn't to be humiliated again, that's for sure. When he thought of those minutes, then hours, then months after she ran out on him, humiliating him before the entire village, he could—

As he grabbed the handle of the front door in order to leave the house, he stepped on something. When he looked down, he saw that it was a Crayola crayon.

Picking it up, he looked at the crushed tip. When Temperance had been in Scotland, she had had her mother send boxes of these things to the children in McCairn. And after Temperance had seen the pictures that one of the children drew, she'd written some letters to a couple of art schools in New York. But nothing had come of the letters because James hadn't married Temperance as he'd planned and Temperance had left McCairn forever.

Turning, he looked at the closed door to the parlor. When she'd walked out on him in the church, she'd said that if he'd just *asked* her to marry him, she would have. It was too late for that now because now she was married and had a child. She had a business helping her down-on-their-luck women, and she was happy. While he was...

James took a deep breath. Pride was a cold bedfellow. He knew that very, very well.

With his shoulders back, he opened the door into the parlor, walked in, and closed it behind him. She was still sitting on the sofa, and he could see that she'd been crying. She turned away, wiped her tears, and tried to hide her face from him.

"I have something to say," he said softly.

"It's all right," she said. "I think you've said everything."

"No," he said, and for a moment he thought again about turning and running. If she was already married, what he had to say wouldn't make any difference. Right now he could save his pride and walk out that door and...and what? Go home with his pride intact? But, then, wasn't it his pride that got him into this in the first place?

"I broke the mirror in the library in a rage. In fact I broke a lot of things after you left."

"You don't have to tell me any of this," Temperance said as she stood up.

"Yes, I do," James said. "And if I can travel all the way to this hot city and put on these itchy, confining pants, then you can bloody well *listen* to me. So sit!"

Temperance blinked at him, then sat back down.

Putting his hands behind his back, James began to pace as he talked. "Grace left McCairn. She took her new husband, her daughter, and her *business* and left McCairn. But she didn't go before she gave me a piece of her mind. She said she couldn't stand what McCairn had become. She said that my bad temper and my sulking over what had happened with my first wife, then later over what I thought that *you* had done to me, was just an excuse for me to stay on that mountain and not face life. So she took her child and her business and she left.

"Actually," he said, "most of the people

376

of the village gave me a piece of his or her mind."

Pausing a moment, James stared at the wall in front of him. He was remembering the lassitude that had taken over the village after their new, modern business was taken from them.

When he spoke again, his voice was softer. "Others besides Grace left too because they said they couldn't see any future in McCairn."

James stopped pacing and sat down on the chair across from Temperance, but he didn't look her in the eyes. Would he see pity there? The great McCairn hadn't been able to save his own people.

"As for Colin, he didn't want the place. He said he was sick of the whole family treating him like a monster because he liked a card game now and then. He said he was happily married, loved his children, and he was on the board of directors of three banks, so his gambling urges were taken care of there. He said McCairn was just a liability and that he wanted nothing to do with it."

James looked down at his hands. It was hard to admit to this failure, but at the same time, there was something that was being released inside him. To say these things out loud made him feel as though a huge boulder inside him were being dissolved.

He looked up at Temperance, but there was no pity in her eyes, only interest. It encouraged him to go on. "I went to lawyers and talked to them about the will. It took a couple of years, but in the end several people came forward to testify that I *had* married for love once, and there was nothing in the will saying what to do if she died."

James gave Temperance a weak smile. "Since Colin didn't want the place, my work with lawyers meant nothing except that now I'm the real owner of the McCairn—such as it is—and I can pass it on to my descendants."

"To Ramsey," Temperance said softly.

"Yes. To Ramsey." For a moment James didn't say anything, but then he looked up at her and there was no longer any shield in front of his eyes, nothing guarding him, protecting him, and Temperance knew that she was looking at the inside of him, a place he didn't allow people to see.

"All those years," he said softly, so quietly that she had to lean forward to hear him. "I thought that the problem with McCairn was money. If I just had enough money, I could bring my land and my people back to what they once were. When you said McCairn was a laughingstock of all Scotland, you were right."

When Temperance opened her mouth to apologize for that thoughtless statement, he put up his hand to stop her. "No," he said, "you were right, and you hit a nerve when you said it. I was ashamed of my family's history of gambling and the resulting failure of my homeland. Grace was right: I was hiding in McCairn, staying away from the world."

James couldn't sit still any longer but again stood and began to pace. "But I was content all those years before you came, content with what I was doing, content with being alone. I now realize that I did heavy, manual labor fourteen hours a day to keep myself from thinking."

He stopped pacing and looked at her. "But then you came along and you woke all of us up. You made me laugh. You made me want the company of a woman. I hadn't been lonely until you showed up, then I was sick with loneliness."

James sat back down on the chair and looked into Temperance's eyes. "But I never told you. I never told you how much having dinner with you meant to me. Or how much pleasure I received from the hours we spent in the cave. You were so generous and kind to the people of McCairn, more generous than I ever was. You were kind to them on a personal level. I didn't have to do anything because I was the McCairn."

When he looked at her, there were tears starting to form in his eyes. "You were right to leave me. You should have. If you'd stayed, I would have—"

"Taken me for granted?" she said.

At that James smiled. "You always did have the ability to make me laugh. Yes, if you'd gone through with that wedding, I think I would have come to treat you abominably. We don't prize what's easily won."

He took a breath and looked away for a moment, then back at her. "I came here today to..."

"To what?" she prompted.

He smiled at her. "To tell you that I'd forgive you and take you back. Looks like I didn't learn much in these last years, does it? I don't think it ever occurred to me that you'd be married and have a child. I think I thought that you were—"

"Crying in loneliness over you every night, as you were over me?"

"Yes," he said, smiling, then had to take another breath to calm himself. He'd lost. His damned, insufferable pride had lost him everything.

But when he looked at Temperance, he smiled. "I can't believe this, but I feel better now. It's odd, but I thought that if I ever humbled myself, I'd crack right down the middle, but instead, it feels kind of free. I feel lighter."

Temperance smiled warmly at him. "I guess they don't have the saying in Scotland that confession is good for the soul."

"It wasn't a saying we had in laird school," he said, making her laugh; then he withdrew another box from his pocket. "I want to show you something else."

It was a ring box. "James, I don't think—" she began, but he cut her off. It was obvious that she was going to tell him that he didn't have to humble himself any more.

"No, I *need* to tell you something," he said. "I need to do this for myself. At the altar you said that you wanted a ring and—"

"James, please," she said. "You don't have to do this."

"But I *do,*" he said. "I want to show you

something. I did, as you said, trick and manipulate you, but maybe I had some good intentions. After I walk out that door today, I promise that I'll never bother you again, so I need to leave you with some good thoughts about me."

Opening the little box, he pulled out a gold ring and handed it to her. "Can you read the inscription?"

Taking it, she held the ring up to the light.

"At the wedding you said that if I had just come to you on bended knee with a ring in a pretty box, you would have said yes. I wanted to show you that I meant to, I really did, but I also wanted to hand you riches, so I waited until the last minute with Kenna to see what she knew."

He handed her a receipt from a jewelry store. It was dated weeks before she left McCairn. The receipt said that the ring was to be inscribed with, "To Temperance, with all my love, James."

As Temperance looked inside the ring, she could see engraved inside, "To TM with all my love, JM."

"It was too long, so they had to abbreviate it," James said, smiling. "And they didn't have last names, and they knew that I was demanding the ring be ready within twenty-four hours, so they made do."

Temperance handed the ring back to him, then sat back against her chair and looked at him in silence.

As James looked at her hands, his stomach

clenched. There was a wedding ring on the third finger of her left hand.

When he spoke, he tried to sound as though his heart weren't breaking. "So who is he?" James asked.

"Who is whom?"

"Your husband. If my uncle found him for you, I'll kill Angus."

Temperance smiled. "Don't have one. I tell people that I was widowed, and they accept that. Truthfully, I don't think anyone believes me, but the lie makes me more human. Kenna's been a great help. She's good at business, and she says she likes earning money much more than, well, men."

James was staring at her, his mouth open. "But the child," he said.

"He's yours," Temperance said cheerfully, as though she were announcing a party.

"What?"

"My son is your son. I never was good at numbers, and so much was happening in those last weeks that I didn't realize that I was going to have a baby."

It took James several minutes to comprehend what she'd just said. "No husband?" he whispered.

"No husband."

The next moment James was fumbling for the ring and almost dropped it twice before he got to Temperance; then he went down on one knee and grabbed both her hands in one of his. "Will you marry me? Please? We'll live wherever you want. Here in New York, so you can run your business. And now I can afford to buy you anything you want—not that I think you can be bought, but I—"

Temperance put a finger over his lips. "I'd like to go back to McCairn. I'd like my son...*our* son to be raised there, with his big brother, Ramsey. And as for this place, Kenna can run it. She doesn't need me."

"*I* need you," James said, his eyes pleading. "We all need you. Desperately."

"And I need you," Temperance said softly. "And our son needs us both." Bending, she softly kissed his lips. "Would you like to meet your son? *Really* meet him?"

For a moment James looked as though he were going to cry; then he stood up and Temperance could see a change come over him. He had discarded his pride to win her, and now she had given it back to him. And he had given her back her pride also. These last years had been difficult. Being a single mother was hard, and—

"Shall we go?" he asked, as he held out his arm for her.

"Yes," she said. "Yes."